KT-558-427

C153543661

DUTCH COURAGE

A Max Rydal Military Mystery

The truth must be told; blinkers removed from eyes. That's the message sent anonymously to Sam Collier, a helicopter pilot decorated for bravery in Afghanistan. When a campaign of harassment is then mounted against his wife, she turns to Max Rydal of Special Investigation Branch for help. As Max probes into the lives of this seemingly ideal couple, he discovers dark undercurrents, which are liable to engulf him...

*Elizabeth Darrell titles available from
Severn House Large Print*

Czech Mate
Chinese Puzzle
Russian Roulette
Shadows Over the Sun
Unsung Heroes

DUTCH COURAGE

Elizabeth Darrell

Severn House Large Print
London & New York

This first large print edition published 2010
in Great Britain and the USA by
SEVERN HOUSE PUBLISHERS LTD of
9-15 High Street, Sutton, Surrey, SM1 1DF.
First world regular print edition published 2008 by
Severn House Publishers Ltd., London and New York.

Copyright © 2008 by E. D. Books.

All rights reserved.
The moral right of the author has been asserted.

British Library Cataloguing in Publication Data

Darrell, Elizabeth.
  Dutch courage. -- (A Max Rydal mystery)
  1. Rydal, Max (Fictitious character)--Fiction.
  2. Veterans--Fiction. 3. Afghan War, 2001- --Fiction.
  4. Detective and mystery stories. 5. Large type books.
  I. Title II. Series
  823.9'14-dc22

ISBN-13: 978-0-7278-7879-3

Except where actual historical events and characters are being
described for the storyline of this novel, all situations in this
publication are fictitious and any resemblance to living persons is
purely coincidental.

Severn House Publishers support The Forest Stewardship Council
[FSC], the leading international forest certification organisation. All
our titles that are printed on Greenpeace-approved FSC-certified paper
carry the FSC logo.

Mixed Sources
Product group from well-managed
forests and other controlled sources
www.fsc.org Cert no. SA-COC-1565
© 1996 Forest Stewardship Council

Printed and bound in Great Britain by the
MPG Books Group, Bodmin, Cornwall.

Acknowledgements

My thanks are due to the following gentlemen who were so generous with their time and knowledge whenever I asked for information for this novel. Colonel Stephen Boyd and Lt Col (Retd) John Nelson, Royal Military Police. Dr Mark Adams, Royal Army Medical Corps. Lt Col (Retd) David Patterson and, most importantly, Captain Gus Aylward, Army Air Corps.

KENT LIBRARIES	
C153543661	
Bertrams	25/02/2013
	£19.99

One

There was a light knock on his open office door, but Sergeant Major Tom Black continued checking the report he had just written.

'Unless it's bloody urgent, come back in ten,' he grunted.

Phil Piercey's West Country burr announced, 'Mrs Collier to see you, sir.'

A cultured female voice added, 'And it *is* bloody urgent.'

Tom glanced up, then struggled to his feet, colour rushing to his cheeks. This tough, experienced detective, this devoted husband and father felt his heartbeat accelerate with excitement in a manner he had long forgotten. The young woman with Piercey was absolutely stunning. Blushing like a schoolboy, Tom skirted his desk to pull out a chair for his visitor and shot a venomous look at Piercey.

'Coffee, Sergeant!'

He would have the man's balls for this. All his staff knew better than to usher visitors to his office without first informing him of their identity and their business with Special Investigation Branch. Phil Piercey's ga-ga expression suggested a lapse of rational thought, hence the breach of protocol. Rational thought appeared also to have deserted Tom as he wondered why this gorgeous woman wanted to see him.

'I don't make a habit of riding roughshod over people, Mr Black, but the situation has become potentially criminal,' she said, sitting and crossing eye-catching legs. 'It needs to be sorted before one of us is hurt.'

'One of whom, ma'am?' Tom queried, overwhelmingly conscious of her perfume and the swell of her breasts in the straw-coloured silk shirt that contrasted so sharply with her blue-black hair and golden tan. She must have spent the winter months well away from Germany. Unbidden desire was overriding his concentration and, for the first time since he was bludgeoned by a crazed woman just before Christmas, Tom was uncomfortably conscious of the scar running down his left cheek. His daughters said he looked villainous; their mother maintained it added to his rugged attraction. Right now, he felt those deep, dark eyes were fastened on it assessingly.

'Myself, or my husband.'

Sanity, professionalism, recollection of where and who he was providentially returned to mentally highlight the name *Collier*. It should have rung an immediate bell. There had been comprehensive media coverage nine weeks ago; pictures in newspapers and on TV. *Click, click, click.* Tom's brain sifted through what he knew of the young pilot celebrated as a national

8

hero. He now recognized his visitor. Margot Collier was far more striking in the flesh than in photographs.

'Your husband is Lieutenant Samuel Collier?' At her slight nod, Tom added, 'You believe you could both be in danger? Why?'

She eyed him frankly. 'Sam's received some threatening letters. He laughed them off, refused to take any action. For several weeks since then I've been regularly harassed. I have not told Sam, but just now someone tried to run me off the road. That's enough. I want him caught and punished.'

Tom frowned. Wives living in the shadow of successful men often courted attention by exaggerating incidents to turn them into dramas. He did not believe it of this wife. She had no need to draw attention to herself. To enter a room was enough.

He retreated behind his desk, still too aware of her aura to remain beside her. He sat and adopted a more official tone to ask where the attempt to run her off the road took place.

'Just outside town, where the road bifurcates.'

Unusual word. Most women would say the fork in the road. 'Please tell me exactly what happened, Mrs Collier.'

Piercey then entered with coffee in the bone china cups and saucers reserved for VIPs, and a plate of fancy biscuits. He must have raided Heather Johnson's desk. He still wore a ga-ga expression.

Accepting the coffee with an abstracted smile,

9

the visitor took several sips, then said, 'I'd entered that straight stretch where men like to indulge their craze for speed. It was surprisingly empty today, and I confess my mind was wandering. Before I was aware of it a light-blue Audi came up beside me and stayed there. At first, I thought it was a new arrival from the UK who had forgotten which side of the road he should be on. I signalled him to overtake. When he didn't, I speeded up. He did the same.'

Tom leaned forward, forearms along his desk. 'Did he make any signs to you, shout across to tell you to pull over?'

Margot shook her head. 'He was grinning as he eased closer and closer. Beneath the baseball cap pulled low over his face I saw two rows of exposed teeth. That made me mad, so I called his bluff.'

Fascinated, Tom invited her to explain.

'I knew we were coming up to that track that leads off to the pumping station, so I trod on the accelerator to force him to do the same. The Audi was mere inches away when I made a skidding turn on to that track. He raced on before he realized he'd lost me. I then reversed intending to follow and get his reg. number, but he was way ahead and the road had grown busy with traffic.'

'So we have no way of tracing this maniac.'

'You won't have to look far. It'll be someone from the Squadron,' she said with conviction. 'Whoever owns a blue Audi.'

Studying her as she sipped her coffee – she

even did that enticingly, Tom thought – he began to feel there was a great deal more to this affair than at first seemed likely.

'You said you wanted him caught and punished. To do that we have to know the full story. These threatening letters your husband received, for instance. Why did he treat them as a joke? You've been harassed for several weeks. Give me specific instances. Why are you certain you're being targeted by someone from your husband's squadron? Will you also tell me why you've come to SIB without first consulting him? Surely that would be the natural thing to do.'

She set her cup and saucer on his desk and gave a faint smile. 'Are you married, Mr Black?'

'Yes.'

'Then you must know there are times when a wife, especially an army wife, has to take matters in her own hands.'

Tom thought of how frequently Nora dealt with problems he only heard about when they had been fixed. Yet he knew she would share anything that posed a threat to all or any one of them. Of course she would! So what kind of marriage had the Colliers?

'You want us to investigate, but unless we have full details we can't do that, Mrs Collier. Any action we take must involve your husband.'

She sighed. 'Foolish of me to believe otherwise.'

Tom waited as she visually wrestled with her decision, wondering why she was so protective of a man of proven courage. Her next comment was a surprise.

'I'm only going ahead with this now because I'm pregnant. I've had two miscarriages and couldn't bear to lose another.'

Tom put her age at no more than twenty-one. Sam Collier was clearly a man of action in the bedroom as well as on the battlefield. So why must his beautiful wife fight this battle for him?

'We'll do our best to get to the bottom of this, but you must tell us everything,' he insisted.

There was no longer any hesitation. Tom heard that there had been resentment from one or two of Sam Collier's colleagues all along, but this had intensified following the action that had hit the headlines. Sam had attributed the anonymous notes he had found on the doormat to this not unusual reaction to public acclaim.

'Envy, resentment, I'd go along with, Mr Black, but the writer of the letters mentioned "letting the truth be known" and "removing the blinkers from everyone's eyes". To me, that constitutes a threat of some kind, although what he means I've no idea. What truth? When I asked Sam he shrugged it off as some squaddie talking off the top of his head.'

'Do you still have the letters?' Tom asked.

'Sam shredded them with some old bills and bank statements.'

'How many did you receive?'

'Four or five.'

'Handwritten?'

'Block capitals, red felt-tip, text phonetics.'

'Did they come through the base mail system?'

'No, they turned up overnight.'

'We'll keep a watch on your quarter.'

'No need. They stopped coming two weeks ago. That's when the harassment began.'

'Go on.'

For the first time her poise faltered. 'On medical advice I take a long walk each day. I drive to the playing fields and go round the perimeter. At this time of year there are shrubs in bloom and the trees have their spring leaves. There's invariably some kind of sporting activity going on, and I enjoy the open aspect. The day after getting the last of the letters, I returned to my car to find it had been moved two hundred yards from where I'd parked it.'

'Had you left it unlocked?'

'*No*, Mr Black,' she responded sharply. 'I *never* do.'

So the beauty had claws. Even more intriguing, thought Tom.

'Two days later, the car was nowhere in sight after my walk. I had to call a taxi to get home. There it was, neatly parked in our driveway. For the next few days I hid in the bushes to watch, but I suppose he guessed and changed tactics. The following afternoon I came out of the NAAFI to find both rear tyres had been let down.'

Tom was incredulous. 'And you still didn't

13

say anything to your husband?'

'No.' It was almost defiant. 'He's a pilot. If he makes an error of judgement, he and the men he's transporting could fall out of the sky. He doesn't need more pressure than he's under at present. The media hype, photographers popping out of doorways. He hates it and it's getting to him.'

'Some men would revel in it,' Tom commented.

'Sam's not like that. He says he was just doing his job. It's only being puffed off because the MoD wants to compensate for the bad news about this unpopular war. Hurrah for our brave boys, and all that.'

Tom kept his views on the subject to himself. He knew a faint sense of envy; not of Collier's undoubted cool courage, but of his ability to win such devotion from this woman who could surely have any man she chose. Was she allowing hero-worship to govern her feelings for him?

'Mrs Collier, he will have to cope with this the way other husbands do, whatever their job entails. He'll surely want to protect you as much as you're trying to protect him.'

'I know, I know. That's why I'm here. Sam's ... well, he's hasty. If SIB handle it no one will get hurt.'

For hasty, read violent? 'Are you suggesting...?'

She waved her hands in a negative gesture. 'I don't know why I said that. An official approach will be better, is what I meant. You can more easily check on those nuisance phone calls, smashed eggs on the doorstep, skull and crossbones posters under the windscreen wipers.'

'All *that* has been going on without your husband's knowledge?' he exclaimed, almost accusingly.

'But the bastard's gone too far with that stunt this morning. He has to be stopped before something really drastic happens.' Her brown eyes appealed to him. 'Please help me.'

Out in the Incident Room Phil Piercey was gazing moodily at Tom's office door. 'She's been in there long enough to set it on fire!'

'Go in with more coffee. Catch 'em at it,' suggested Connie Bush with amusement.

Heather Johnson, always at odds with Piercey, concentrated on her computer, saying with a bite, 'She's married to a commissioned hero, who's also a hunk and a half. Highly unlikely she'd take a carnal interest in our 2IC. As for a gawky, goofy sergeant, she wouldn't even have noticed you, Phil, believe me.'

'She's right,' Connie agreed. 'We're women. We know.'

'Yeah, and you've both got the hots for her so-called hero. I saw you both growing orgasmic over his pictures in the papers.'

'Grow up!' snapped Heather, punishing her keyboard in her annoyance.

Connie's attention remained on their col-

15

league. 'Why the *so-called* hero?'

Piercey shrugged. 'I read between the lines of some newspaper accounts. While the "hunk and a half" was all too ready to recount what had happened, a few of the men he operates with have been tight-lipped on the subject. Guys like him get my shackles up. Jump on the fast track and keep on running.' Addressing the backs of the two women sergeants' heads, he added, 'You know who that bit of crumpet in there is, don't you? The daughter of Major General Sir Preston Phipps. So how did a spotty-faced student pilot come to take her fancy, eh?'

'Because he's a hunk and a half?' offered Derek Beeny, Piercey's friend and frequent working partner.

'Balls! Girl like that can choose from any number of brawny Hooray Henrys at polo matches or horse trials. Why waste herself on someone from the wrong side of the tracks?'

Connie Bush chuckled. 'You must be a closet reader of Catherine Cookson. *Wrong side of the tracks*, for God's sake!'

'Didn't you see the TV interview with his people when the news first broke? They run a fish-and-chip shop. Two young lads go to the local comprehensive, and their daughter does doorstep deliveries in a van with their name on the side. Hardly silver spoon territory, is it?'

'So yours is?' challenged Heather, swinging round to confront him. 'I'd put used car sales on a par with fish-and-chips. They're both high street businesses. If Collier's a kettle, you're

16

the bloody pot, Phil!'

Clearly stung by this attack – unusual in the frequent wordy confrontations with Heather – Piercey offered a weak defence. 'I've nothing against his family background. I'm just saying he's a jumped-up nobody who's wallowing in the attention he's getting over something that's being blown up out of all proportion.'

'So maybe his wife wants us to give him round-the-clock protection,' murmured Beeny with a smile.

'From men like Phil, I imagine,' said Heather with sarcasm.

Connie stirred things further. 'I'll volunteer as his personal bodyguard, like Kevin Costner with Whitney Houston in that film. They grew *really* close.'

The interchange abruptly halted as Tom's office door opened and he ushered his visitor between the desks to the main entrance, then on out to where she had left her car. The eyes of the two women assessed the cost of Margot Collier's clothes; the four men in the room were lasciviously assessing the shape beneath the clothes as they watched her departure. When Tom re-entered, his team appeared to be hard at work.

'Piercey, my office!'

Heather gave a malicious smile. She knew the summons was not to give the bumptious sergeant a special assignment. He was about to get a blast from a tongue well-known for its ability to reduce men – and women – to little

17

more than dust on the ground. Even so, she was as eager as the rest to discover what Margot Collier had divulged to their boss. Surely, she was one woman who could have no problems in her life.

Years of practice enabled Max Rydal to come from the depths of sleep when all his senses were urging him not to. Someone was moving stealthily about his room. He lay perfectly still, opening his eyes to mere slits. Then he sat up abruptly as recollection returned, and switched on the bedside light. Livya Cordwell, the woman he had spent the last three days and nights with, turned from the wardrobe to face him.

'Sorry. I should have remembered this door squeaked.'

Max took in the fact that she was fully dressed, with her suitcase at the door. A swift glance at the clock had him tossing aside the duvet. 'You were going,' he accused. 'Going while I slept!'

She did not deny it. 'We said our deliciously long, lingering goodbye last night, Max. Airport farewells are dire.'

'Dire or not, I want that extra time with you.' He headed for the bathroom. 'Give me ten and we'll go together.'

Swiftly performing the basics in the bathroom, he returned to pull on pale slacks and a burgundy roll-neck sweater, before snatching up his wallet and car-keys. As Livya made to open the door, he stopped her and drew her against him.

'Can't do the job properly with an audience of thousands,' he murmured, proceeding to 'do the job' very thoroughly.

The hotel corridors were quiet as they made their way to the vestibule, where a girl in a button-front overall was vacuuming and dusting. She gave them a knowing look.

Livya smiled up at Max. 'She thinks you're an errant husband and I'm your bit on the side.'

He squeezed her hand as they walked to his car. 'You couldn't ever be any man's bit on the side. You'd always be the main course.'

There was very little traffic about that early in the morning. Max was tempted to drive slowly to spin out the period of intimacy before arrival, but it was vital for Livya to catch her flight and there could be a snarl-up nearer to the airport.

He wished she had not to leave. The long weekend with her had been comprehensively stimulating. Half Czech, darkly attractive, Livya was intelligent, warm, funny and challenging. After three years of emotional hiatus following the death in a car crash of his pregnant wife, Max very much wanted to pursue and strengthen this relationship. There was much to hamper that desire. To paraphrase Gilbert and Sullivan, a soldier's life was not a happy one when it came to romance. The demands of duty overrode all else. Meetings had to be abandoned, promises invalidated, important occasions missed, all at very short notice when military

19

orders so demanded.

A soldier who was also a policeman had the frustration of being on call day and night during a vital case. On their first serious date Max had been summoned on the very point of taking Livya to bed. The mutual attraction had nevertheless flourished, perhaps because she was herself a soldier and understood the unavoidable disruptions to personal plans.

An additional problem was that she was based in London, which meant one of them having to fly to or from Germany in order to meet. All in all, it was a hit and miss romance. Livya had chanced her arm in opting to stay for another night and take the early flight to Heathrow. Providing it arrived on time she could dash to her flat, change into her uniform and reach the small unit commanded by Brigadier Andrew Rydal at the appointed hour. The fact that his lover worked for his father was a small cloud on Max's horizon, because she had a better understanding of the man than his son had ever had. Although loath to admit it, Max was jealous of Livya's high regard for the talented, charismatic widower; resentful of the many hours they spent together when his own with her were so scattered and few.

The flight was listed to depart on time, but the check-in clerk broke the news that thick fog over London and England's east coast made a diversion to Southampton necessary. Livya was highly annoyed.

'Even if I decline the coaches laid on to bus us

to Heathrow, and take the train at my own expense, I won't make it to the office until after lunch. What bloody ill luck!'

Max said soothingly, 'Can't be helped. If London's fogbound it'll be obvious that flights will be diverted.' He smiled at her. 'Southampton's more convenient than Birmingham.'

'I should have flown back last night,' she declared, unappeased by his attempt at consolation.

'It was probably foggy then.'

She flashed him a look full of irritation. 'Always got a pat response, haven't you.'

'Not always, no,' he said, stung by what he saw as an undeserved snipe at him.

She laid her hand on his arm. 'Sorry. I warned you airport farewells are dire.'

'Only when flights are delayed and there's nothing left to say.' Was that another pat response, he wondered. 'We have thirty minutes. Long enough for a coffee and croissant. Come on.'

He took her arm, led her to the small cafe near Passport Control, and ordered for them both while she settled on a high stool beside a pedestal table. When he joined her he broached the subject of their next meeting.

'If nothing serious breaks I should be able to get over for a couple of days in three weeks' time. We could do dinner and a show, or drive up to overnight in the Cotswolds and enjoy some interesting walking.' He smiled. 'Your turn to choose, ma'am.'

21

'Both would be nice, but the weather is sure to be the deciding factor. It usually is.'

She sounded distracted and merely played with her croissant. Max felt she had already departed in spirit. He was disappointed and grew defensive. 'Surely he's not such a martinet he won't make allowances for a diverted flight.'

'He's not aware of my intention to come here,' she replied, knowing Max was speaking of his father.

'Oh, I understood...'

'I lied.'

'You *haven't* told him about us?'

'My personal life is divorced from my work.'

'So why are you in a state about being diverted to Southampton?' he challenged, curiously shaken by her confession. 'Are you loath to tell him you're being bedded by his son?'

'Why would I be?'

'I can't think of a reason, but maybe there's one I don't know about.'

She stood, picking up her cabin bag. 'You should have stayed in bed, Max, then this pointless conversation wouldn't have taken place. I'm concerned by the delay because I take my job seriously and I'm meticulous about being where I should be during the specified hours. If you weren't so concentrated on bedding me you might have understood that by now.'

He made to follow her, but she joined a fast-growing queue leading to the passport controller's desk and made no attempt to glance back. Cursing his clumsy handling of the situation,

Max watched Livya vanish beyond the screens. He did know she loved and valued the work she did for the élite Intelligence unit headed by his father. He also knew she willingly sacrificed personal plans on demand. Her surprise decision to stay for one more night had delighted him, and what a night it had been. Yet she had allowed an unavoidable fact of life to demolish that pleasure. Or had it been his own jaundiced attitude towards her professionalism, he wondered as he plodded back to his car.

Driving moodily to the hotel where they had stayed together, he went up to their room for the lengthy shower he had bypassed to drive to the airport. Her perfume hung in the air in the bedroom; the scent of her talcum and some discarded tissues bearing her lipstick that sat in the small bathroom bin, all served to exacerbate his sense of loss.

Once more he pondered the notion of applying for a transfer to the UK, but it could be to somewhere so far distant from London the journey to meet up could be equally lengthy. In any case, he was not sure enough of Livya to make a serious career move at this stage.

Still experiencing a sense of anti-climax, Max decided to head for the restaurant where breakfast was now available. Nothing but a mountain of paperwork awaited him in his office, so he lingered over a substantial meal eaten while reading the English newspapers he had picked up on leaving the airport. All the usual crises and idiocies bumped up by newsmen anxious to increase circulation. Max put the papers aside in continuing dissatisfaction.

Back in his room in the Officers' Mess he unpacked his bag, then dressed in a white shirt, a dark suit and a tie sober enough to match his mood. Lacking Livya's zest for getting to work, he drove slowly around the perimeter road to where 26 Section Special Investigation Branch had moved in to new premises four months ago prior to Christmas. The heating system was still playing up. From past experience Max guessed it would be an ongoing problem.

A glance at the clock on the wall of the Incident Room showed that Livya's aircraft should be nearing Southampton. Was she counting the hours until she could get behind her desk ready to do Andrew Rydal's bidding? Why had she lied about revealing their relationship to his father?

'Good morning, sir.'

Max came from his thoughts to see Tom Black emerging from his office. His second-in-command looked serious, which explained why he had not bidden him good afternoon with his usual sly reference to a late start to the day.

'Good morning, Mr Black,' he responded formally. 'Something I should know about?'

Tom followed Max in to the Section Commander's office and shut the door. 'We've a tricky one here.'

'Oh? In what way tricky?'

'Harassment that began with moving the car from place to place, increased to incapacitating the vehicle, then putting threatening images under the wipers. Today he tried to run her off the road.'

'Sit down, Tom,' said Max, trying to concentrate. 'Who *her*?'

'Wife of Lieutenant Sam Collier, Army Air Corps.'

'The hero pilot?'

'The same.'

'Nothing tricky about that. We've come across it before when a guy gets a gong. There's always someone who resents it, has to demonstrate the fact by creating aggro. Has to get it out of his system. Picking on the wife is easier. Doesn't usually last long.'

'He tried to drive her off the road,' Tom repeated emphatically. 'That's bloody dangerous kind of aggro, sir.'

Max was surprised by the other man's passion, and his use of sir when they were alone. They were friends as close as their respective ranks allowed them to be.

'She probably exaggerated, Tom, shaken up by the earlier intimidation. Someone drove a little closer than advisable and she imagined the rest. Give the gen to George Maddox. It's a job for Uniform, not us.'

'No, sir,' said Tom with determination. 'Mrs Collier's not the kind of woman to imagine something like that. She asked for our help and I said we'll investigate.'

Max leaned back in his chair and studied Tom's face, which now bore the scar from an

25

attack by a crazed killer. Aside from the deep cut in his cheek, the blows had inflicted serious damage to his skull which kept him under medical supervision for a considerable time. He had been cleared as fit for duty five weeks ago, but Max now wondered if Tom was truly back to the man he was before the injury. It was unlike him to be so fiery over something that had occurred several times in their careers.

'What kind of woman is she?' Max asked quietly.

With slightly heightened colour, Tom said, 'She's suffered from dedicated harassment ranging from deflated car tyres, to smashed eggs on the doorstep, to death's head posters on the car – all that without telling her husband because she didn't want to add to the stress he's under as an operational pilot. Told me if he makes an error when flying it endangers his passengers' lives as well as his own.' He paused for breath. 'She could have been killed or injured this morning if she hadn't kept her head, and used her obvious intelligence by making a sudden sharp turn on to that track leading to the pumping station. She reckons the guy who tried to force her off the road is a member of Collier's squadron.'

'It's always one of the victim's colleagues, if you recall.' Further study of Tom's expression made him add, 'Doesn't this obviously intelligent woman realize her stressed husband will have to be told all if we do as she wants?'

'I made that very clear, but this morning's

attack has left her afraid it wouldn't stop at that. She believes someone means to kill her next time ... and she's pregnant.'

They stared at each other across the desk. It was a direct goad and they both knew it. Max was disappointed that his old friend should employ such a tactic, but it was to good effect.

'Then you had better keep your word and investigate, Sar'nt Major.'

There was an uneasy pause before Tom said, 'Sorry, that was a bit below the belt, sir. It's her fear of miscarrying a third time that has led her to act now. I do honestly believe this is more serious than cases we've come across before, because she revealed that her husband has also been receiving anonymous threatening letters. I'm confident this is a case for SIB not Uniform.'

Max gave a nod and turned pointedly to the paperwork in his tray. 'Collier doesn't sound much of a hero if he lets his missus fight his battles for him.'

Tom walked to his car feeling uncomfortable about the conversation with his boss, with whom he had a long-standing, warm relationship. They had served together in the past and both had welcomed the chance to do so again when Max was sent out to command 26 Section after double tragedy struck the former OC. The reference to the pregnant Margot Collier perhaps meeting death in a road accident had been out of order, Tom knew, but it had been born of his eagerness to chase up a situation he found highly intriguing. Besides, he had assured the victim SIB would act on her information.

678 Squadron, Army Air Corps had its hangars, workshops and operational pad way out on the furthest extremity of the base. Pulling up outside the Admin offices, Tom went in to ask the present whereabouts of Lieutenant Collier.

The blonde lance-corporal at the desk gave this apparent civilian in a dark-blue suit a straight look. 'Not another reporter! There can't be anything more to be squeezed from that story. Don't you people realize the lads are doing things like that all the time on active service – except they aren't married to bloody generals' daughters.'

So the resentment was pretty widespread, was it? Tom followed up on her words. 'You think that's the only reason Collier's being hailed as a hero so extensively?'

'Stands to reason,' she agreed with a nod. 'He's being pushed to the top by "Daddy" so he'll be worthy enough for the family. Feel a bit sorry for him, really. He's basically a nice guy. But he *must* have seen the writing on the wall before they got hitched, and he still went ahead.'

'Probably couldn't help himself,' mused Tom, thinking of the impact of the woman he had met a few hours ago.

'You can say that again. She homed in on him and marched him up the aisle before he knew what had hit him. Daft sod!'

Tom swiftly held up his SIB identification. 'If I was from the press you'd have just committed a chargeable offence, you brainless individual.'

The girl paled and got to her feet. 'Sorry, sir, I didn't know ... I just thought...'

'That's exactly what you *didn't* do! Blabbing to press or media is strictly not on. When it concerns a person of higher rank it's insubordination. The tabloids would have made a meal of your inane gossip. I'll report you to the Squadron Commander and ask that you work in future in a small back room. Now, where will I find Lieutenant Collier?'

Shaken by the ferocity of this attack and by the truth of his accusation, she pointed at the window. 'That's his Lynx coming down now, sir.'

A helicopter was approaching and losing height, so Tom went out to his car and drove across to park near the Control Tower. That stupid girl's comment gave him food for thought. He could not wait to meet the pilot who had been marched up the aisle by the gorgeous, cultured woman who had been in the office this morning. Tom could not imagine any man having to be dragooned into marriage with her.

The two pilots eventually climbed from the cockpit and walked to the Ops Centre deep in conversation. Tom watched them enter, gave them a good ten minutes, then crossed to seek his quarry, who should have cleared the debrief by then. It must have been swift. There was no sign of the pair. Introducing himself, Tom stated his business to the corporal on duty and was told Lieutenant Collier had gone to the crew room for a coffee.

'First right along the corridor, sir,' the man added helpfully. 'He's just got in from a patrol.'

The small airless room was full of noisy aircrew holding mugs of coffee and putting the world to rights in the way of men when they assemble. A sergeant pilot glanced across at the intruder and asked if he could be of help.

'Yes. I'd like a word with Lieutenant Collier.'

'Sure thing. That's him by the window.' He turned back to his voluble group. Next minute, one of them, wearing the single pip of a second-lieutenant, called out, 'Sam! Another guy here to chat up the conquering hero.'

Tom was a six-footer and sturdily built, but the unsmiling man who approached was six-four, at least, and impressively muscular. He was also deeply tanned, with crisp hair bleached almost white by the Afghan sun, which made his dark-brown eyes seem all the more arresting. He looked like a man who could fight any battle totally unaided. So why was his wife so afraid he could not?

Two

Sam Collier jammed his foot on the brake and came to a halt at the roadside where he sat staring ahead and breathing heavily, his hands gripping the wheel so tightly his knuckles were white.

'Calm it! Calm it!' he muttered through clenched teeth.

It was impossible. Rage surged through his body and senses. He had just been utterly humiliated. Not only by the scar-faced Redcap, but because the bastard had turned the screw of Margot's betrayal.

Sam could still picture the disdain almost amounting to contempt in the man's eyes as he had listed what she had suffered in silence over the past few weeks. How *could* she have kept him in ignorance? Worse still, how could she have run to some other man for help? Sam heard again the caustic tone of Black's comment that she had not wanted to stress her husband. As if he was a total wimp!

Fresh anger and humiliation washed over him. How could she have allowed herself to be subjected to that catalogue of persecution, and the suggested threat it carried, without giving him the opportunity to defend her? He had a shrewd idea who might be behind it; the writer of those bloody letters. While he could ride out that situation perfectly well, attacks on his wife had to be countered with action.

Resting his forehead on his hands still gripping the wheel, pain formed a lump in his chest. Not only the supercilious detective, but Margot's tormentor must believe he was not man enough to face up to and deal with any threat to his wife's safety ... and she must also believe that. Dear God, whoever tried to drive her off the road this morning could have killed her, and their unborn child. Yet she had appealed to a stranger. It was a public denial of her husband of three years.

With an unsteady hand Sam took from the glove box the flask he kept there, and drank deeply. Vodka, undetectable on the breath, would counteract the familiar shakes. Tilting his head back he closed his eyes. He was on a roundabout whirling faster and faster, out of control. One day his grip on the handrail would slip and he would be flung out into a dark void.

He had stepped on it with eyes wide open, because they had seen only a girl so dazzling he was blind to all else. An international air show: Sergeant Collier had performed aerobatics with the Blue Eagles team. Back on the ground he was walking to the marquee where he could shower and change on this sweltering day, when he turned to acknowledge a colleague's shouted message then turned back to collide

32

with something very soft and very voluble. His hefty boot had landed four-square on a small foot shod with a pale-lemon strappy sandal. The exposed gold-tipped toes began immediately to bleed.

The girl was clearly in pain, but she was so stunning Sam's normal self-assurance deserted him. The first-aid tent was all of five hundred yards away. His victim could not possibly walk that far, yet he could not leave her there bleeding profusely while he fetched medical help. He stood mumbling apologies until he acted on the only solution he could come up with. Picking her up in his arms, he strode purposefully while demanding ease of progress through the milling crowd.

The incident should have ended when he handed responsibility to St John Ambulance staff, mumbled another apology, and went off for the much needed shower. However, fresh and spruced-up, he could not resist returning to check on the most tantalizing girl he had ever encountered. Having been bewitched into obeying her command to carry her to the VIP enclosure, young Sergeant Collier immediately realized that he should have bowed out after that first meeting.

Coming face-to-face with a handsome military man wearing red tabs and a major general's badges of rank, he was introduced to 'Daddy' by the enchanting creature still happily in his arms. Sam had been given a cool, optical head-to-boots assessment; had been told to set Miss

Phipps on one of the upholstered chairs. Then, with a toneless but meticulously polite word of thanks, he had been dismissed. Obliged to straighten and salute, Sam was further discomposed by the sight of the girl smilingly blowing him kisses from behind her father's back.

Margot Phipps was used to getting what she wanted, so she soon traced the blond pilot who had taken her by storm. Unable to resist her, Sam embarked on a passionate affair, ignoring his alter ego who warned of hazards ahead.

Sir Preston Phipps took his daughter aside to persuade her that an NCO with a broad Yorkshire accent, son of fish-and-chip shop parents was not the right partner for her. As usual, she had disarmed him with persuasive affection and told him she would never be happy again if she could not have the man she adored.

He then talked to Sam, but it was soon apparent that it was impossible for a major general to have a man-to-man discussion about his daughter with a sergeant. Sam responded to everything with a crisp 'Yes, sir' or 'No, sir', which stole the older man's thunder and increased his dislike of someone he regarded a social climber.

Margot's first pregnancy settled the issue. They drove to Cornwall and were married by special licence in an old village church with a backdrop of wild, craggy moorland. On learning a grandchild was on the way, Preston Phipps acted swiftly. Sergeant Collier's name was put forward for a commission. Then came Sierra Leone and Margot's miscarriage. Sir

Preston laid the blame for this at Sam's door, not only because he had been careless enough to be captured by teenage mercenaries, but because he clearly came from weak stock. No credit was given to Sam's subsequent daring escape from captivity.

The second miscarriage had strengthened Phipps's claim. Quite when it had dawned on Sam that Margot was desperate for him to prove his worth to her father he could not pinpoint, but the obligation to excel began to dog his days. It became essential to father a child – preferably a lusty son – and as pilot, soldier and fighting man he must stand head and shoulders above his peers. At six feet four it was physically true in many instances, but it was his personal resilience and procreative ability being questioned. Margot loved him madly, but she was obsessed by the compulsion to make her widowed father love him, too.

In addition, Sam had to deal with resentment from a few of his colleagues. Who could blame them? There was no denying his father-in-law's influence had secured the sudden elevation to officer status. That he would most probably have been commissioned within a year or two was discounted. Sam, himself, would have been prouder of his new rank if it had been earned in the usual way.

Unscrewing the flask, he took another long drink to combat his reviving anger. Had Margot no idea what she was doing with her conflicting desires for him to excel and yet protect him from the stress of doing so? Her overwhelming delight with the publicity and squadron pride over the action in Afghanistan which had earned him an MC, took no account of what it had cost him then, and what it was costing them both now. She had her way. Major General Sir Preston Phipps was impressed. Keep up this level of excellence and, providing this third pregnancy ran its full term, the fish-and-chip boy might meet the full criteria.

More vodka to boost the resolution to drive home now and tell his wife they could not go on as they were; warn her that what she had built up could easily come crashing down. Yes, and make her aware of his anger over her lack of confidence in his ability to champion and protect her. Running to the bloody Redcaps instead!

Max moodily flipped through stuff that had accumulated in his in tray over the four days he had been with Livya. Most of it was routine paperwork issued to every officer on the base, which they were expected to peruse and memorize. They could not, of course, because they were too busy to plough through pages detailing such things as alterations to the siting of fire hydrants, new regulations governing the size of replacement office desks as from January 2008 and memoranda on maintenance and repairs of washing machines in Other Ranks' accommodation blocks. Unfortunately, when they were away in a war zone, or even on a military exercise, this 'bumf' mounted up to await their return.

Max had a cupboard where he stacked these papers under appropriate headings, so that he could hook out the relevant pages if he needed to bone up on the subject. Sod's Law decreed that the most mundane information would be needed the moment it became buried at the bottom of a huge pile.

A glance at the clock told him it was lunchtime. After his large breakfast he was not hungry. He supposed Livya was by now swiftly donning her uniform prior to taking a taxi to her office, there breathlessly to offer his father a lying explanation. Just as well he had no contact with Andrew Rydal. He might be tempted to tell him of the game Captain Cordwell was playing.

Heavy-hearted over the airport parting this morning, and the clash of temperament with Tom Black just now, Max was deciding to go in search of alcoholic stimulus at a small hotel just outside the main gate when Sergeant Maddox, senior NCO of the uniformed branch, appeared in the office doorway.

'Are you busy, sir?'

Max smiled and indicated his in tray. 'Only with this lot. Happy to be interrupted.'

The burly Redcap entered and carefully closed the door, which surprised Max somewhat.

'Problem, George?'

'One for SIB, I think. No, I'm sure it is.'

'Sit down and outline what you've got so far,' Max said, his spirits rising at the prospect of some real work.

A large man passionate about golf, rugby and hot-air ballooning, Maddox had appeared unshakable until a family massacre at Christmas had affected him deeply. Childless himself he nevertheless deplored crimes against minors more than any he handled. He spoke in harsh tones now.

'Corporal Melcher was called to her quarter by Mrs Laine this morning. Stacey, her daughter, was in a state of near hysteria. She claims Major Clarkson indecently assaulted her.'

'What?'

'I know,' he agreed with raised eyebrows. 'He was called by the mother yesterday because the girl had a very high temperature and severe pains in her stomach. He examined her, said she had a viral infection that could be treated at home, and gave medication to ease the discomfort. This morning Stacey threw a wobbly and told her mother the MO had put his fingers between her legs and stroked her intimately, while whispering suggestively in her ear.'

'He surely wasn't alone with her.'

'Not during the examination, but Mrs Laine admits she left him in the bedroom writing a prescription while she went downstairs for a glass of water to dissolve the powder he had given for the patient. Stacey claims he pulled back the duvet and did it then.'

'So why wait until the morning to report it?'

38

'She told Melcher she was shocked and too frightened of the consequences if she said anything. She worried about it all night, wondering what best to do. Seems she's a bosom pal of Ginny Clarkson. Said she couldn't believe her friend's father would do such a disgusting thing, but she decided to keep quiet for the sake of her friendship with Ginny. In the morning she realized she couldn't bear to face him again and confided in her mother.'

Max knew the Medical Officer well. Charles Clarkson had a brusque manner but he was a first-rate doctor. The word was that he had distinguished himself as a young medic in Bosnia, dealing with the horrendous inhumanity of that campaign with compassion and iron nerves. Had the stress of what he had seen and done there tardily overtaken him, as it had many men who had served in that campaign, and led him to act out of character? Clarkson was married to an attractive Portuguese, a devoted father of four. Surely not the type of man to molest a young patient, yet Max's profession had taught him anyone was capable of anything when driven to it.

'Is she lying, George?'

He shrugged. 'Melcher said she was putting on a good act, if she was, but teenage girls can make high drama of anything.'

'If he did it, it *is* high drama,' Max pointed out. 'He'll have seriously damaged his career. I can see why you want us to take over.'

'It's a serious charge, sir.'

39

'One that'll be the devil to deal with. Her word against his. No physical evidence if he simply stroked her with his fingers, as there could be if he had actually penetrated her, and there's no way of proving he spoke dirty words to her.' He sighed. 'We'll investigate, George. The Laines have made an official charge that has to be dealt with.'

'Mrs Laine was ready to lynch the Doc. Said she'd warn every mother there's a sex maniac in our midst.'

'Bring him in. I'll interview him right away. The last thing we want is a swarm of maternal vigilantes marching to his house. The girl's father is away, I guess?'

'Small Arms course. Back at the weekend.'

'What rank is he?'

'Sergeant, sir. Steady, reliable, collects suits of armour. He'll be hot on this.'

'Like any father. Pity he's away. He might have put a clamp on some of the hysteria while we look into the charge.'

After detailing Connie Bush and Heather Johnson to interview Stacey and calm the mother, Max felt more himself than he had since Livya walked away from him this morning. Shifting forms and pamphlets from place to place had left him too much time to think and to question his actions. Now he must question another man's.

Major Charles Edwin Clarkson was a tall, swarthy, decisive man. When George Maddox brought him in fifteen minutes later, he was pale with shock, his dark eyes staring stonily as if at something beyond reality.

'Sit down, Major,' said Max briskly.

The MO remained standing. 'Was it really necessary to bring me here under escort, like a criminal? I thought you'd have the decency to afford me the privilege of rank and deal with this fiction in my surgery or home.'

'Sit down, Major. The charge made against you is a serious one. The more you cooperate the sooner we can get to the bottom of what happened yesterday at the Laine house.'

'*Nothing* happened!' he said forcefully.

When Max remained silent, Clarkson sat in the chair facing him. 'I don't believe this. Why would she tell such lies? Christ, she's one of Ginny's little coterie of schoolfriends. Stacey's been to us for tea and for my kids' birthday parties. Jean Laine and my wife often chatted when she came to collect Stacey. We're all on easy terms. *Why* would she tell such lies?'

'You were called by Mrs Laine to attend her sick daughter. Did she greet you in a friendly manner – on the easy terms you claim there are between you?'

'Of course.'

'First names?'

'No, that's never been the case.'

'But she was as friendly as she had always been?'

'She was overly anxious. Since we had that meningitis scare on the base, all parents fear the worst when their child ails. Jean Laine betrayed all the symptoms of panic when I arrived.'

'You just now said she was friendly.'

'In as much as she gripped my arm and said she knew she could trust me to help her through this with Jeff away.'

'Isn't that what most anxious mothers would do in the absence of their husbands?'

Clarkson glared. 'I can't see the relevance of this. It's my treatment of the patient that's being questioned, isn't it?'

'The patient was upstairs in her bedroom?'

'Yes.'

'In her nightclothes?'

'Yes.'

'Describe them.'

Anger flashed in the dark eyes still reflecting shock. 'Not being a connoisseur of children's sleeping attire, all I can say is they were pyjamas similar to those my daughters wear.'

'How did Stacey greet you?'

'As always,' he replied pugnaciously.

'And that is?'

'She said "Hello, Major Doc." It's what all my kids' friends call me. Then she put on something of an act I imagined was to impress her mother, and said she was feeling "utterly grotty". There was a bit of head-rolling on the pillow and a few faint moans.'

'You believed it was to impress her mother, not you?'

'She knows me well enough to be sure it wouldn't.'

'Go on.'

'I knew immediately that she was suffering from the viral infection affecting ten other children at the school. It induces aggravated colic which drastically raises the temperature; symptoms that alarm the kids and their parents into believing it's something far more dangerous.'

'And?'

'*And*, I examined Stacey's abdomen, checked her pulse and temperature, asked if she had any pain in her limbs or her jaw, although I was certain of my initial diagnosis.'

'Was her mother present during the examination?'

'Of course, damn you,' Clarkson retaliated heatedly.

'Did you lower the girl's pyjama trousers during the examination?'

Clarkson glared again. 'How else could I feel her abdomen?'

'It was necessary to do that?'

'She had severe stomach cramps. Of course it was bloody necessary.'

'How far down did you pull her pyjama trousers?'

'I didn't expose the pubic area, if that's what you're getting at,' he snapped.

'After the examination did you adjust the trousers, or did she?'

'I nodded and said something like, "That's fine, thank you, Stacey." Then I turned to Jean and told her there was nothing to worry about, it was simply a virus going the rounds. When I looked back at Stacey she...' He stopped and frowned. 'She was still lying there with her body exposed.'

'What happened then?' asked Max.

'Nothing *happened*! What d'you take me for? I told her she could get under the duvet again because I'd finished my examination.'

'Did she cover her stomach before pulling up the duvet?'

'I've no idea. I explained to Jean that the sachets I took from my bag and gave to her contained a powder to be mixed with tepid water, and assured her they would alleviate the stomach cramps quite swiftly.'

'Did you then send her downstairs to fetch a glass of water?'

'No, I did not! I began to write a prescription for further sachets, but Jean rushed away to fetch water so that Stacey could take a dose immediately. As I said, parents panic unnecessarily.'

'So you were alone with Stacey in her bedroom for around five minutes?'

Clarkson gazed at Max during a lengthening silence as the shock of what was happening hit him anew. 'You don't believe these lies, do you?'

'What I believe or not has no bearing on the case. A serious charge has been laid against you and I have to uncover the truth. You were alone with the girl long enough to act as she claims. Yes or no?'

'*Yes*. I had time enough to ravish her, steal her

44

junk jewellery, strangle her teddy bear, STAND ON MY HEAD,' he said, voice rough with anger. 'But I continued writing the prescription for further medication while reassuring my daughter's friend she'd be bouncing back in a couple of days. *Nothing happened!*'

'When Mrs Laine left the bedroom why did you stay there?'

'I was writing the prescription.'

'That could have been done downstairs. Why stay alone with a young girl in her night-clothes?' probed Max.

'I was in a room with a *patient*,' he said, thoroughly rattled. 'I'm a happily married man with four kids, not a closet paedophile! Why, in God's name, have they invented such a damaging story? *Why?*'

Hiding his personal conclusions, Max asked neutrally, 'Has there been any bad blood between your family and the Laines? Has your daughter fallen out with Stacey? Perhaps the little coterie of friends you mentioned has ostracized the girl for some reason.'

Clarkson sank back in his chair, saying bitterly, 'Does it matter? The blow has been struck, for whatever reason.'

Max got to his feet. 'My two female sergeants are presently interviewing the girl and her mother in depth. When they report back I'll decide what action is necessary. Meanwhile, we'd like the clothes you wore yesterday for forensic examination, and there'll be a brief personal one.'

45

'What!'

'If you had gone downstairs with Mrs Laine you'd not have left yourself open to these charges. I'll inform you of what action will be taken after discussing your professional duties with the Garrison Commander. Until a decision has been reached I suggest you go home and break the news to your wife.'

Connie Bush and Heather Johnson were friends who enjoyed pairing up on investigations. They sat on chairs in Stacey Laine's bedroom where the walls were covered in posters of pop stars and five-minute-wonder 'celebrities'. On a shelf alongside the bed were a family of teddy bears, a panda, a giraffe and an elephant, all well-cuddled judging by their condition. Signs of emerging adolescence still clinging to the comfort of childhood.

Stacey looked flushed and belligerent; her mother was bristling with anger one minute and fussing over her daughter the next. Both woman and girl were badly overweight; they had similar podgy features and pale eyes. There appeared to be a good mother–daughter bond between them.

Having opened the interview with comments on the obvious subjects of the fourteen-year-old's admiration, and shown fond interest in the stuffed toys, the SIB sergeants determined Stacey's exact age, her favourite subjects at school, and who her friends were. Connie carefully picked up on the mention of Virginia

Clarkson.

'The Medical Officer's daughter?' At Stacey's nod, she asked, 'How long have you two been friends?'

'All the time we've been in Germany.'

'Which is?' put in Heather.

Jean Laine said harshly, 'Two years, but that's the end of it. Stacey's been in his house often, had invites to Ginny's parties. When I think he could have taken Stacey in one of the bedrooms and done God knows what to her! He should be struck off the medical list and kicked out of the army. I hope you're going to lock him up meanwhile. He's two girls of his own, you know. They're not safe.'

Better at keeping her cool than Heather, Connie said quietly, 'We're here to establish exactly what happened last night, Mrs Laine. Perhaps you'd let Stacey tell us in her own words.' She smiled at the girl well hidden beneath a red and black patterned duvet. 'Take your time, Stacey. Try to remember the details as clearly as possible.'

The girl gazed at the ceiling for a moment or two before answering. 'I trusted him. He's my best friend's dad, so I never expected him to be so beastly. I've seen him lots of times at Ginny's, and he's been all right. Mrs Clarkson's been around then, of course, so I s'pose he had to be nice ... except...'

'Yes?' prompted Heather gently.

Stacey brought her hands from beneath the duvet and concentrated on them as she mum-

47

bled, 'He ... well, he once patted my bottom as I went past his chair.'

'*What?*' cried her mother. 'Why didn't you tell me? I'd have sorted him then and this would never have happened.'

'How did he pat your bottom?' asked Connie. 'Was it a fatherly gesture from someone you know well?'

Stacey's head rolled a negative on the black pillow. 'It was sexy.'

Against Jean Laine's snort of disgust, Heather probed further. 'It was more than a light pat?'

'More of a grope, really. And he touched my breast at their Christmas party.'

'*What?*' cried her mother again.

Connie intervened swiftly. 'In what circumstances did he touch you, Stacey?'

'We were playing charades and dressing up. He made an excuse to help me put on an old feather scarf and he brushed his hand over my breast. He smiled and said, "That's nice, Stacey."'

'And you didn't mind that he'd touched you?' asked Heather.

The girl looked up from her twisting hands to meet their eyes. 'Of course I minded. It was disgusting. But I couldn't say or do anything, could I? Mrs Clarkson was there. So were Ginny, Zoe, James and Daniel. They wouldn't have believed me, anyway. And *he* would have denied it. He only does things to me when no one can see what he's up to.'

With her pen poised over her notebook, Connie said urgently, 'There were other occasions like that? Was there any time when Major Clarkson suggested you went with him to another room, or met him somewhere on your own?'

Again a shake of her head. 'He knew I'd never do that. But he made it plain it's what he wanted.'

'How?'

'You know. Secret smiles, always looking at my breasts, trying to get me in the front seat when he ran a group of us home, so he could touch my leg when he changed gears.'

It was too much for Mrs Laine. 'Stacey! Stacey, love, how could you have kept all that from me?'

'I just told you. He would have said I was making it up. Nobody would have believed me. Besides, Ginny would have turned them all at school against me and the whole base would think I'd encouraged him. I couldn't face that, Mum.' She began to cry and her mother gathered her up to rock her comfortingly.

The sergeants looked at each other expressively, then Connie explained the situation. 'You'll have to face a great deal of gossip now, Stacey. It's inevitable, and your friendship with the Clarkson children will be over. You do understand that?'

The sick girl emerged from her mother's embrace, red-eyed and tear-streaked. 'He put his fingers there. He *felt* me there. Tickled between my legs,' she confessed in a rush. 'He said he

49

wanted to see me naked, touch me all over. He said he wanted *me* to touch *him* where it would excite him the most. He said he thought all the time about making me his slave who would do anything he wanted.'

Jean Laine was now crying, saying over and over, 'Jeff'll *kill* him when he hears about this.'

'Neither you nor your husband must do anything, Mrs Laine. We will handle it from now on,' Heather told her sternly. 'Stacey, are you willing to repeat all you have just told us during an official recorded interview?'

The girl looked wildly at her mother. 'I don't feel well, Mum. I can't answer any more questions.'

'Someone else will come to see you tomorrow,' Connie told her reassuringly. 'Stop worrying and concentrate on recovering from the nasty bug you have.'

'I won't have to see *him*, will I? He'll say I'm lying.'

'You won't have to see Major Clarkson or any of his family while the case is being investigated.'

They left Stacey burrowing under her duvet with a teddy bear clutched against her, and walked out to sunshine and fresh air. Seated in their car they exchanged impressions.

'Can you imagine the Doc doing that?' Heather asked.

'He's a bit of a cold fish, but that doesn't mean anything,' Connie said frankly. 'Men of his age can get indecent urges that shock even

50

themselves. Let's *assume* he's going through a mid-life crisis. Married eighteen years ago; sired four kids. Life now seems to revolve around them and their occupations. His free time is spent driving them to ballet lessons, football practice, swimming, tennis, youth club, parties. The house is constantly swarming with their friends who invade every room and play pop music in conflicting styles at full volume. His wife is forever preparing food for the horde, washing football gear, sewing sequins on tutus or helping them rehearse their lines for a school play. She has no time or energy for sex. He's fast losing his libido, so he gives himself some stuff from his surgery to pep it up. Result: the nearness of tender young female flesh drives his inhibitions away. He's tormented by his daughters' schoolfriends; can't stop himself from touching them and dreaming of initiating them to the pleasures he rarely gets these days.'

'Mm, add to that the fact that he spends his working days dealing with sickness and injury, listening to the moans of young, virile lads who have sex as often as they have weekends, and you have a man bursting to break out from the sober, responsible guy he's always been.'

'So why doesn't he go to a brothel in town where girls are willing to act as a sex slave?'

Heather shook her head. 'Not the same. It would lack the excitement of tasting forbidden fruit. However, I'd guess if he found himself alone with a teen virgin, he'd back off.'

'You don't see him as a potential rapist?'

51

'Do you?'

'No. If what Stacey says is true, he's probably just using her as stimulation before slinking off somewhere quiet to masturbate. A pathetic bid to console himself his virility isn't on the wane.'

'OK, let's pursue that theme,' said Heather. 'Why that lumpy girl we've just seen? She's not looking her best right now, of course, but there are others around her age, slim, gorgeous and flirty, who would inspire a great many men to fantasize about making them their sex slave.'

'Sure there are. Teen teasers who encourage middle-aged admiration just for kicks, and the Doc's quite a dish to look at.'

'But a cold fish,' Heather reminded her with a grin.

'Adds to the challenge for some.'

'But not for Stacey?'

'She's lying.'

'I think so, too.' Heather switched on the ignition. 'The test will come when we ask her to record her damning evidence.'

'Even if she backs off then, it'll be too late for Clarkson. His name'll be mud before the sun sets tonight.'

Three

At the briefing late that afternoon, Tom led off by detailing his interview with Sam Collier. 'On the surface, he's what you'd expect of a guy who's twice distinguished himself. I checked his record. Three years ago, on detachment in Sierra Leone, he and three others were captured by trigger-happy teen mercenaries high on some kind of opiate. Our guys were subjected to sadistic humiliation and semi-starved for a week, until Sergeant Collier conceived and led an escape.

'We've all read about his recent rescue of four wounded men at risk to his own life. Action his colleagues should surely applaud, yet it appears that one of them resents the public acclaim and has mounted a campaign of harassment against Mrs Collier that culminated in attempting to drive her off the road this morning.

'She identified the rogue car as a light-blue Audi. Beeny found one parked outside an accommodation block. The owner is on UK leave, so anyone could have borrowed it. That means a hell of a lot of questioning. The anonymous letters sent to Lieutenant Collier threatening to "tell the truth, remove the blinkers from

53

everyone's eyes" he shredded. They were printed in red felt-tip and couched in text-speak. So no clues there to aid us.'

Tom glanced at the faces watching him and saw a leer on Phil Piercey's. It put a bite in his tone. 'I want this given top priority. Four months ago, before Christmas, we had to deal with two murders. We can be quick off the mark on this opportunity to prevent a tragedy by removing the threat as soon as possible. Mrs Collier was composed enough to escape danger today. I want this sorted before the worst happens.' Giving Max a swift glance, he added, 'This isn't merely a case of a person expressing resentment. Someone out there intends to harm the Colliers, perhaps fatally. I've asked Sergeant Maddox to mount a guard on their house and, first thing tomorrow, I want you all out questioning the whole squadron.'

'Question them on what, sir?' asked Piercey with feigned innocence.

Tom countered his taunt deliberately. 'Not on how much they fancy Margot Collier, Piercey. We need to pinpoint anyone with a more than understandable resentment or dislike of her husband. A person eaten up with jealousy of his high-ranking father-in-law's influence which brought swift commissioned rank, and whose money probably paid for the Jag the Colliers drive around in together. Someone like you, Sergeant.'

They all laughed, and Tom continued. 'That any number of men envy Lieutenant Collier for

54

having such a beautiful, wealthy wife doesn't come into the equation. If the attacks were solely on him I'd include it, but they've been aimed at her. The intention being to make him pay for his golden-boy status, and pay as dearly as possible.'

Sergeant Olly Simpson, idly doodling on a scratch-pad, glanced up as Tom fell silent. 'The anonymous letters, sir. Did you discover from Lieutenant Collier what they referred to? What was the truth that should be told? Whose eyes must be cleared of blinkers? It suggests to me that the writer believes him to have done something that's been hushed up. By the top-brass dad-in-law?'

'That was my first thought,' Tom said. 'I don't think there's any doubt Sir Preston Phipps raised his daughter's husband to an acceptable rank by plenty of arm-twisting, although that promotion would surely have come in the normal way soon after. But I don't see a distinguished general covering up a military transgression serious enough to set in motion a lethal campaign.'

'Did Lieutenant Collier give you any info on the letters? You didn't say, sir,' put in Staff Sergeant Melly.

Tom shook his head. 'He claimed to be puzzled by them. But he knows what's behind them all right.'

'It has to be something the writer knows about but can't prove; something detrimental to a man hailed as a hero,' said Piercey. 'He's ignored the letters, so the threats to his wife are designed to make him spill the beans.'

Tom frowned. 'If your kids' comic language means you think Collier is being pressurized to reveal something that would destroy his heroic status, I thought we established that belief five minutes ago. Haven't you been listening, Sergeant?'

'Can we be certain of the number of letters received?' Sergeant Roy Jakes asked. 'Could be he's had blackmail demands. Getting at his wife is inducement to pay up.'

'A strong possibility,' Tom agreed. 'I'm about to run a check on his recent financial trans-actions, but the money is all on his wife's side and he refuses to have a joint account. He was very uptight on the subject when I spoke to him today.'

Undaunted, Piercey said, 'That's for public effect. You can't tell me he doesn't let her pay for anything he wants.'

'I'm not telling you that,' Tom snapped. 'I've had enough of your inane input. Shut it!'

Max had been sitting quietly throughout this discussion, but he now entered it. 'Let's consider another slant. The letters are the result of common resentment by someone who's been passed over for promotion; whose wife or girl-friend has cheated on him or walked out; who's recently smashed up his car and can't afford to buy another because the insurance had run out. Sam Collier appears to have the Midas touch and deserves to have something to worry about for a change. But this double hero ignores the slyly threatening letters, so eggs are smashed on his doorstep, the tyres of his wife's Jag are let down, silly skull and crossbones flyers are put under her wipers. Maybe *that* will spoil his complacent life.

'This morning, some German druggie in a blue Audi has a bit of sport putting the frighteners on a lone female driver in a jazzy car by side-swiping it on a straight, empty stretch of road. A quick check with Klaus Krenkel on whether he's had other reports on this nutter could sort that, and a couple of you doing a bit of casual questioning could soon pinpoint someone going through a tough enough period to spark malice against a colleague who seems not to put a foot wrong.'

Tom was annoyed, but he hid it to agree that a more innocent interpretation *could* be put on the facts. 'It's up to you all to investigate and come up with the correct one.'

'Now let's consider the charge of indecent assault that's been levelled against Major Clarkson,' said Max in a positive change of subject. 'He denies it vehemently. I saw no sign of guilt in his manner. He looked genuinely shocked. It's a messy situation. No evidence; no proof. It's the girl's word against his.'

'We interviewed Stacey at length,' offered Connie Bush. 'She maintained the MO had touched her intimately on several other occasions at parties for his children. We're all familiar with kids' reluctance to tell anyone about

57

behaviour of that kind, because it's too embarrassing and people will think they encouraged it, but Heather and I both think the girl is fantasizing. If he really did feel her bottom and her breasts in his own home, surely she would make excuses not to go there. She thought it disgusting, so she's unlikely to give him opportunities to do it again.'

'Also,' said Heather, 'if he has been touching her up whenever he can, she would surely have done all she could to keep her mother in the bedroom so that she'd not be alone with him. In our opinion, Stacey has a heavy crush on the Doc and is easing the yearning by imagining he has the hots for her. Being examined intimately in her bedroom brought her adolescent passion to the boil – the virus induces fever – and she fantasized overnight until she believed her fantasy. The prospect of facing him again with these erotic thoughts ruling her brought panic, so she turned to her mother, with whom she has a solid relationship.'

Connie said, 'Now Mrs Laine's brought us in, Stacey's embroidering her story to justify her claim. She has no real notion of what she's doing to the Doc and his family. She's totally self-absorbed, like many teens.'

Max nodded. 'A very balanced summation. I'm handing this to our Joint Response Team who'll video their interview with the girl and deal with the sensitive side of this case. The Commander, Army Medical Services will act for Major Clarkson in harness with the Garrison

58

Commander. At best, I imagine they might rule that he deals only with male military personnel during this investigation. To suspend him from all duty could suggest the MO is guilty as charged.'

'We warned Mrs Laine not to spread slanderous gossip, but she will,' said Connie.

'Of course she will. We can't tape up her mouth. As I said, it's a messy situation that will encompass Mrs Clarkson and their children. It's certain to be all round the school by tomorrow. They'll have to be posted elsewhere as soon as the dust settles, of course, but doubts on his probity will follow them. The unique military grapevine will see to that. Young Stacey Laine has a lot to answer for.'

When Tom entered his rented house a short distance outside the main gate he was irritated to find Hans Graumann halfway down the stairs with his daughter Maggie in tow.

'Hi, Dad,' she greeted casually, but the German boy was, as always, strictly formal.

'Good ee-ven-ing, sir.'

'Where's your mother?' Tom asked brusquely, causing Maggie to frown.

'Still sewing that hideous dress-and-coat thing for Major Rhodes' wife, of course.'

Taking exception to her tone, Tom said, 'There's no *of course* about it. She makes wedding outfits because she enjoys it. It's light relief from looking after you three.' He glanced up the stairs. 'Are Gina and Beth up there?'

'*Yes*, Dad, we've been perfectly chaperoned.'

'Don't be cheeky!'

'I'm not. That *was* what you wanted to know, wasn't it?'

He walked through to the dining room without another word. His eldest girl had grown pert and difficult to approach over the past four months. Since her friendship with the German boy living across the road. Tom could pinpoint the exact cause for the change in Maggie. She was just two months into her teens, that was all, and that boy appeared to have taken her over. What was Nora thinking of to let them go upstairs together?

She was, indeed, busy at her sewing machine in the room they used for dining only when they had guests. The rest of the time they ate at the breakfast bar in the kitchen.

'Hallo, love.' She greeted him without looking away from her work. 'I want to finish these buttonholes before supper. A glass of wine would help it along.'

'Maggie and Hans were upstairs together.'

'They're all upstairs. Rehearsing some kind of drama for parents' evening at the school.' Nora turned then to study him. 'Bad day?'

He walked to the sideboard for glasses. 'I've had better.'

'Don't tell me you're starting a big case just as we plan to go home and visit the parents.'

'It won't stop you and the girls from going.'

'So what's new?'

He poured ruby-red wine in two glasses and

took one to her. 'What's for supper?'

'Grilled lamb chops followed by summer pudding, *sir*.'

He looked away from her challenging eyes. 'Just asking.'

'If you can't wait another half hour, I won't get in a huff if you put on your chef's hat.'

'I can wait.'

He stood moodily sipping wine and watching Nora's sure fingering of plum-coloured silk. This was her hobby, as model steam engines were his. She was good at it, and orders for bridal and evening wear flowed in. It was a useful addition to their finances, particularly with three girls fast growing up and demanding the latest fashions. They did not always get them when the price for fancy trainers or some gadget was ridiculously extortionate, but they were able to hold their own with their peers often enough to satisfy them.

Tom had never objected to his home frequently being festooned with silk and satin, although he would give a lot to see dirty football gear or windsurfing boards somewhere around to level the balance in this female-dominated family. He admired his wife's skill at elaborate dressmaking. He studied her now as she swished the plum material from side to side with expertise. She wore a loose checked shirt and purple trousers – comfortable working clothes. Her brown hair was drawn back in a scrunchie. It shone with health. He loved to feel its softness against his skin in bed; found pleasure in stroking it.

When she wore it swept up in a sophisticated style, he enjoyed wrecking the complicated arrangement to let it fall long and straight as soon as they returned home.

Nora had a slim, neat body. No page three top-heavy bimbo, she, but Tom had always been aroused by her gentle curves. Unbidden came a memory of full breasts pushing against a silk shirt, and a fall of blue-black hair around a beautiful tanned face. And those legs!

He moved to the sideboard to top up his glass. Sam Collier was a big, bluff man with a broad Yorkshire accent and no obvious charm. How had that pair ever got together? Two miscarriages and a third pregnancy in three years. Taking account of Sierra Leone and his spell in Afghanistan, the bastard must have been at her non-stop.

'If you're just going to prowl around and not talk to me, you might as well grill the chops.'

Tom came from his thoughts almost guiltily. 'Don't you think Maggie's getting too familiar with that Graumann boy?'

'She's doing what all girls her age do. Right now Hans is number one. Next week, next month, it'll be a different lad.'

'This one has lasted four months, which makes nonsense of that.'

Still expertly edging buttonholes, Nora said, 'If she had a different one here every week you'd worry that she was becoming a tart. There's no pleasing you, Tom.' She slid the material along to the next buttonhole. 'Go and take your bad mood out on the lamb chops.'

Although he frequently cooked, he now told himself he would be damned if he would make supper when he had three daughters capable of doing it. 'I'll have a shower and change before we eat.'

Taking chinos and a polo shirt to the bathroom, deaf to the usual giggles and shrieks from the bedrooms, Tom stripped off then did something he had not done for a long while. He looked critically at his naked body in the full-length mirror. Was his waist starting to thicken? Had his thighs lost some of their muscular power? He unconsciously pulled in his stomach. Maybe he should pump iron more regularly. Mmm, nothing wrong with the essential tackle, but a flatter belly would enhance the profile. His gaze lifted to meet the eyes of the mirror image. He sighed heavily. That scar!

Charles Clarkson determined to get drunk. He was officially on call, but he knew no one would demand his attention tonight. He had left his surgery on Max Rydal's advice and driven home to warn Ria of what was sure to come. She had been deeply upset, not least because she had always been kind to Stacey who lacked the budding attraction of Ginny's other teen friends. She found it hard to accept that the girl could tell such lies, and that Jean Laine could believe them.

It was a harrowing afternoon, ending with the painful necessity to break the news to their children on their return from school. Although Ria limited her words to saying their father had been wrongly accused of giving their friend Stacey Laine incorrect treatment, so it would be best if they did not go to school tomorrow, all four met the news with silence. Even seven-year-old Daniel sensed that his parents were holding something back. They all went to their rooms and remained there until the meal nobody really wanted was served. The children then departed to their rooms again to do homework and watch TV, but it was when his two fond daughters said goodnight without their usual kiss that Charles decided to get drunk.

Max drove from the base to a restaurant he often used. His bid to escape the conviviality of dining in the Officers' Mess in his distracted mood rebounded on him, because he had several times brought Livya to this eating place run by the Russian family Pashkov and those memories were strong.

Max also patronized the restaurant because the piped music was Russian and, on special occasions, three of Yevgeny Pashkov's grand-children played balalaikas and sang to the diners. Livya had known Max's taste – bala-laikas, mandolins, Paraguayan harps: what she called 'plunky musik' – but she had been charmed by the children and had given him a CD of Czech folk tunes at their next meeting.

'Not precisely "plunky" but the music of my

homeland bears a strong resemblance to some old Russian airs. Broaden your horizons,' she had teased.

Despite Yevgeny's fulsome embrace and his promise of a superb stroganoff, Max brooded on the uncertainty of his relationship with Livya. He had punched in her number on his mobile three times already and was invited to leave a message. He had not. It was essential to speak to her, gauge her mood.

Pouring more wine from his carafe he told himself yet again he had been a fool to suggest she might have some kind of personal attachment to his father. Yet would she have fired up as she had if their relationship was purely professional? Women were the very devil to deal with. Even wearing his detective's hat Max found them tricky to assess. They deceived more successfully than men.

Pushing away his empty plate, Max turned his thoughts to the charge against Charles Clarkson. The MO had surely been genuinely shattered, and Heather and Connie were sure Stacey was lying. A good, straightforward man could be badly damaged by a fourteen-year-old child who could not live her fantasy.

Max drank more wine. Did Livya fantasize about the charismatic Andrew Rydal? Pulling out his mobile he looked hopefully for a text message. Blank! He would try her home number again when he got to his room. The situation must not be left as it was. Livya Cordwell had put light in his life again. He needed that light. Without it his days would return to the bleakness following Susan's death. All work and no play.

Already he had found today totally lacklustre. The Clarkson business was very negative, and Tom Black was making a meal of a commonplace example of regimental resentment. Max could not fathom why he should be treating it with such determined priority. Was the man losing his touch?

Sudden desire to return to base and at least leave a placatory message for Livya led Max to wave away Yevgeny's eulogy on nut and red berry pancakes, and ask for his bill. He drove fast along the straight stretch of road where Sam Collier's wife alleged she had been fazed by a blue Audi. He kept a lookout for the *Polizei*. Although he was completely in control, he had imbibed freely. A two-man German patrol would doubtless be delighted to pick up a senior British Redcap and haul him in.

Reaching the main gate without incident, Max turned on to the perimeter road. It was that time of evening when the base seemed quiet. Supper was over and the troops were either in the various leisure facilities, or relaxing in their quarters. It was a moonless night with a rising wind that lowered the temperature enough for Max to have the heater on as he drove. His thoughts were so concentrated on what he would say to Livya, he was almost on the lump in the road before he stamped on the brake.

Peering through the windscreen at the dark

mound, he realized it was a human body bunched in a tight ball. Turning the headlights to full beam, he clambered out to approach the motionless man. Squatting beside him, Max searched for a pulse and found one. It was faint, but regular. He rang for an ambulance, explaining that the victim was alive, but that there was a lot of blood around his head and his body was excessively chilled.

Returning to his car he took from the back seat the sheepskin rug kept there in case he was ever stranded overnight in winter conditions. Throwing the rug over the injured man and tucking it as close to him as he thought wise, Max spoke urgently in an attempt to raise a response. He was still trying when the ambulance came up.

A man and a woman crossed to where he squatted. 'Hit and run, sir?' asked the man, also squatting with his partner to feel the pulse.

'Looks like it. I'll have men checking every car on the base in the morning. It must have sustained some damage.'

The paramedics pulled aside the rug and began their careful assessment of the situation, all the while vocally trying to get a response from the huddled man. After checking for dangerous injuries they fetched a stretcher and carefully lifted the patient, whose head they had immobilized in a clamp. Max walked beside them to the ambulance, noting that the man barely fitted on the stretcher. His large feet in safari boots projected over the end of it.

'How bad is it?'

'Difficult to say until we get him to the sick bay,' the girl replied. 'He's in shock and slightly hypothermic, which is our first concern.'

'Right. I'll follow you and get his ID when you remove his clothes.'

It took ten minutes to reach the base Medical Centre. When Max entered, the patient was under several blankets and receiving an injection. It was now possible to see that the areas of his face visible through the congealed blood were very tanned. They still had not succeeded in breaking through his unconscious state.

Max picked up the slacks they had removed and searched the pockets. In an expensive-looking wallet containing a wad of Euros there was a service identity card. Max gazed at the photograph of a broad uncompromising face with brown eyes and crisp blond hair, and at the name Samuel Frank Collier.

He was drawn from his sober contemplation of what had actually happened to this publicized hero by a noisy entry, and he turned to see Charles Clarkson standing hollow-eyed at the foot of the examination couch.

The male paramedic said, 'We brought him in as a hit and run, sir, but we think there's some doubt. We thought you should be called.' He then added a mouthful of medical jargon that meant nothing to Max. Probably details of what they had done and given to the injured man.

Clarkson moved to the far end of the couch to examine the head still held immobile, and then caught sight of Max. 'Come to see fair play?' he snapped.

'I found him in the road,' Max answered quietly, as unhappy to see Clarkson as the doctor was to see him.

Silence fell while a full and careful examination of the unconscious pilot's injuries was carried out. During this procedure Max did some positive thinking. What was the man doing taking a lone walk so far from the junior officers' quarters on a gloomy evening like this one? The accident had occurred near the Armoury and the REME workshops. Not a much-frequented spot at ten thirty p.m. He was in civvies, so there was no question of his performing some late duty. Anyway, Max had not noticed a car parked anywhere near that spot. In view of the supposed harassment of his wife, and the threat to run her off the road this morning, surely he should be at home with her tonight.

The facts produced at the briefing a few hours ago began to take on new meaning for Max. Maybe Tom was right; there was a real threat to the Colliers. Had this hit and run been deliberate, not the result of a driver with too much booze under his belt? Which prospect brought back the question of why Sam Collier was walking alone around the perimeter road, and also of how the driver of the car had known his target would be there at that time. No, it surely had to be an accident; a coincidental one, to be sure. When the car was traced by George Maddox's team things would become clearer. It seemed unlikely that Collier would be fit for questioning tonight. He looked to be in a very gory state right now.

It was almost eleven thirty before Clarkson stripped off his sterile gloves, murmured instructions to his staff, then crossed to Max who had been waiting on a hard chair. Rising at his approach, Max smelled whisky on the other's breath. It was so strong, he wondered at the steadiness of Clarkson's hands during the examination.

'Something *undeniable* to occupy yourself with here,' he said in colder than usual manner. 'I'm not an expert, but I'd say the injuries were not caused by collision with a car. More likely from an extremely brutal beating. I'll reassess that opinion in the morning. He's a big, strong guy who'd not be easily overpowered by a single assailant, so you'll be looking for a couple or group who decided to punish him. There are signs that he was restrained while the beating took place. Dark bruising on the upper arms.' Clarkson's mouth twisted. 'If you'll accept the conjecture of a condemned man, I'll offer it.'

Max met that jibe with a straight answer. 'You're the medical expert and I'm the man who has to seek justice. Go ahead.'

'The attack would have been prolonged and noisy, which leads to the supposition that it is unlikely to have been inflicted on the road where you found him. Too public.' He began

70

removing his blood-smeared white coat. 'I'll keep a twenty-four-hour watch for signs of intracranial bleeding. If that occurs, he'll be rushed to the hospital for immediate surgery.'

Max frowned. 'Please inform me if that happens, whatever the hour. I'll now contact the Duty Officer and go with him to inform Mrs Collier that her husband has met with an accident.'

'Won't she be alarmed by the presence of someone from SIB?'

'Not as much as if you went smelling like a distillery.'

Their eyes met and held. 'If this had happened to a young girl it wouldn't matter. I'd have stayed at home, and she could have bled to death waiting for a replacement doctor to attend.'

The Duty Officer was Ben Steele of the Royal Cumberland Rifles, who had involved himself in a complex case concerning his regiment last year. A likeable young man who fancied himself a private detective, which strengthened Max's decision to represent the situation as a hit and run to both him and Mrs Collier. Safer to wait for the victim's account of what happened before spreading alarm.

Lieutenant Steele was waiting in a Land Rover outside the Collier house, and greeted Max like an old friend. 'I knew you had moved to the base at Christmas, but our paths haven't crossed until now. Is he seriously hurt?'

'He's certainly not walking wounded.'

'Give the bastard who drove off and left him

71

the works. Those were four of our guys Collier rescued in Kandahar, so the regiment owes him a big debt. If I can be of help...'

'Thanks, but no,' Max said with a grin. 'Not learned a lesson from your last foray into detection?'

Ben grinned back. 'I did help, though, didn't I?'

'And put yourself in danger.'

'Not half as much as Sam Collier risked to lift our men to safety. As I said, if I can...'

Max laid a hand on his shoulder. 'Let's break the news to the lady.'

Just before midnight and lights were still on on the ground floor. So, if they had quarrelled and he had walked out to cool his temper, she had not gone to bed in a huff. This husband would not have returned to a house in darkness and his pyjamas on the floor outside their bedroom door. Interesting!

Margot Collier opened the door seconds after Max knocked. She was still fully dressed in midnight-blue trousers and a matching sweater. Large, apprehensive eyes took in the sight of the uniformed Ben beside Max before she collapsed in a faint on the hall carpet.

Instructing the dumbstruck Ben to fetch a glass of water, Max picked up the unconscious woman and carried her through to a sofa in the sitting room. Setting her down on it, with a cushion beneath her head, he switched off all the lights save what he judged to be a Wedgwood table lamp beside the sofa.

In the soft glow, Max then grew aware of the disturbing beauty of Margot Collier. Long black eyelashes curled against golden skin, apricot-tinted lips were enticingly full, her throat was slender and her tan continued down to the full swell of her cleavage visible at the base of the sweater's low vee neckline. She must have sunbathed topless to get that unbroken colour. Unable to stop himself, Max let his gaze absorb the seductive curves of waist, hips and thighs in the snug-fitting trousers. A goddess fit for a hero?

Ben, still looking bemused, arrived with the water as Margot's eyes opened. The impact of their dark lustre on Max's heightened senses gave him the cause for Tom's keenness to pursue this woman's claim of persecution. Surely only a man of stone could refuse to help her.

'It's Sam, isn't it?' she whispered. 'Is he...?'

Max denied her assumption. 'I'm not a padre, Mrs Collier. Your husband is receiving treatment in the base sick bay.' He nodded to Ben to offer the glass. 'Please drink some water. It'll help to revive you.' He paused while she drank, then said, 'I'm Max Rydal, SIB. I found your husband lying in the road as I returned from dining out. He appeared to have been the victim of a hit and run accident.'

'Oh, God!'

'Because I actually found him, and in view of your disclosures to Sar'nt Major Black this morning, I've come with the Duty Officer to get some information about what might have happened tonight. Then, Lieutenant Steele will take you to see your husband, if that's what you'd like to do, although he won't be aware of your visit and you won't be allowed to stay long. It might be better to wait until morning.'

'No, I *must* see him.'

'Fair enough.'

'You *are* going to investigate this situation, then?'

'A situation you kept secret, I gather. Now Mr Black has made your husband aware of the campaign of harassment against you, surely only a very urgent reason could have led him to leave you alone this evening. Can you tell me what that was?'

She shook her head setting long, silky hair swinging. 'It's all my fault.'

'Explain, please.'

'Sam was so angry. *So* angry. He has a hot temper. I've seen him in a rage several times, but never with me before. I wanted so much to help him, make things as easy as possible for him. Is that so wrong?' she appealed.

'He's a fully trained soldier. He'd be competent to deal with most things. From all I've heard recently, he's dealt with rather more than many men would attempt.'

'I know, I know. *That's* why I tried to spare him additional stress.' Her eyes grew bright with tears. 'He said I'd made him a figure of ridicule and derision; caused him to be humiliated by the military police.'

'I'm sure that wasn't Mr Black's intention,'

said Max, resolving to have a word with Tom on that score.

'I went to SIB because I knew I couldn't help Sam on my own any longer. I intended to tell him what I'd done, in a loving fashion, this evening. Then he'd be ready to talk to you about it. I didn't dream Mr Black would tackle him on his own, during working hours, before I'd had a chance to prepare Sam.'

'Your account of the dangerous road encounter led him to act right away.' He smiled to soften her concern. 'We don't hang about in cases like that.'

'I didn't *think*, you see. He's been so uptight about all the publicity and fuss, I tried to ... I just made things worse.'

Max frowned. 'Your husband dislikes having *praise* heaped on him, as well?'

She avoided his eyes. 'He wants to be ... I think it's that he dislikes being in the limelight, for *any* reason.'

'Because it creates resentment, envy in others?'

That brought her gaze up to meet his. 'Sam never boasts, throws his weight around. He's just not like that, so why...?'

'Yes, Mrs Collier?'

Adroitly changing direction, she said, 'We never row. It was love at first sight for us both, and that hasn't changed, but he was deeply hurt because I'd not told him what had been happening.'

'Understandable.'

'I didn't *think*,' she repeated. 'Men have idiotic attitudes about things like that. It's perfectly acceptable for Sam to put his life on the line and say nothing to me, so that I learn about it from the TV news, but not for me to protect him from anxiety.'

'Sounds familiar.'

'I then compounded my crime by asking you people for help.'

'That was the right thing to do,' Max said firmly. 'We know how best to deal with problems like yours. If you had taken your husband into your confidence he'd have come to us much sooner.'

'You're wrong. He was so angry because I'd brought you in instead of allowing him to deal with it his own way.'

'Is that what he was attempting to do tonight?'

'I don't know. He came home early, ranting and raging over the interview with Mr Black. We kissed and made up before he returned to work. I prepared his favourite stew with dumplings, and things seemed to have settled down until he spotted a Redcap strolling about outside the house. He got angry again and intended to go out and move him on, but the phone rang and he took the call.'

'Who did he speak to?'

'He didn't say. Just told me I'd be safe with the guard outside and left by the back door.'

'What time was that?'

'Nine fifteen, nine thirty. Somewhere around

then.' Her voice broke. 'When I opened the door and saw the Duty Officer with another man, I thought you'd come to tell me Sam was dead.'

'You believed that to be a possibility?' Max probed.

She nodded. 'As Sam left he said, "I'll sort the bastard out once and for all."' Tears now ran down her cheeks. 'I'm to blame for what happened to him tonight.'

'You mustn't think that, Mrs Collier,' said Ben Steele earnestly. 'It was a hit and run accident.'

'But who did the hitting and running?' she countered thickly. 'If they kill him, *my* life will end.'

Max got back to his room in the early hours. Far too late to call Livya, even to leave a message. There was not one from her, either. He lay in bed thinking about the Colliers. A golden couple who fell in love at first sight. Life should be a bed of roses for them, but they had known the tragedy of two miscarriages, and they were now caught up in some dark plot to destroy their idyll.

He realized his bad mood over the spat with Livya had soured his professional judgement this morning. Tom had been right to prioritize the Collier case. Charles Clarkson might suffer slights and doubts on his moral probity, but young Sam Collier was in actual mortal danger.

Four

Max awoke at seven and called Livya's number in London. He was invited to leave a message. The receiver went down with a bang. He knew she rose early because she liked to be fresh and impeccably dressed, whatever she was doing that day. He took a perverse delight in wrecking that perfection the minute they reached a bedroom. Frustrated, he called the number again.

'Please pick up, Livya. I tried several times last night to contact you. Come on, let's talk.'

Silence. He slammed the receiver down again and took a shower. It did nothing to ease his mood of mixed anger, frustration and concern. Why wasn't she there? If she was, why refuse to speak to him? Surely such a small, unwise comment from him could not have put an end to something so good; a relationship she had pursued without guile from their first meeting here in Germany.

Livya had come to participate in the Inter-Services Chess Championship just prior to Christmas, and mutual attraction had been instant. The three days they had just spent to-gether had been warm and wonderful. A tiny

78

flash of jealousy could not have put an end to that, could it?

Dressing in a dark-grey suit, with a white shirt and a red and silver tie, Max then picked up his telephone again. On the point of punching in Livya's number, he changed his mind and called Tom.

'Are you undergoing the usual morning chaos?'

'Well, there are assorted females in various stages of undress wandering around upstairs, but I'm in sole, peaceful possession of the kitchen at the moment.'

'Grab some breakfast while you can. Tom, I owe you an apology. I came upon Sam Collier lying in the road last night. Clarkson dismissed the notion of a hit and run. Claims he'd been given a severe going over by a couple, or even a group. And I do mean severe. He looked a mess. You're right, there's something deeper than resentment behind the campaign against the Colliers. We have to sort it before there's a tragedy.'

'Has his wife been told?'

'I went to the house with the Duty Officer. She took one look at us and dropped in a faint. Thought I was a padre and we'd come to tell her her husband was dead.'

'Think she's aware of what's behind the campaign?'

'Do you?'

'It's possible, I guess, but unlikely.'

'I'm going to question him first thing, and I

suggest you call on her to suss out just how involved she is.'

There was a fractional pause before Tom said, 'Right.'

Max grinned. 'Don't bother to put bread in the toaster, chum, just hold it between your hot little hands.'

After his breakfast Max surrendered again to the urge to call Livya. Same invitation to leave a message. He tried her mobile number. It was switched to voice mail. So she did not want to speak to him. Or to anyone else. That was her privilege, but it was curious. As he drove to the Medical Centre he worried about her inaccessibility. Had something happened to her? He knew her parents' number, but he would only call them in an emergency situation. The swiftest means of checking on her safety would be to call his father, but that would be his last resort. He would tackle the problem this evening.

Because he had been on call last night, Charles Clarkson was not officially on duty today, the daily sick parade being taken by the civilian doctor who served the base in harness with his military counterpart. However, the Major was in the small ward when Max arrived, and he came from it with no greeting other than an unsmiling nod.

'He came through the night without a problem, then?' Max asked.

'He won't be out of the woods until tonight. We're still watching his pupils for signs of dilation. Most of the visible blood came from his nose and mouth. Good dental work will repair the damage to his teeth, and the sutures I put in his lip and cheek should ensure he's left with only faint scars. There's a curious element to the damage to his torso, however.'

'In what way curious?'

Clarkson frowned. 'There are raised stripes across his back that suggest flogging.'

'Flogging!'

'Mmm, like the good old days of military and naval service. Fifty lashes as the sun goes down.' Seeing Max's expression, he gave a grim smile. 'No, no, if he'd suffered fifty he'd be in hospital. The bruises on the upper arms indicate to me that he was restrained while being lashed with something like thick rope. The weals are too broad for a cane or a riding-crop.'

'Poor bastard!'

'Indeed. If they'd bared his back, he'd now be in a life-threatening condition after being left on the road in such a low temperature. I'd guess the blows to his head were designed to stun him enough to prevent resistance to being held against a wall and thrashed. The back of his sweater is roughed-up and torn in places, but it gave him some slight protection. I shall monitor his kidney function today. That area appears to have taken the brunt of the attack.' His mouth twisted. 'Will that indicate the height of the assailant?'

'It'll be a strong pointer in that direction,'

Max told him thoughtfully, missing the slight sarcasm. 'The most natural swing of his arm. If you can pinpoint the areas where the weals are the most damaging, it could tell us whether the man was right or left-handed.'

'I'm not a bloody pathologist!'

'OK, forget it. How soon can I talk to Collier?'

'Tomorrow. His complete system has been traumatized. He needs time and peace for recovery. David Culdrow has agreed that I should follow the case through as I dealt with it last night. I take it you have no objection to that?'

'No, this is best kept within military circles, especially in view of all the recent hype concerning Sam Collier. We don't want the press getting hold of this.' Max considered further. 'In fact, the finer details of his injuries should be kept under our hats. Can you trust your orderlies not to blab?'

Clarkson pursed his lips. 'I can mouth-off about patient confidentiality and hope for the best, but the guys here when he was brought in last night might already have spread the news as fast as the other titillating piece of gossip.' He gave Max a straight look. 'We've stopped answering the phone, and we've kept the children home from school. Ria and I don't see why they should suffer the taunts and abuse created by their lying friend.' He made to leave. 'I'll check on Collier at regular intervals. Between visits I'll be at home and available on my

82

mobile number, should you need to contact me.'

Tom experienced a ridiculous sense of excitement at the prospect of seeing Margot Collier again. She had appealed to him for help yesterday morning. How much more anxious for reassurance would she be today? The physical attack on Sam Collier must have been the next step in the campaign against them and it seemed, to Tom, to send a message of either-or.

It also vindicated his own assessment of the seriousness of the harassment. Max had clearly imagined he was swayed by the beauty of Margot Collier, hence the comment about bread being toasted by his body heat. Yet Tom sensed there was another reason for Max's present mood, and it was not hard to guess it also concerned a woman. They played havoc with a man's concentration on his work.

Tom knocked and was struck anew by the arresting quality of Margot Collier's features, when she opened the door almost immediately. Her healthy tan belied the fear and anxiety in her eyes and the tenseness around her mouth. Yesterday, she had been worried. Today, she was deeply afraid.

'Mr Black! Has something happened? Is he worse?'

'No, no, nothing like that. I'd like to talk to you about what happened last night. May I come in?'

She stepped back to allow him to pass, and he

was immediately aware that this was unlike the usual junior officer's abode. A graceful, exquisite bronze ballerina stood on a marquetry table in the hall, both of which screamed *wealth*. Hanging on the sitting-room walls in pale frames were what looked like the images on the paper dress patterns that Nora used. Hardly pictures, though.

'I'm a costume designer.' Tom swung round at her words. 'Those are some I created for Ballet Romayne's production of Eugene Onegin.' She gazed steadily at him. 'I'm not just a poor little rich girl, you know.'

'My wife would love to see those. She makes wedding and evening dresses. Just a hobby,' he explained awkwardly. 'She's had no professional training.'

'You wanted to talk about last night. I wish you had waited before tackling Sam yesterday. Couldn't you realize how humiliating it would be for him before I had had time to break the news in gentler fashion?' She sank gracefully on to a padded stool Tom reckoned had come from an antique shop in Chelsea. 'I went to your office directly from the incident on the road. I was shaken and maybe too hasty. I didn't dream you'd race off to confront Sam the minute he landed. I told you his job is very hazardous. Are you aware of the number of lives lost in Lynx crashes? Taking to the air has the underlying factor of risking one's life. Being safely on ground, I suppose you don't understand that.'

Admonition from this tantilizingly lovely woman brought unwelcome colour to Tom's cheeks. It also brought ready defence. 'Since we last spoke, I've met Lieutenant Collier. Aren't you badly underestimating him? He struck me as a man well able to assess the risks he faces. He's a soldier, Mrs Collier. Joining the Army is in itself an acknowledgement of the dangers of that profession. He's a former member of the Blue Eagles display team – a *voluntary* member – and he very successfully brought men out from a hostage situation in Sierra Leone shortly after your marriage. He's a man of courage, and this latest proof of it in Afghanistan should calm your doubts on his capability.'

This reasoning brought a staggering reaction. 'I don't doubt his capability *or* his courage, you fool! It's *because* he's so daring that I tried to keep the petty details of deflated tyres and smashed eggs on the doorstep from him for as long as I did. You then blundered in heavy-footed and undid all my careful work. He was fighting mad.'

Tom seized on those last words, tingling with awareness of how passion heightened her electric beauty even further. 'What happened when he received the telephone call last night? Captain Rydal told me you'd indicated that your husband said something about sorting the bastard out once and for all. Did you know what he meant by that?'

The flush receded from her cheeks, her eyes

lost their angry glitter, her voice resumed its low cadency. 'I suppose he intended to sort out whoever has been harassing me. Sam needs this pregnancy to go full-term as much as I do.'

'All the more reason for you to have confided in him from the start,' Tom pointed out, noting the emphasis on the desire for a child and the use of *need* rather than *want*. Had Sam Collier a compulsion to prove himself in that one area as yet unfulfilled? 'So, you think the call came from your tormentor?'

'Why else would Sam have gone straight out like that?'

'And all he said was that he would sort them out?'

'Yes. Oh, only that I'd be safe because there was a Redcap outside the house.'

'Which suggests to me that he knew or suspected more than one person being behind all these incidents, including the sending of threatening letters. That call must have given him a strong notion of who they might be. If he had reported that suspicion to us instead of trying to tackle it alone, he wouldn't now be in the sick bay. Have you really no idea who attacked him?'

'Don't you think I'd tell you if I did?' The flash of passion again.

'Did your husband take his car when he responded to the call?'

'Your boss asked me that last night. Don't you share information?'

Stung by this further criticism, Tom said, 'Not

always in the middle of the night when the crime has already been committed and dealt with. I'm here this morning to get any further evidence before the general briefing on your case. We believe the phone call was to lure your husband to a chosen spot so they could leave him in no doubt of their messages in those letters they sent. Mrs Collier, I have to tell you he wasn't injured in a hit and run accident, he was set upon and severely beaten up by several people, then dumped out on the perimeter road.'

'Oh, God!' she whispered, stricken. 'It's my fault. I should have left well alone. It's because I came to you that they've punished Sam.' Getting to her feet, she said wildly, 'Forget everything I told you. Keep out of this from now on.'

'SIB can't ignore a brutal attack on a military officer based within our area of jurisdiction, regardless of what you have or haven't told us about previous incidents,' Tom said firmly. 'Surely you want whoever hurt your husband traced and brought to justice?'

'And have everything reported in gory detail in the press?' She looked near to tears. 'They've bumped him up as a hero. Think how they'd love to knock him off his pedestal.'

Tom's eyes narrowed. 'That could only occur if there was evidence to support such action. I ask you again, do you know what lies behind this campaign against you both?'

'*No!* Now, please go!'

Tom left, knowing in his heart of hearts she was lying.

The atmosphere in the Incident Room was unusually charged. This case had an intriguing quality. A pilot awarded an MC two months ago who last night had been overpowered and flogged, and his breathtakingly gorgeous, wealthy, pregnant wife who appeared to hero-worship him. Such titillation rarely came the way of 26 Section, and the team was relishing it.

Max outlined what they had to work with. 'Lieutenant Collier took a phone call, then rushed out vowing to sort out the bastard once and for all. His wife told me last night that he left by the rear door, which explains why George Maddox's man watching the place didn't see him go. This should also indicate that the RV given in the phone call was not far from the Collier house.

'I think we have to assume he was not expecting to meet with violence. A man of his calibre is unlikely willingly to have walked into the arms of men liable to administer physical punishment of that severity, without any means of self-defence. It's my guess he either believed an undertaking of some kind, or a cash payment, would settle the affair. His wallet did contain several hundred large denomination Euros, which could be evidence of an anticipated payment.'

'But would he have had an amount large enough to silence a blackmailer kicking around the house?' asked Connie Bush.

'Yes, if he was expecting that call,' reasoned

Beeny. 'His comment about settling it finally could support the theory that he was prepared to do so with the sum they had demanded.'

'So why do him in and leave the money?' demanded Piercey. 'All we know of this is what was reportedly in the anonymous letters. Guff about the truth being told and blinkers removed from eyes. Cash wouldn't satisfy that.'

'The truth about what?' asked Roy Jakes.

'If we knew the answer to that it would've already been told, wouldn't it?' declared Piercey.

'OK, let's have some *intelligent* input,' ruled Tom testily. 'Facts.' He held up a finger for every point he made. 'The campaign against the Colliers began after his spell in Afghanistan. The anonymous letters were shredded, so we have no way of checking what Mrs Collier told me. If we believe her there are two options. "The truth" concerns something questionable that happened in Afghanistan *or* during the two months since Collier returned to base. The letters failed to shake him, so pressure was put on his wife. When he failed to rise to that – because she kept it from him, although they could not have known that – they decided to give him a persuader even the stubbornest of men would heed.' He glanced at the bright faces around the room. 'Let's hear some opinions on that.'

Piercey, ready as ever to theorize, said, 'There's no proof the letters ever existed, and we have only the delectable Margot's word that her tyres were deflated and eggs were broken on her doorstep. What if that's a load of bollocks?'

'To what end?' demanded Heather.

'Hero Sam was having it off with some American GI Jane at Kandahar, so the wife who thought he was God's gift solely for her paid a trio of squaddies to teach him to keep his flies zipped when out of her sight.'

There was silence for a while. The volatile Piercey had put forward a working theory. They had been basing their brief on Margot Collier's unsubstantiated account, and husbands on active service consoling themselves with the local talent were a common specie. Add the fact that 'the delectable Margot' could probably persuade most men to do anything she wanted, especially if backed by generous payment, and the theory was eminently feasible.

Max broke the silence. 'She was genuinely shocked when I broke the news to her last night. Fainted at our feet.'

Piercey's lip curled. 'Because she didn't mean them to half kill him, just to make him very sore in the offending area.'

Tom was unhappy. 'I've had two conversations with her and she didn't strike me as the type of woman to do anything of that nature. As the Boss said just now, she hero-worships him.'

'A woman scorned. They've *murdered* the object of their lust for less than a battleground fling,' offered Piercey, unwilling to abandon his theory.

'OK, Piercey, we've had enough of your edification,' Tom snapped. 'Can we have some fresh input?'

Olly Simpson glanced up from his doodling. 'If we accept all she told us, then the letters did arrive. This demand for the truth to be told: If the sender knows there's been a cover-up, that lies have been spread around, why can't *he* reveal the truth? The campaign of harassment ending with last night's brutality suggests that only Collier can, so he has to be forced to give the facts.'

'About what?' asked Roy Jakes again.

'If we knew, it would already have been told,' repeated Piercey with a grin.

'You're all going around in circles,' declared Max irritably. 'Discussion is getting us nowhere. I suggest we address Mr Black's options. Something questionable happened in Afghanistan, or during the two months Lieutenant Collier's flight has been back in Germany. Both possibilities can be investigated by interviewing all the crews who form A Flight, and the Colliers' neighbours.

'One thing we are certain of is that a military officer was last night lured to a lonely spot near his house, severely beaten around the head and face, thrashed with something akin to a length of thick rope, then taken to a quiet stretch of the perimeter road and abandoned. The vehicle used for this will surely have splashes of blood on the rear seat or in the boot. I also want the area within reasonable walking distance from the junior officers' quarters searched for evidence of that attack. The victim bled from his nose and mouth, so there would be signs of it there, and search for fibres from his sweater. It's probably too much to hope that we'll trace the rope, but keep your eyes peeled for anything resembling a weapon.

'Collier's clothing has been sent off for forensic examination, which will give us more to work on when the results arrive. You all know how long that can take. I want someone to question NAAFI staff about Mrs Collier's deflated tyres. Maybe there's a nutter going around doing that on a regular basis, and surely someone would have noticed a swanky Jag in that condition. In short, I want corroboration that the lady is on the level with us. Get out there and make things happen.'

Tom shot Max a significant glance at this evident winding-up instruction. 'Until we evaluate Mrs Collier's claims we should maintain protective vigilance. She's presently alone in her house, and she's pregnant. In view of the attack on her husband, there are potentially *two* lives in possible danger from whoever has it in for them.'

Max nodded. 'We need to move fast on this before there's an avoidable tragedy.'

Left alone, apart from Sergeant Jakes who was doing headquarters duty until relieved by Heather Johnson, Max motioned Tom to his office and closed the door.

'What did you say to Collier yesterday?'

'I told him his wife had asked for SIB intervention in the dangerous harassment campaign against her.' Tom frowned. 'What's this about?'

'She says he was livid after being ridiculed and humiliated by you.'

'Oh, really? Any ridicule and humiliation would have been self-induced by learning how he was being babied by his woman, I imagine.'

Max looked him over thoughtfully. 'Tom, don't let yourself be swayed by personalities after all these years. A woman is being targeted by someone bent on making her life anxious and unpleasant. An officer has been grievously harmed in a deliberate assault. That's all we're dealing with. Two straightforward charges.'

'What are you trying to say, sir?'

Max perched on the edge of his desk. 'Get off that high horse, man, I'm talking as an old friend. I have to say I don't warm to the lady. There's something about all that overt passion I can't entirely trust, try as I will, but I have to take her claims seriously until my doubts are corroborated.'

'Or disproved.'

'Yes, or disproved. I've not yet met her husband, apart from finding him bleeding and unconscious in the road, so I reserve judgement. Nevertheless, he's a serving officer who's the victim of a crime and deserves justice whether he's a hero or a wimp.'

After a moment or two, Tom said woodenly, 'I checked their finances yesterday. No clues there, unless they drew out a large sum just before the bank closed last evening. I'll check again today, but I think blackmail is unlikely.'

'So do I. No regular sums going out of their accounts?'

'His is like you'd expect most subalterns' to be. Pretty straightforward. Hers is different altogether. Large sums going *in* fairly regularly. Without probing any deeper, I'd guess she has an allowance from her father and from other close relatives; grandparents, great aunt, godfather, something along those lines. And she's a professional theatre designer of some note.'

Max was surprised. 'You *have* been busy. So we've a tangent leading into the unknown in this case, although I doubt the answer lies in that direction. My guts tell me he's at the core of this nasty business.'

'And I don't warm to *him*.'

'I think I already deduced that,' said Max with a hint of a smile. 'So let's go and find out how others feel about him.'

Once in Max's car, the awkward moment behind them, Tom asked casually, 'How's Captain Cordwell?'

'Fine.'

'Have a nice time during her visit?'

'Very nice.'

'Good.'

They were silent until they approached 678 Squadron's hangars and offices, then Max murmured, 'Keep your eyes open for anyone with bruised and cut knuckles.'

Tom grunted. 'There'll be one or two of those following the weekend.'

'When you were a squaddie did you have a mill every Saturday?'

'No, I spent all my free time trying to charm Nora into taking me seriously. They enjoy keeping you guessing, don't they?'

'Mmm,' agreed Max non-committally, knowing what Tom was getting at.

They split up, Max heading for the Squadron Commander's office, and Tom making for the crew room where he had sought Sam Collier yesterday. Spurred by their last comments, Max swiftly checked his mobile for texts. There were several, none of them from Livya. Yes, she was enjoying keeping him guessing.

Major Rex Southerland was a sandy-haired Scot, genial but brisk to the point of abruptness. He invited Max to sit. 'I trust your people will be discreet with their questioning. What news of Sam?'

'He's being kept under constant observation today, but...'

'Yes, I got that from the Doc first thing. Any idea who did it?'

'Too early for that.'

'There's a rumour that it was a whipping they gave him.'

Max sighed. 'So much for my hope of keeping that quiet.'

Southerland's eyes sparkled aggressively. 'Bastards!'

'Major, can you give me any clue as to why

anyone would treat Sam Collier in that manner?'

'God, no! Sam's an easy-going guy, a true
team member. Not the sort to provoke such
aggro.'

'His wife claims he's hot-tempered,' Max
pointed out.

'Oh aye, along with the rest of us trying to
operate with old equipment, lack of spares, lack
of trained personnel and lack of sleep. Sam's a
first-rate pilot who never loses it when he's on
the job. He'll rant and rave – with justification,
man – but the moment he walks out to his aircraft he's calm and totally professional. Only a
man of his calibre could have done what he did
recently. Whoever attacked him should be
based out there until we're allowed to leave the
devils to their own devices and pull out.'

Knowing full well how many men felt about
the situation in Afghanistan, Max steered the
conversation in a fresh direction. 'You'll appreciate that our first task is to investigate the
victim's relationship and standing with his
colleagues, who are the most likely suspects in
a case like this.'

'Much as I deplore that reasoning, I'll cooperate as much as I can. We want this cleared
up fast and with as little disturbance as possible.' He smiled. 'Six Seven Eight is bloody
pleased with itself right now. Sam and his crew
did us proud. We don't want the gilt tarnished.'

'Completely understandable. What I'd like
first from you are the names of his particular

friends, men who regularly flew or socialized with him. I'd also like to know about any incident or unpleasantness that occurred in Afghanistan during his recent tour.'

Southerland shook his head. 'I wasn't out there. A Flight deployed with Apaches to form part of the Joint Helicopter Force based at Kandahar. The Flight Commander was John Fraeme, a close friend of Sam. He's aloft right now, but he'll be glad to talk to you about those four months. As to who flies regularly with Sam, the most prominent of them is Staff Richards. Andy was wounded during the rescue that earned them all recognition. He's grounded until a decision is made on his future as a pilot. Unfortunately, there's some doubt about the flexibility of his hand.'

After a brief pause, Southerland said, 'In any unit there are men a wise commander will only put together when he has no other option. I daresay you also have perfectly good, competent soldiers who lose their cool when they have to work together.'

Max nodded. It was a common problem in any workplace. In the armed forces, where people lived as well as worked closely with each other, it was even more important to recognize and deal with it.

'So there are squadron members who prefer not to fly with Sam Collier?'

'There's nothing significant in that,' Major Southerland said firmly. 'It's not just Sam Collier. Personalities frequently clash, and it's essential for a crew to be in complete harmony. Any aggro, any hasty or impulsive action, particularly in a hostile situation, can send an aircraft into the ground. If men tell me they can't gel with certain others I respect their regard for all-round safety.' Seeing Max's expression, he added even more firmly, 'It doesn't mean they'll waylay a guy and give him a thrashing.'

'In my experience a bosom pal is just as likely to offer violence when provocation grows beyond containment.' He got to his feet. 'If you'll list Collier's friends as well as those who are chary of flying with him, I'll join my sergeant major in the crew room and talk to them.'

At mid-morning on a working day, aircrew who were not in the air or sleeping-off night-flying practice were checking equipment, discussing problems with their aircraft with ground staff, studying charts for their forthcoming flights or attending lectures on what to expect on deployment to Middle East war zones. There were just two men with Tom when Max entered.

Introductions were made, coffee poured and biscuits offered. Tom then revealed that they had struck lucky in having with them the crew of the Lynx that had flown in harness with Collier's on the day of the daring rescue. Expressive eyebrow movement told Max more than Tom's words. There was a lead here.

Second Lieutenant Baz Flint and Sergeant Pilot Jerry Lang were disturbed by the punishment assault last night. That was what they called it: a punishment assault.

'Punishment for what?' asked Max.

'What happened to Andy, I guess,' said the tall, lean subaltern with a shrug.

'But surely he was shot by snipers, and Sam Collier flew back with him after extricating four wounded men.' At their silence, Max said, 'I only know what the media puffed off. Give me your version.'

Clearly too edgy to sit, the two men shifted from foot to foot beside the coffee machine as they relived that sweltering morning at the start of the year.

'We go out in pairs to give aerial protection to convoys running essential supplies from Kandahar to Camp Bastion,' Baz Flint explained. 'There's only one traversible route for laden trucks. The Taliban know this and consistently place roadside bombs in what look like broken down vehicles.' He gave a faint grin. 'Not difficult. Most of them in that area are last-breath wrecks tied up with rope or strips of cloth.'

Jerry Lang said, 'It's not always car bombs. They're fond of siting explosives with timers, knowing full well when a convoy will be passing.'

'Our task is to watch out for lone parked vehicles, or several ramshackle cars that could contain suicide bombers heading in the opposite direction to the convoy. We warn the lead escorts and they investigate.'

They were like a double act, relating their

story in alternate passages. Lang took up the narrative again. 'From our overview we can spot potential hazards way ahead.'

'Where we're stymied is in the built up areas. We can't identify a bloody thing in narrow overcrowded streets with flapping awnings and carts piled high with melons or vegetables,' Baz explained.

'That's more or less where it happened,' said Lang. 'The trucks had cleared the centre of the city and were winding through the outskirts when we saw the last one and the rear Land Rover disintegrate. The convoy put on a spurt to clear the area, and people ran to the locals who had been caught in the blast.'

'There was chaos. Through the smoke we then saw our guys crawling, staggering, trying to help each other away from the burning wrecks,' Baz said with an echo of the tension of that time. 'Then Sam's on the radio saying they're going down and asking for cover. It was ... well, as a helipad it had zero advantages and smoke-hazed ground visibility. But he was the boss.'

'So they went down and you did give them cover?' asked Tom.

Baz nodded. 'I've never seen anything so determined. As soon as the skids hit the ground, Sam was out and running to a guy who was on fire. He rugby tackled him, rolling him in the dust to smother the flames, then picked him up and carried him to the Lynx. We circled low, eyes peeled for signs of further hostility, but the place was fast emptying of people.'

Jerry Lang took up the account again. 'When Sam was bringing the second man across, gunfire burst from one of the buildings, bullets raking the ground just ahead of them. Joe Binney, their air door gunner, set up return fire on bastards well hidden. Rounds flew back and forth while Sam continued bringing the wounded across. The third guy was then hit in the leg and collapsed, but Sam hauled him up and appeared totally unconcerned with the danger of what he was doing.'

'He's a large, hefty guy,' said Baz with an appreciative shake of his head. 'Even after half-carrying four men, he threw out some packs of water and supplies on board to allow for the weight of an additional passenger to the normal three. Tossed it out as it were lightweight stuff. I couldn't believe what I was seeing. He was like a man gone beserk.'

'Yet he flew the Lynx back to Kandahar single-handed,' prompted Max, who had read the newspaper accounts.

'Andy, in the left-hand seat, was nearest to the snipers,' Jerry explained. 'He was unlucky to be hit as they left the ground. Made a mess of his hand. Two fingers all but severed. So Sam took control. Andy passed out from loss of blood before they reached base.'

'They all survived, although two needed serious medical care. The guy whose legs and arms were badly burned, and the one with a smashed kneecap. We always collect our wounded, and the dead, because these people don't recognize the rules of engagement,' Baz put in emphatically, 'but what Sam did was exceptional. He was captured in Sierra Leone, then subjected to mental torture and humiliation before escaping. He and the other captives have no doubt they'd have been killed eventually. Sam had been married three months earlier; Margot was pregnant. He swears her fear for him led to the miscarriage. He has a fierce hatred of captivity or any form of helplessness in the hands of an enemy. I'm sure that's what drove him to do what he did.'

Tom made a point. 'Yet you believe last night's assault was to punish him for his daring rescue.'

They both looked uncomfortable. 'We didn't say that.'

'You suggested retribution for his co-pilot's injury, which might end his career as air crew,' Max reminded them.

Baz looked even more uncomfortable. 'Look, Sam's a real team player through and through, never acts solo.'

'Except...' Lang hesitated.

'Yes?' Tom prompted.

'It's nothing really ... but he seems to be pushing himself to the limits lately. It's as if he's trying to prove something. Crazy! What's left to prove?'

Five

'Our bleeding squadron hero?' said the pugnacious corporal. 'Yeah, I've flown as his air door gunner once or twice.'

'Not regularly?' asked Phil Piercey, satisfied by the obvious disparagement in the man's response. Piercey mistrusted heroes, feeling instinctively that they were too good to be true. When they were also physically attractive all his hackles rose in a desire to expose a serious flaw. He sensed that Corporal Fleet was about to oblige in that respect. He was wrong.

'We like working with the same pilots whenever we can. Means we have a good understanding. It's important when RPGs are flying around.'

Having no experience of rocket-propelled grenades flying around him, Piercey glossed over that. 'You didn't have that understanding with Lieutenant Collier?'

Fleet shrugged. 'Some of the cockpit guys are prima donnas. Fancy theirselves. When all's said and done we're a team. They need the guy with the gun as much as he needs them.'

'You're saying Collier throws his weight around; treats his crew as subordinates?'

'Nah, I'm not saying that,' came the contradictory response.

Piercey was getting annoyed with this character. 'So what *are* you saying, Corporal?'

At that moment they were practically deafened by the nerve-jangling screech created by engineers working on a Lynx at the far end of the hangar. Piercey had tracked down this gunner of A Flight inspecting the gun-mounting on the helicopter he was due to fly in later that afternoon. Not ideal interviewing conditions. He jerked his head towards the hangar doors.

'We'll continue this outside.'

Fleet went willingly enough, but Piercey now recognized the game the other man was playing. *They* called it Buggering the Redcaps; SIB called it perverting the course of justice. Piercey acted accordingly as soon as they left the hangar and stood in the freshness of mid-morning.

'Where were you last night, Corporal?'

'Eh?' He was unsettled by the direct question. 'At home. With my missus.'

'From what time and until when?'

'Here, you don't think I had something to do with that business?' His knowing expression had vanished, the sly gleam in his grey eyes had dimmed.

'So you *are* aware that I'm investigating a serious crime against a serving officer?'

'I don't know anything about that. What d'you take me for?'

Piercey gave a grim smile. 'Since you ask, I take you for a cocky little know-all who thinks it's clever to run rings around anyone in authority. Can you prove you were at home for the whole of last night?'

The expression was now wary. 'She'll tell you.'

'She?' snapped Piercey.

'The wife.'

'No one else?

Real anxiety now. 'Christ, what're you saying?'

Piercey's smile grew even grimmer. 'Which is exactly what I was asking you back there.'

Even in the open air they were disturbed by the sound of two Lynx coming in, but Piercey could detect the hint of nervousness in Fleet's voice.

'When I said that about prima donnas, I didn't mean Lieutenant Collier. As I said, I don't often fly with him, but he's all right. I got no grudge, like some have.'

'Like who?'

A quick nervous smile. 'Oh no, I'm no snitch. I got to work with them. But there's one or two not happy about his upper-crust connections and flashy lifestyle. Not that I'm saying they'd beat him up,' he added swiftly. 'Can't think who'd do that.'

The downdraught from dual rotors hit them, ruffling their hair and flipping Piercey's gaudy tie over his shoulder. 'You were in Kandahar recently. Was there any incident, unpleasant or controversial, involving Lieutenant Collier during those four months?'

'Not that I knew of,' Fleet replied above the screaming of the rotors. 'I mostly flew with Captain Fraeme and Staff Benedict or Lieutenant Fields and Sergeant Benbow. Off duty I was with the other gunners and NCOs.'

'Any of them have a knife to grind with Lieutenant Collier?' asked Piercey, tucking his tie back inside his dark jacket and smoothing his hair.

'If they did, it weren't obvious. Look, Sarge, I've got nothing useful to tell you, and I've to check that gun before I go for my dinner.'

Piercey moved to block his path. 'The base at Kandahar is run by the US, isn't it? How were the Yankee women? Friendly?'

'What you getting at now?'

'Just answer the question.'

The knowing expression returned. 'What did our grandparents say? Overpaid, oversexed and over here? Not much has changed, but the women weren't interested in us berks. Lieutenant Fields sometimes wandered over to their lines, but in the shop and coffee bars we maintained armed neutrality. That special relationship we're always being told we have.'

Knowing he had probably exhausted this man's usefulness, Piercey let him go. Fleet was not the type to lambast an officer – verbally behind his back, but not with a length of rope. Yet he had avoided giving his opinion of 'our bleeding squadron hero's' courage. Well, Fleet

106

was not going anywhere so there was always the prospect of a second go at him.

Connie Bush took an instant dislike to Sherilie Fox and not simply because of the soapstar name for a woman she labelled a hard-faced bitch. Second Lieutenant Ray Fox had been allocated the house next to the Colliers, which Connie thought most unfortunate for Sam and Margot. She had not met Sherilie's pilot husband, but any man who had willingly married this woman was unlikely to earn Connie's favour.

Aside from personal dislike of the size zero, brassy, overdressed, loud-mouthed Sherilie, Connie found her a fount of knowledge about everyone connected with 678 Squadron, the Colliers in particular. How much of her high-octane gossip was true was debatable, but Connie was adept at sifting the possible from the airy-fairy.

Contrary to the habit of most people to say as little as possible to a military policewoman – Connie refused to call herself a policeperson – Sherilie's tongue ran merrily on any point raised.

'That snooty cow next door? I'm not surprised someone let down the tyres of her bloody fancy Jag. Top marks for whoever it was. I've wanted to do it for yonks, only I'd've stuck a knife in them. Thing is, I knew it wouldn't bother her. Phone Daddy, ask for another car. Easy-peasy. Don't know why she bothers living in these grotty quarters. I had her money, I'd rent a villa outside the base. Have you seen inside next door? Antiques, silk cushions, crystal lamps. Haven't seen their bed, but it's sure to be double king size with satin sheets and quilt the colour of champagne. You know, like the people in *Hello!*' A wide knowing smile. 'Not that he'd notice the colour of the sheets. Hero? Got to be with stamina like that.' Even more knowing smile. 'I wouldn't say no to a taste of it.'

'Ever any chance of that?' Connie asked swiftly.

'Huh! Our Margot has him firmly to heel. There he is, a six foot four hunk of sinew and muscle with all the guts in the world as a fighting soldier, yet he's a lapdog when she's around. Practically sits up and begs for her.'

'You're saying she wears the trousers?'

A dirty laugh. 'I'm saying she has his off him the minute he walks through the door. Nympho, she is. Common knowledge. Ask around.'

Connie hid her distaste to ask, 'How do your husband and the other men regard that set-up?'

Sherilie's expression changed. 'What d' you think? *Men!* If she was cross-eyed and obese they'd call him a wimp, but they all secretly lust after her.' She nodded vigorously. 'Oh yes, even my Ray. Caught him watching her through binocs once, dirty devil.'

'While she was undressing?'

Smirk. 'He knows better than to do *that*. Claimed he was trying to identify the plants she was digging-in. Ha! She was gardening in small, tight shorts. He was drooling over her bum as she bent over.'

'Does Mrs Collier ever respond to the admiration of other men?'

'Just the reverse, I'd say. She's got her pet dog who'll do anything she wants whenever she wants it.' Sherilie's tongue ran over her bronze-glossed lips. 'She calls him *Samson*. Heard her one day when I was on the other side of the dividing hedge last summer. And she's a right Delilah, if you ask me.' She ran a hand over her cropped apricot-coloured hair. 'I feel rather sorry for him, matter of fact.'

Surprised at such a sentiment after her abusive comments, Connie asked her to explain.

'If it was just her it'd be different. Men are such fools over big eyes and big tits,' she said, unconsciously smoothing her T shirt over her small ones, 'but Daddy has him on a tight lead, too. What Delilah doesn't demand, he does.'

'Isn't that perhaps an advantage? High-ranking influence can boost a man's career. It's already secured for him the move to officer status.'

'Umm, but I think Sam's the sort of guy to want to *earn* everything he gets,' Sherilie said, revealing more thoughtful insight to men's characters. 'I could name a few who'd happily accept promotion to *general* overnight and strut their stuff, but Sam's not like that. There's also a lot who'd enjoy the hullabaloo over that

109

rescue of his. Sam hates it.'

Connie regarded her shrewdly. 'You know him that well?'

'I wish,' she said, with a slight smile to give her words a light-hearted quality. 'No, it's what Ray told me.'

'Does your husband admire that, or decry it?'

Sherilie shrugged. 'He takes the general view that the press has made too much of a meal of it. It's what's going on all the time out there. It's their job. It's what they do. It's only because bloody Margot's father is a "sir" and knows government ministers.'

'This is why Collier is unhappy about it?'

'I guess. He's a nice guy ... when he isn't doing doggy tricks for her.'

Tired of this salacious gossip, Connie then asked if Sherilie or Ray had any knowledge of smashed eggs on the Colliers' doorstep or threatening images under windscreen wipers, but they had only noticed Margot's shapely bottom in tight shorts, apparently.

Connie took her leave from a room where bottles of nail varnish, gossip magazines, several boxes of chocolates, a couple of empty beer cans and a pile of clothes awaiting ironing were strewn. No satin sheets and quilt the colour of champagne in *this* house. She sat in her car for a few moments studying the Colliers' home, imagining herself between the satin sheets with the hunky Sam. Ah, well!

A tap on the car window heralded Heather Johnson, who had been interviewing the

Colliers' other neighbour. Sliding on to the passenger seat, she sighed with frustration.

'God, what a difficult woman! She began by saying "I'm not one to indulge in scurrilous tittle-tattle, Sergeant" in an oh-so-superior manner. When I pointed out that I was conducting an investigation into a vicious attack on a serving officer, she made to shut the door in my face, saying, "We had nothing to do with that."

'I eventually persuaded her to let me stand in the hall while I asked about smashed eggs etcetera. She hadn't seen or heard anything suspicious. Nobody delivering letters very early in the morning, for instance, or putting leaflets on the Jag. What she did let slip was that Sam and Margot spent more time upstairs than down. She then qualified that piece of "scurrilous tittle-tattle" by saying they appeared to be very much in love.'

'Mmm, champagne-coloured satin sheets,' Connie murmured.

'What?'

'Go on. Anything else?'

'Yes. Interesting, I think. When Sam went out to Afghanistan, Margot joined a group of theatre people in the Seychelles for those four months.'

'Theatre people?'

'Seems she designs stage costumes for ballet companies.'

'My, my! Not between the satin sheets with our Sam *all* the time.'

111

'Wonder how he felt about her high-lifing it while he was facing the risk of Taliban bullets.'

'He treats her with dog-like devotion, so his heart probably rejoiced at the prospect of her being carefree and happy during his tour of duty in a war zone.'

Heather looked sideways at her friend. 'Men like that exist only in fiction. The real ones are born selfish. It's the nature of the beasts.'

'According to *Sherilie* Fox,' Connie replied with a straight face, 'he sits up and begs on her command.'

'With a biscuit on his nose, no doubt,' Heather added dryly. 'In her dreams!' After a pensive silence, she said, 'The Colliers are beginning to intrigue me no end. We're told by the boss she hero-worships him, and now we learn of his doggy devotion for her. If they're so unnaturally obsessed with each other, how do they each manage to have time to pursue their careers?'

'You think all this talk of mutual adoration is a careful cover for what they really feel?'

'Be interesting to find out, won't it?'

'Not if it proves Phil Piercey is right about her paying squaddies to beat hubby up for dropping his pants in Afghanistan. Think how he'd crow.'

'Heaven forbid!' said Heather with real feeling.

Tom decided to drive home for lunch. It was something he did not often do during a serious investigation, but he felt uneasy over the caution Max had issued after the briefing. He had spoken as a friend, but his words had touched too closely on the truth. Tom knew his approach to Sam Collier had been brusque – OK, it had been blunt to the point of scathing – and he had made no secret of his sympathy for a wife who felt unable to confide in and rely on her man's support. It was unlike him, and it had been unprofessional. Which was what Max had been hinting at. He had also hinted at an unprofessional interest in Margot Collier.

During investigations Tom had come across beautiful women before. He had also dealt with men who were ultra-macho. So why this strong reaction to the Colliers? His present unease was due to the suspicion that his attitude towards the pilot was based on a disturbing interest in the man's wife. Thoughts of her were at the back of his mind ready to come forward when he allowed them to.

He had met Nora fifteen years ago, and there had been no other woman in his life from then on. He was as lusty as any man. He appreciated shapely breasts and legs, come-hither eyes and sexy hips, but his sex life with the woman he deeply loved was totally satisfying. Why then did a faint sense of excitement hover during each meeting with Collier's wife? And between those meetings why was he suddenly question-ing himself, his impact on others, his self-worth?

He was inclined to be short-tempered at home lately, too. The daughters he loved unreservedly seemed concerned only with their own activities and needs, and surely Maggie's new pertness had grown out of the hours she spent with that German boy. The closeness he had once shared with her had been broken up by Hans Graumann. With Easter coming next week, Nora was up to her eyes in wedding dresses, and the girls were expecting shopping sprees for new clothes to wear on the visit to their grandparents during the school holiday.

Ignoring the truth that his family had frequently been obliged to function without him during investigations, Tom drove home bemoaning the apparent uninterest in him they all displayed lately. His decision to return to the rented house for lunch was to demonstrate his right to be there. The girls would be at school, but Nora could put aside those bloody make-believe gowns for sixty minutes.

He walked along the corridor to the dining room to find Nora at her sewing machine. The walls were hung with several long underslips and yards of veiling; the table bore boxes of sequins and rhinestones, handmade rosebuds in various sizes, and reel upon reel of sewing thread. Nothing as exotic as the framed designs on the walls of Margot Collier's elegant room, however.

'Hallo, love, what brings you home at this hour?' asked Nora, very carefully outlining a design of waterlilies with pale lemon thread on cream silk.

'It's lunchtime ... or haven't you noticed?'

She glanced up swiftly; stared at him in surprise. 'What's wrong?'

'I'm hungry. Nothing wrong in that, is there?'

'Nothing *unusual* in that,' she said quietly. 'I planned to have a sandwich when I finished this embroidery. There's a hefty chicken and leek pie for supper, but if you're too hungry for just soup and sandwiches there's a lasagne in the freezer.'

He turned away knowing he had been unreasonable, yet felt unable to compensate. Surely she could have left what she was doing to eat lunch with him. The opportunity to finish the embroidery would still be there an hour hence. Taking the frozen lasagne out he gave it one look and returned it to the freezer. He should have gone to the Sergeants' Mess, or even the NAAFI. 26 Section still did not have the canteen they had been promised. Probably never would have.

He opened a tin of mushroom soup he did not really fancy, and buttered four pieces of bread while heating it. There was a packet of sliced ham in the fridge. Covering half the bread with ham, Tom added thickly sliced cheese and tomato before putting the buttered lids on his fillings. Sitting at the breakfast bar with hot soup in a bowl and the sandwiches on a plate beside it, a curious sense of isolation washed over him. Was that embroidery so bloody important?

He had practically finished his light snack when Nora came to the kitchen, saying, 'Am I glad to see the back of *that*! Ordinarily I'd enjoy tackling something really creative. It makes a nice change from seams, darts and hems, but not when there's a pile of things to do before our trip home.' She stopped short beside Tom, glancing around at the worktops. 'Where are they?'

'Where are what?'

'My sandwiches.'

It was several moments before Tom realized she expected he would have made some for her while making his own. Of course he should have.

'I didn't know what filling you'd want ... or how long you'd be working on that tricky stuff. You wouldn't have fancied dry slices with turned-up corners.'

'No. No, I wouldn't have,' she responded slowly, then turned to take another tin of soup from the cupboard. 'I'll make do with what you had. The aroma lingers temptingly.'

'I'll do you a ham, cheese and tomato to go with it,' he offered guiltily.

Nora shook her head. 'Soup'll be fine. Warm me up after sitting there most of the morning.' Busy at the cooker, stirring her soup, she said, 'It's all over the base that Doc Clarkson's a pervert who can't keep his hands off young girls. What's set that rumour off?'

'A complaint by a teenage patient. No proof, but we have to investigate.'

'I've always found him rather aloof. Knows his stuff, but regards patients as opportunities to practise his profession rather than people to reassure. Still, you never know what men are like deep down, do you? He's the right age to start growing afraid.'

Tom frowned. 'Afraid of what?'

She half-turned to look at him. 'His future. Youth and excitement have become the perogative of his children now. It's all out there waiting for them. What's awaiting him? An endless line of sick complainers, retirement and old age. It's suddenly hit him that he's a member of yesterday's generation. When that happens men can resort to fancying and, in extreme cases, trying to initiate children who're growing into adults. Some women start dressing like teenagers and indulging in girls' nights-out, where they drink to excess and ensure they capture the attention of every male in sight with their antics.'

Tom stared at her as she poured soup in a bowl and came to sit facing him. 'I doubt he's even *forty* yet.'

'It has nothing to do with age, love, it's *circumstances*. Wealthy bachelors in their sixties can still seek fresh fun and excitement in the belief they have eternal youth. Heavily married men with a large batch of children often feel the way I've just outlined. That's when their sexual fantasies can grow too strong to resist.'

Tom remained silent, watching her drink her soup. Her hair was again fastened back with a scrunchie, emphasizing the lean lines of her

117

face, her large hazel eyes and her smooth throat above the open neck of a pale woollen shirt that had seen better days but was comfortable around the house.

'The other rumour I heard this morning from Petra Townsend was that the helicopter hero was hit last night by a car and left in the road badly hurt. His wife must be wondering if the Grim Reaper's sending him a stark message. Is he OK?'

'He'll bounce back.'

'Good. She's pregnant again after two miscarriages, I hear. Shocks like that won't help her condition.' She put her spoon back in the empty bowl. 'There may be a couple of jam tarts in the tin. Fancy one with a cup of coffee?'

Tom declined. 'I was just thinking how nice it is to have the house to ourselves for a change. The girls won't be home for at least another hour. How about going upstairs for something more enjoyable than a jam tart?'

She gave a regretful smile. 'I wish.'

'Do I take it that's a no?'

'Until tonight, love. I must push on with that bridal gown. The wedding's at the end of the week and I've two flower-girls' dresses to make yet.' She gave him her fond teasing smile. 'Have the jam tarts for now.'

Normally he would have an appropriate response to that. Today, he collected bowls and his plate to take to the sink. 'All that froth and fantasy, to say nothing of the bloody ridiculous expense for a pointless spectacle. That's all it is these days. Couples have been having sex, if not actually shacking-up together, for years. Some even have their kids as page-boys or whatever. Weddings are no more than glorified parties where the wife-to-be can flounce around in a copy of something she's seen in a soap or a gossip magazine. It's totally meaningless.'

'Ours wasn't ... and you'd talked me into bed long before we tied the knot,' Nora reminded him quietly.

He swung to face her. 'You didn't wear a bloody great crinoline covered in spangles, and Maggie was only a twinkle in my eye.'

She reached for his hands and clasped them warmly, searching his face with her gaze. 'When our girls marry they'll probably want a bloody great frilly crinoline covered in spangles, or if the fashion then is to wear a virginal white wetsuit, they'll want that. It's the day every woman dreams of from infancy. It's *her* day, whatever the situation. It's special. Don't put on that face, love. All three of your daughters will want the full works when the time comes, so you'll have to keep your opinions to yourself, especially if they want their children to walk down the aisle with them. It's how things are these days.'

Tom drew his hands from her grip. 'You're now telling *me* I'm a member of yesterday's generation.'

'We both are, but I'm too fulfilled and busy with plans to need girls' nights-out to shore up my happiness.' She paused fractionally before asking, 'How about you?'

He forced a smile, conscious of the pull of flesh around his facial scar. 'I don't need girls' nights-out, either.'

Nora smiled back and gave him a swift kiss. 'Must get to the sewing machine. That's a date for tonight, chum. The future's bright.'

So why did he feel so bleak as he left the house and returned to his office?

Max lunched off toasted cheese and tomato sandwiches prepared in the tiny kitchen at their headquarters, which had to substitute for a regular canteen. Staff Sergeant Melly had taken on responsibility for keeping cupboards fully stocked with the makings for snacks, light meals, and comfort eating for when cases reached stalemate. He continually complained that the comfort supplies vanished even when things were going well. The complaint fell on deaf ears.

Max took two chocolate-coated caramel slices to have with another mug of coffee, justifying this on the grounds of being unable to interview Sam Collier and so progress the investigation. The 'comfort' was not needed to offset concern over Livya, of course! He was about to start on the second cake when Rex Southerland rang to say Captain John Fraeme, commander of A Flight and Collier's close friend, was back on the ground and ready to help in any way he could. The cake beckoned, but Max reluctantly returned it to the tin, where its brethren sat invitingly. He could always have it with a cup of tea before the briefing later on.

The sun had appeared to provide warmth and brightness to a dismal grey day. It should have lifted Max's spirits. It failed, even though he told himself he had little to grumble about compared with Sam Collier. Or Charles Clarkson.

Entering the command offices of 678 Squadron Max found, as usual with the Army Air Corps, a more laid-back atmosphere than there was in regimental headquarters. The 'flyboys' had absorbed some of the more relaxed attitudes to military life practised by the RAF, which must be engendered by the fact that airmen mostly left their large parent group on the ground to operate in the vast freedom of the sky. Max was not wholeheartedly enamoured with flying, invariably glad to unbuckle his seat belt and step out to the open air once more. He supposed being occupied at the controls would put a different slant on the activity.

John Fraeme was in a small office reading a report. On his desk were a mug of coffee and a plate bearing two Wagon Wheels. Crumpled foil beside the plate suggested he had already eaten a third. He glanced up and got to his feet, hand outstretched.

'Hallo. Grab a seat while I rustle up some coffee. How d'you like it?'

'Black, no sugar,' said Max, noting his firm handshake and relaxed approach. A man well in control of himself. He studied Fraeme as the pilot wrapped himself around the partition

121

to say to someone in the next office, 'Coffee for my visitor. As it comes, nothing added. Thanks.'

Collier's friend was around five-nine and sinewy, with close-cropped dark curly hair showing grey strands at the temples. He had the kind of intelligent good looks and frank gaze that would do wonders for recruitment on a poster, and old ladies afraid of flying would happily take to the air with him. Max was neither a timid pensioner nor a youth yearning to be an ace flyer, but experience told him this man was not behind or involved in the 'punishment assault' on Collier. John Fraeme was the type to resolve problems with words, not fists ... and resolve them he *would*!

Sitting behind his desk again, Fraeme said, 'I guess you've not yet been able to talk to Sam. I heard he's under observation.'

'That's right. Best for him, a nuisance for us.'

'Bizarre business. Why Sam?'

'Why, indeed, but these things always happen for a reason and I'm hoping you can shed some light on that. All I know of Collier has been garnered from media coverage of his action in Afghanistan, and the horse's mouth account of it by Baz Flint and Jerry Lang this morning. Your squadron commander told me Sam is well liked, a true team player. Can you elaborate?'

Before Fraeme could speak, a pale-faced corporal entered with a mug he put on the desk before scuttling out as Max thanked him. John

122

offered the chocolate biscuits. Max declined.

'I always need a chocolate fix after flying,' the other man confessed. 'The shrinks would have an explanation for it, no doubt.'

Max laughed. 'I can give you that. Chocolate prolongs the buzz.'

'Do you fly?' John asked with interest.

'Only as a passenger.' He waved a hand at the biscuits. 'Those things pep me up when I'm down, and keep me up when I'm up.' He sobered. 'So you get a buzz when you fly. Does Sam Collier?'

'I guess we all do.'

'And in a combat situation?'

He nodded. 'Even more so, I'd say. Fear and excitement meld to produce a state comparable to a drug-induced high. Only when danger no longer threatens do we begin to wind down.'

'That's when you need a chocolate fix.'

The pilot regarded him shrewdly. 'What is it you want from me?'

'Major Southerland told me you're one of Sam's close friends, yet it appears you don't often crew with him. Why's that?'

'Good friends don't necessarily make good flight partners, although Sam and I do. As flight commander I select crews because the character and aptitude of each man makes for good teamwork. I actually have two guys who're so mismatched temperamentally and professionally it would be madness to send them aloft together in a combat situation. Flying helos is a

123

dangerous pastime, Max.'

'So you crew with someone whose qualities suit you better than your friend Collier's?'

The other man frowned. 'No, you're not getting it. A Flight has four Lynx and eight pilots. Within that group are guys who've discovered they operate best with certain others, so they expect to share a cockpit when they're both on duty. When one is away, they pair differently but return to the original arrangement. Sam and I operate well together, but equally well with two guys who are unhappy as a crew. It makes sense to split them, so I normally crew with Ray Fox, and Sam with Andy Richards.'

'Who had half his hand shot away during that daring rescue in Afghanistan.'

John looked uncomfortable for the first time. 'That was bloody bad luck.'

'Particularly when Collier was exposing himself so totally outside the aircraft and remaining unscathed. It's not surprising that some people felt resentful of all the media puff centred on him rather than the whole crew.'

The other man gave Max a level look across his desk, and his manner hardened. 'A Flight operates as a team every which way. In your line you work independently, which is why you're here alone right now and there are SIB guys all over the offices and hangars questioning personnel one-to-one.'

'And the point you're making?' Max asked crisply.

'Is that we're not in the business of flogging

one of our team members and dumping him in the road because we feel *resentful* of something he's done. We're too close-knit to put anyone out of action. We need each other too much. We're drastically undermanned, in case you hadn't heard.'

Max let several moments pass, then said, 'Point taken. So you can't give me a lead on who might have assaulted Sam?'

'None at all.'

'How long have you been close friends? You meet socially? Wives equally friendly?'

John drank some of his coffee which must by now be cold. Max recognized it as playing for time. 'We've always hit it off,' he said eventually. 'When he joined the squadron he was single and a sergeant, heavily involved with the Blue Eagles display team. We didn't meet up much in those days.'

'You got together more often once he was commissioned?'

'Well, he bowed out of the Blue Eagles when he started dating Margot, so he resumed normal squadron duties.'

'And he moved into the Officers' Mess,' Max added smoothly. 'Do you and your wife make foursomes with the Colliers?'

'We have two kids. A girl of two and a babe of nine months. Not much chance of foursomes of the type you mean.'

'Your close friendship operates mostly on professional lines, then?'

'I guess so,' he agreed after a pause.

'So tell me, what has your pal Sam done to provoke such a brutal attack last night?'

John Fraeme leaned back in his chair, relaxed once more. 'You'll have to ask him, won't you.'

Six

Charles Clarkson slowly raised the gun, steadied his hand, then pulled the trigger. He did the same five more times. His score came up in lights above the target. Not bad. Anger always sharpened his skill. He signalled that he was reloading, and a fresh target popped up. He wanted to put all six in that solid centre, but two just nicked the side of it. A third target recorded the same. Setting the gun down he then removed the ear protectors. His present anger must be too great for perfect aim.

'Fine shooting, sir,' said the ex-sergeant who issued weapons and ammunition at the Army Rifle Club.

Charles pushed the gun and equipment across the counter. 'I've done better. I'll have another go tomorrow.'

'Tomorrow *afternoon*, sir?'

'Is there a problem?'

'Well, Wensdees, the ladies come from midday to fifteen hundred. They have lunch in the restaurant and a bit of a meeting. Mostly chat, reely. They use the range for around ninety minutes, then go off in time for the kids coming back from school.'

127

'I'll give it a miss, then. Thanks, Joe.'

He walked through to the bar knowing very well what the man was telling him. If he was using the club to hide out, tomorrow would be a great mistake. The female members would not allow him through the door. Ordering a double whisky from the barman, who today seemed too busy with paperwork to yarn like he usually did, Charles took his drink to a window over-looking the busy road running past the base and stared at the passing cars. All those people heading somewhere! How many of them were facing public vilification and professional censure? How many had children who had suddenly become tongue-tied in their presence? How many had working colleagues who tried too hard to pretend nothing had changed?

Ria had agreed it would be best to keep their four children at home until SIB completed the investigation into Stacey's accusation. Easter holidays would close the school for two weeks on this coming Friday, anyway, and both he and Ria were setting Zoe, Ginny, James and Daniel work to compensate for lost lessons.

He tossed back half the whisky in bitter mood. He had unplugged the house telephone, but they all had mobiles. These used constantly to be ringing – in different tones to identify which one – but they were all more or less silent now. His lovely daughters and bright sons had lost their friends. The house used to resound with laughter and teen music. The bedrooms were hushed, occupied by bewildered, whispering children since yesterday afternoon.

It was particularly hard on Ria. Having a husband who molested underage girls and made explicit suggestions to them was more humiliating than having one who kept a mistress, or even a male lover. They were consenting adults. A husband who used his status as a doctor to abuse children was beyond the pale.

Hearing voices, Charles glanced round at the doors to the bar. Oh God, three members of the Royal Cumberland Rifles had arrived. Time to go. Time, also, to look in on Sam Collier again. Mishandling the recovery of an acclaimed hero would finish him off, for sure.

Renewed anger surged through him as he remembered the mortification of the body search for evidence of sexual tampering, eighteen hours after leaving the Laine house! They still had his outer clothes. His underwear had been washed, of course, and he had showered twice since that visit, but they reckoned it was still possible to find proof if it was there. The girl was undergoing investigation by a team trained to handle underage victims. God knew what she was telling them; what their conclusion would be. It could be a week or more before SIB were notified of it. Meanwhile, he had to ride out hostility and innuendo wherever he went.

He had urged Ria to take the children to Portugal now, but she refused to be seen running away and insisted they would all go next week, as planned. He was unmanned by her love and faith in him.

At the Medical Centre David Culdrow greeted him in normal manner and said he had looked in on Collier every hour. No dangerous signs of internal bleeding, and the patient's kidneys were functioning normally.

'No serious physical damage, I guess. As for the rest, who knows? His wife sat beside him for two hours drawing coloured patterns on sheets of paper. He slept the whole time. Bit pointless, but she's fiercely protective and behaved herself. It would be sensible to talk to him quietly about his situation and who brought him in last night. Prepare him for what's to come.'

'I agree, but I'll not allow SIB to question him until tomorrow.'

Culdrow nodded. 'Give him some breathing space to come to terms with what was done to him and why. How was the target practice?'

'Worked off some of the stress, but it hasn't changed anything.'

He went through to the small ward where Sam Collier lay on his stomach, apparently deeply asleep. Best to come back after dinner to prepare him for a probing interview in the morning. As David had just said, give him some breathing space to get his mind around what had happened. In his own present mood, any hindrance to Max Rydal and his team would give Charles great satisfaction.

Tom tracked down Andy Richards awaiting a

session at the controls of the Lynx simulator. A sturdy, square-faced man with wings on his breast, he was not pleased to see Tom.

'I'm just about to get up there, sir,' he said, nodding at the mock-up of the cockpit from where two whey-faced youngsters were emerging. The instructor had clearly given them a rough ride.

'I'm investigating a serious crime,' Tom replied brusquely. 'The training session can go on hold for ten or fifteen minutes. We'll talk outside while these two hear the list of the things they did wrong, and how they'd be dead if they'd been flying for real.'

Out in the welcome warmth of the sun, Tom looked at Richards' hand hanging by his side. 'Getting full control back yet?'

The pilot raised his injured hand to display the puckered flesh at the base of his palm. 'Not quite. They managed to stitch the fingers back in place, but movement isn't what it should be. I'm having regular physio, but they say I'm not ready to go aloft.' His eyes burned with eagerness. 'I know I could bloody do it, but until I've had enough sessions in the simulator to prove I can cope with anything the instructor throws at me, I'm stuck on the ground.'

'Better on it than in it.'

Andy sighed. 'You want to talk about what happened to Sam last night? I can't tell you anything about it.'

'You don't know of anyone who'd have it in for him to that extent?'

'God, no!' He looked genuinely aggrieved. 'OK, so there's a couple of officers in the squadron who like to put it about a bit. "Look at these pips on my shoulder." You know the sort of thing, sir. Lieutenant Collier's not like that. He came up through the ranks and knows what's what.'

'But he had a helping hand along the way, didn't he?'

'Well ... yes, but what I'm saying is he's still the guy he used to be before he got that leg-up.'

Tom probed further. 'He's also got a very beautiful wife and enough in the bank to live the high life. That *has* to change a man, Staff.'

Richards looked mulish. 'The money's hers. So's that Jag. You won't find him wearing designer gear or a gold Rolex. Those things don't interest him.'

'What does?'

The reply was immediate. 'Flying. He was in the Blue Eagles team before he met her. Gave it up then, but he'd do it again like a shot. Know that for a fact.'

'Mmm, you appear to know him very well.'

Andy gave a faint smile. 'Should do, we got our wings on the same course. We were best mates in the Sergeants' Mess before Cupid came along' He shook his head. 'Never seen a guy so instantly smitten. Couldn't talk any sense into him. He was gone away.'

'He lost his head?'

'Don't we all when women come on the scene?'

'You're married?'

'Last year. Baby on the way. Sam's really desperate for it to go right this time. It won't help if Deena's and mine arrives safely in September and they lose another one.'

Tom pursued this line. 'You're hoping to continue crewing with him?'

'Of course.'

'You don't blame him for your injury? You don't think he made too rash a decision to go down after the bomb took out those trucks?'

Richards' eyes hardened. 'You think we shouldn't have gone down for the wounded? One was a human torch, for God's sake!'

'Have you had the feeling that Collier has become overly reckless lately? Several of your colleagues have offered that opinion.'

'Have they?'

Tom read into that non-committal reply a loyalty that would not be shaken, so he changed direction. 'Those months in Kandahar would have been stressful. How did you relax?'

'All the usual ways. Only difference was it was like sitting in an oven to do it.'

'Many women out there?'

Richards stared Tom right in the eye, saying deliberately, 'It was *much* too hot for that, sir.'

'The excessive heat must have shortened tempers.'

'Yes, we got real annoyed when the Taliban lobbed rockets at us.'

Tom's mouth tightened. 'You're being deliberately obstructive. Wise up! I'm trying to

133

discover who half-killed your friend and fellow pilot last night.'

Richards sobered. 'If I knew, I'd have been over to your headquarters first thing, believe me.'

'Someone has suggested the assault was punishment for causing the injury that might have grounded you permanently.'

'That's balls, sir,' he countered emphatically. 'What Sam did was bloody brilliant. He was bringing the second of the wounded across when enemy snipers began firing, taking us by surprise. Joe Binney – our air door gunner – raked the building non-stop in retaliation, and a right royal gun-fight was maintained while Sam continued fetching the wounded over to the aircraft as bullets were flying. That took real guts, sir, and I don't care if he *was* pushed up the promotion ladder by his father-in-law, because he demonstrated that's right where he deserves to be. In command. Without hesitation he rescued four wounded men who would have fallen into Taliban hands. You know what would have happened to them, don't you? Guys who support the practice of stoning women to death have very inventive ways of killing infidel enemy captives.' He glanced briefly at his hand before adding, 'We're all in it together out there, so we look after others the same way they'd look after us when things get bad.'

Tom knew he was dealing with a genuine team player, so he posed a final question. 'Dismissing the punishment theory, you can't think of anything Sam Collier has done that could drive someone to such brutal retaliation?'

'No, sir, and I don't believe he ever would. They got the wrong guy. It's the only explanation.'

At the end of that day they had no lead on the attack on the young pilot, nor had the scene of the crime been identified despite the search mounted by George Maddox's team. Tom's suggestion of a constant guard on Margot Collier had been scaled down to a night patrol of the house where she would be alone. Max and George shared the opinion that the harassment towards her had been designed to force Collier into decisive action. It failed because he was unaware of it, so he was then left in no doubt of his options. Submit or face dire consequences.

The team reported the results of their interviews and Max summarized the evidence so far. 'Two facts appear to be constant. Let's take the first. The Colliers are a more than usually devoted couple. According to neighbours and colleagues, Sam is easily manipulated by his wife. He surrendered his place in the display team after meeting her, but would love to rejoin it. He's adamant about maintaining his own bank account, but he allows Margot to spend her family wealth in their home, on her clothes, cars and holidays. The couple spend more time upstairs than down. She suffered two weeks of unsettling and unexplainable harassment without telling him, because she wanted to protect him from stress. When I called with the Duty Officer to tell her her husband had been hurt, she fell in a dead faint at the sight of us. I hear she has been sitting at his bedside for most of today, although he's still only half conscious.'

Tom took over the summation. 'The second constant fact is that we've not detected any violent dislike of Collier, or corrosive resentment of the man. There were two instances of refusal to comment or offer any opinion on his decision to go down for the wounded. The crew of the partnering Lynx thought it excessively risky, but his own crew, including the co-pilot shot in the hand during the action, backed him to the hilt and said they would do the same again.'

Seeing the expressions on the faces around him, Max said, 'Yes, there is an element of closing of ranks, but these AAC guys are being deployed to war zones. Experience has told us that facing an enemy draws men more strongly together. Individual issues are put aside while danger threatens.'

Piercey could remain silent no longer. 'They have been back here for two months, sir. Long enough to revive individual issues.'

'I agree, Sergeant, but I still maintain the evidence we've gathered today gives little credence to the theory that Collier was attacked by members of his squadron.'

'Mrs Collier seemed certain the blue Audi that side-swiped her belonged to a squadron member,' Beeny pointed out.

'Unfortunately for us it did *not* side-swipe her, so there are no helpful marks on her Jag, or on the only squadron blue Audi, owned by Lieutenant Maine who is presently in the UK.'

Olly Simpson, doodling as usual, offered his own slant on that. 'The lady didn't note the car's reg number, nor did she get a look at the driver's face. Why be so certain someone from Six Seven Eight was crowding her? Does she know something she's not telling us?'

'Almost certainly,' agreed Max. 'She'll have to be questioned again. Meanwhile, we have to consider the possibility that Collier was attacked by *any* of the personnel on this base, which will be a real pain in the arse to investigate unless we discover where it took place and gather forensic evidence. Fibres, footprints, blood samples, tyre marks. Nothing definitive, of course, but these things often point us in the right direction.'

'Sir, isn't it possible that Collier went to the rendezvous given over the phone, but was taken from there near to where he was dumped?' said Connie Bush.

'Why would he get in a vehicle with people he had told his wife he would sort out once and for all?' challenged Piercey.

Heather Johnson spiked his guns very quickly. 'He arrives on foot at the appointed spot. They come out of the darkness, grab and hood him, then bundle him in their vehicle to drive him along the perimeter road. We should search the area where he was found. Doc Clarkson reckons the victim was stunned by punches to the head, then held against a wall or other solid surface to be flogged. On that side of the base are the Armoury and the REME workshops. Plenty of solid walls to spreadeagle a victim against.'

Max nodded. 'A workable theory. I'll have George Maddox set up a search there tomorrow. Collier can be interviewed in the morning, which should set us well on the way to dealing with this distasteful affair. After an assault of that viciousness, he's unlikely to hold back on the reason for it.'

The truth has to be told,' murmured Piercey. 'We'll hear what it is before it's made public.'

'Maybe it'll *remove the blinkers from your eyes* and allow you to look beyond your prejudices,' Heather Johnson murmured back.

Max drove to the Mess tired and frustrated. The dramatic events last night had made it difficult to fall asleep, and anxiety over his relationship with Livya had kept him tossing and turning once he had. Even after living for four months on the base, he was not used to the single bed. His former lodging in the house of an elderly German widow and her brother had contained an old-fashioned double bed with brass fittings at head and foot. A large, restless man, he had slept well there, but now he was forever having to retrieve the duvet from the floor during the night. Occasionally, he found himself there in the morning.

Planning to have an early dinner, then bed with the biography of Sir Edmund Hillary he was reading, he vowed to resist the impulse to attempt to contact Livya again. Reviewing the Colliers' relationship with the team, he had silently disparaged the man's apparent willingness to allow his wife to dominate him. Beautiful, classy and seductive she might be – she certainly *was*, he had seen for himself last night – but she was the only child of a wealthy prominent widower who had most probably doted on her to the same extent.

Oh no, Max Rydal was not going to emulate them over Livya Cordwell. If she wanted to end an affair that had seemed to be heading into seriously long-term territory, then so be it. Plenty of years ahead to enjoy close encounters with a succession of women.

Parking at the rear of the long building, Max walked round to the main entrance and headed upstairs to the bedrooms. Every week he resolved to seek living quarters outside the base, but they were not easily come by. The surrounding area offered houses like Tom and his family occupied, which were too large for one person, or smaller apartments. Max had viewed a few, but his former experience of a rented flat made him cautious. He had lived next to a swinging couple who played loud music, had noisy sex, and hosted riotous parties. They had driven him to the German widow's house, where he had found peace and motherly consideration from Frau Hahn. He needed to find another elderly widow with a large bed-sitter to rent, but they were thin on the ground so he was still a cuckoo in this nest of regimental men who were never entirely relaxed with someone they rated a policeman, not a real fighting soldier like themselves.

Nodding briefly at a couple of fellow residents as he walked the corridor, Max entered his room to look immediately at the telephone. The red light was winking evidence of a message, and the jolt of anticipation came despite his resolution a few minutes ago. Pushing the door shut with his foot he walked to the desk and pressed the replay button.

'It's eighteen hundred hours on Tuesday. I know you have a heavy case on the go, but call me when you can. I'll be here for the rest of this evening. As the Yanks say, missing you already, Steve.'

Max gazed at the telephone still hearing her voice saying the words that had turned his mood around. He smiled at the answer machine and played her message again. On the night of their first real date, when wine had flowed and her every gesture, every look had told him the coming night together would be all he hoped for, he had been bewitched into confessing he was a devotee of classic World War Two films. Further encouraged, he had revealed an ongoing student desire to emulate Steve McQueen's famous motor-cycle dash to reach neutral territory and freedom. At Christmas, he had taken UK leave and arrived unannounced at the Cordwell family home on a rented Harley Davidson, to Livya's delight. When she used the name to tease him, he knew all was right between them.

Pausing only to remove his jacket, tie and shoes, he swiftly punched out the number he knew so well.

'Livya Cordwell.'

'This is another of those times when I wish I could slide on to the saddle, rev up and jump a few hedges to reach you.'

'Believe me, I wished for a fast means of transport yesterday, even a motorbike.'

Not quite the response he hoped for, but she sounded warm and friendly. 'You'd better explain that statement, madam,' he said in SIB manner, then added gently, 'I've been concerned. What happened?'

'Are you sitting comfortably? Remember saying to me that diverting to Southampton was better than to Birmingham? There was a suspected terrorist incident at Southampton, so we were sent on to Bournemouth where we had to wait on the tarmac while two of their regular incoming flights went through the system. On finally reaching the terminal we were told our baggage would be held until the coaches waiting at Southampton had been driven to Bournemouth. I ask you!' she said, yesterday's exasperation still evident.

'Could only happen in the UK.'

'There's more. My bag was missing. They

141

were prepared to hold one of the coaches while I completed all the paperwork, but I told them I'd catch the train. Should have known better. All the taxis had been taken by the earlier arrivals. I waited forty-five minutes for one. Just missed a London-bound train. Next fast one in an hour. Spent half a week's salary on a Continental breakfast while we sat on the line for fifty minutes due to an "incident" at Basingstoke station. Hoodies had thrown bottles on the line. I rang the office on my mobile to say I'd be late. Queue for taxis at Waterloo was a mile long, so I took the Tube. Only a limited service due to industrial action.'

'You poor love,' murmured Max in sympathy.

'Here's the crunch line. Hurrying from the tube station to my flat, I was calling the office again when a kid on roller blades came up behind me and snatched the phone from my hand. He was off round the corner before I registered what had happened.'

'Did he hurt you at all?'

'No, but I'd have hurt him if I could have caught him. Couldn't have been more than twelve.'

Sorry that she had had such a bad time, Max was nevertheless glad her silence had not been because of their tiff at the airport. 'Has your bag turned up yet?'

'Five minutes ago. Delivered to the door by a Lufthansa lackey with Germanic apologies. It had been to New York and back.'

'Everything intact?'

'Except my temper, yes.'

About to say something along the lines of 'all's well that ends well' Max thought she might consider it one of his pat responses and changed direction. 'I've been calling your mobile. The yob didn't answer.'

There was a smile in her voice now. 'His antennae must have warned him the old bill was on the line. I've a new mobile. Here's the number.'

Max wrote it down, then asked as neutrally as he could, 'I hope you've not been put off coming over here.'

'I'm a soldier, Max, not easily discouraged by failures in the system. But I won't again risk an early morning departure, however great the temptation to stay for an extra night.'

'You'd like me to ease up on temptation?'

A moment's silence. 'Don't you dare!'

They talked for almost an hour on the easy, intimate terms of lovers, and Max felt the tension drain from him. To hell with early bed and a book. He would instead listen to his CDs of balalaikas and remember the three days he had just spent with this wonderful woman. Remember them without a cloud of uncertainty hovering. Only as they were saying goodbye did Max recall the message she had left on his answer machine.

'You said you knew I was on a heavy case. How come?'

'Your fame is widespread,' she teased.

'As a lover?'

'You wish! General Sir Preston Phipps is a member of our select committee. His daughter has caused him serious concern because her hero husband was attacked and badly hurt. I'm afraid you're liable to feel the weight of our noble general's influence if you don't get to the bottom of it swiftly.'

The Black house was buzzing with activity when Tom arrived there. The usual squeals and laughter could be heard from the girls' bedrooms, which left their father unprepared for the shock of discovering in the understairs alcove his eldest locked in the arms of Hans Graumann as they kissed in adult fashion.

'What the hell do you think you're doing?' he shouted.

The pair sprang apart, presenting a picture of guilt. Maggie's youthful cheeks burned scarlet. The German boy's face grew pale. Neither spoke as they gazed at this very large, very hostile man.

'Go! *Now*,' he told the blond, blue-eyed boy, striving to keep his hands from cuffing him around the ear. 'Go on, take yourself home!'

Maggie found her voice. *'Dad!'*

Tom rounded on her. 'I'll talk to you in a minute.'

The sounds from two girls upstairs had ceased. Tom felt rather than saw them peeping over the banisters. Then Maggie began shouting. 'We weren't doing anything *wrong*. Hans was saying goodbye, that's all. They're going to

144

spend Easter with his grandmother, leaving tomorrow. *We were just saying goodbye.* There's nothing wrong in that. *Everyone* kisses goodbye.'

'Not the way you were,' snapped Tom, shutting the front door very forcibly as Hans stepped outside. 'And *everyone* doesn't hide under the stairs to do it.'

'How could we hide?' came the emotional challenge. 'It's all open. There's no door. We weren't in a cupboard. Anyone could see us. He was just saying goodbye,' she cried again, more defiantly.

'Then why go under the stairs? Why not at the front door, where it's usual to say goodbye? You're getting far too friendly with that boy,' Tom continued fiercely. 'Yesterday you were both in your bedroom when I came home.'

'We were *not*,' his daughter contradicted, turning even redder. 'We were all in Gina and Beth's room rehearsing for the school play about the origin of Easter eggs. We were hearing each other's lines.'

'Don't raise your voice at me,' roared Tom. 'Does that boy go to your school? Is he in the play? *No!* So what was he doing upstairs in the bedroom with you and your sisters?'

Nora came from the dining room holding a pair of dressmaker's shears. 'What's going on?'

'He sent Hans away; made me look like a naughty *child.*'

'Don't point at your father, and don't refer to him as *he.*' She walked through to the hall. 'Can

145

we discuss this in normal voices?'

'I'll never forgive him. *Never!*' Maggie ran for the stairs and thundered up the flight as only an overwrought adolescent girl can, sobbing as if the world was about to end. A bedroom door slammed and the one sound from the otherwise silent first floor was muffled weeping. Gina and Beth had become uncannily quiet.

Nora waited for Tom to speak, but he was too shaken to embark on an explanation. Instead, he walked in to the kitchen, saying, 'I need a drink.'

He was unscrewing the whisky bottle when Nora came up to take it from his hand. 'Let's talk first, Tom. Before I go up to Maggie I need to know why you sent that boy home.'

He took the bottle back, but made no attempt to pour a drink from it. 'If you weren't so all-fired determined to do those bloody fairy frocks you'd see what's going on here between those two. Your daughter, who's barely thirteen, was being mauled by that youth old enough to know what sex is all about.'

'*Mauled?*'

'Pressing himself against her as they kissed. Under the stairs, where they wouldn't be seen. They were too far gone to hear me come in.'

'*Too far gone?*' she quoted incredulously. 'Whatever does that mean? Were they on the floor, half-undressed?'

Her sarcastic attitude fanned the flames. 'Would you know if they were? Would you care?'

There was a stunned silence because neither of them could believe he had just said that. Tom made a helpless gesture with his hands in lieu of a withdrawal of such wounding words. 'She's too young to be alone with him. He's *sixteen*. I know what lads of that age get up to, if you don't.'

'And *I* know what girls who're just discovering the joys and misery of adolescent passion go through. I don't expect you to understand that, but I *do* expect you to respect my superior knowledge on the subject.' Her eyes flashed with rare anger. 'Why is it that when you consider the girls have done something wrong you refer to them as *my* daughters? They're *our* daughters, Tom, ever and always, even though the greater burden of their upbringing is borne by me. Because it is, I trust and respect them. I believe they feel the same way about me. If you humiliated Maggie in front of someone she feels great affection for, you're in danger of losing her trust and respect for *you*.'

Shocked at how swiftly the harmony of his family had shattered, and dismayed by this sudden discord between them, he said from the depth of his hurt, 'Whose side are you on?'

'D'you know, Tom, I often wonder that myself. I have to keep the peace between three lively, talented girls without showing any favouritism, and I have to keep things sweet between them and a father whose work frequently sends him home in an unreasonable frame of mind. I sometimes get sick of mediating between you all, so I keep my sanity by sewing bloody fairy dresses. If that means you have to make your own lunchtime sandwich, and Maggie experiences her first real kiss, too bad. Right now, chum, I'm on *my* side.' She indicated the whisky bottle. 'Drink the bloody lot. Once you're dead to the world, the evening will be a hell of a lot pleasanter.'

Phil Piercey was deeply disgruntled. Gerda had sent a text message cancelling their meeting at the Red Goblin Club and offering no alternative date. For once, he was in no mood to go on the prowl and chat up the local talent in town. Gerda's dismissive message somehow highlighted the reported adoration of Sam Collier by his gorgeous, sexy wife – a woman who could have anyone, but who apparently could not wait to tear the pants off her fly-boy husband.

Phil's grandfather had flown a Spitfire in the 1940s. Brylcreem Boys they were dubbed, and women threw themselves at them. From the first days of flight, aviators had worn the gloss of glamour whether they were tall and handsome, or short and ugly. It was the daredevil element of what they did that had the women goo-goo-eyed, and young lads envious. Phil had considered joining the AAC or the Royal Military Police on signing up for military service, but chose the RMP. When people asked why, he told them investigating made greater use of his intelligence. He had once been in an off-duty fist fight with an airman who had overheard his remark in a pub. Actually, more than once. Fliers were a very sensitive breed.

Eating supper in the Sergeants' Mess, where Connie Bush and Heather Johnson were talking animatedly together at a nearby table, Phil guessed they were gushing over fish-and-chip Sam once more. His hackles rose. Collier was no bloody hero if guys were prepared to beat the living daylights out of him to get at the truth. Looking at the flushed expressions on his female colleagues' faces, Phil's hackles rose further. How he would enjoy exposing the bastard as a fraud. Worse. A guy was not given a flogging for simply telling a few white lies.

When Connie and Heather glanced his way, then conspired in obvious merriment, Phil pushed back his chair and walked out, his mind made up. Walking to his car, he got in and headed around the perimeter road towards the Armoury and its surrounds. Max had said he would talk to George Maddox about searching that area in the morning, depending on what he learned from the victim that might make it unnecessary. Why not look around now; steal their thunder?

Tuesday evening, at the hour when soldiers were either eating, cleaning their kit, phoning girlfriends or chilling out together. Only the Duty Officer and Sergeant were liable to be in the vicinity of the Armoury after dark, checking for intruders and examining the security system during 'rounds'.

When Piercey arrived there it was deserted.

149

He left his car, taking up the powerful torch kept in it, and skirted the Armoury well clear of the area within which he would activate the floodlights. Collier's attackers would not have risked being illuminated; they would have taken him to a wall well out of public view to deliver their brutal message.

The REME workshops loomed in the darkness ahead. Piercey exercised the intelligence he claimed was put to better use with SIB than in a helicopter to guess the location of the likely spot. Somewhere only dimly lit by the lights on the corners of the workshops, but not too far from the road. Collier was a big, hefty man to drag or half-carry for a considerable distance if they had punched him almost senseless before conveying him in a car or Land Rover.

Maybe they had merely jumped him, shoved a hood over his head and pinioned his arms. If so, they could have then marched him right to the rear of the workshops. During training sessions, Piercey had been hooded and manacled to demonstrate how even the toughest of men could be subdued and dominated. He had hated the experience; had never forgotten that terrible helplessness.

For a brief moment he felt empathy for Collier, but that was soon superseded by the near-certainty that the man had got his rightful comeuppance. Sam Collier had sinned in a big way, for sure. Eight years of policing told him so.

He rounded the corner of the tall building and

began to search the rough ground with the beam of his torch as he walked slowly alongside the rear wall of the workshop. Next minute, he was seized and thrust against the bricks, his arms outstretched spreadeagle fashion and held in clamplike grips. Fear shot through him, his back already twitching with anticipation of the blows to come.

Sam at first thought he was dreaming. He had recently had a recurring one of being in a strange room that had no door; no escape route. This room had a door that stood open, and he could hear the murmur of male voices not far away. The bed was hard, so he attempted to turn over to a more comfortable position. Pain raking across his back set him gasping, and he froze as memory of the cause of that pain came at him like a rocket-propelled grenade.

Realizing where he must be he fought the nausea rising in his throat. How had he got to the Medical Centre? Christ, it would be common knowledge now. How much time had elapsed since it happened? Had he said anything without being aware of who was listening? Dear God, what had they told Margot? How would he face her; how could he lie his way out of this?

Struggling to calm his heartbeat and his ragged nerves, Sam recollected the events of that evening ... how long ago? It was presently night-time. Which night? The same one? It had happened on the evening of the day Margot had done the unthinkable and betrayed him by going behind his back to SIB. She had portrayed him as spineless and ineffective to that scarfaced warrant officer.

Although Margot had diluted his anger in her usual fashion, the rift had remained through supper. When the phone call came he had no hesitation in going to meet the man he was certain had sent the letters and frightened Margot. He had gone determined to settle the issue with reassurances and a handout, but he had no sooner approached the shadowy figure waiting there than two others had grabbed him from behind and pinioned his arms while the third thrust a sack over his head and tied it tightly around his neck.

Totally unprepared for violence, he had swiftly lost all sense of what was happening when they roped his arms together and forced him to walk. He remembered the alarming sensation of fighting to breathe; a nightmare reminiscent of Sierra Leone. He was then pushed into the boot of a vehicle and taken on a short, bumpy journey.

He was dragged out and marched over rough ground where his head was used as a punchbag until he was almost choking on his blood, and was so disorientated he would have fallen if they had not held him steady.

Nausea returned with a vengeance as Sam's mind shied from recalling the degradation of that final act. They had released his arms and held him spreadeagled against a wall. The pain had grown with each lash. His last cohesive memory was of buckling at the knees and sinking to the ground, awareness fading with the growing anguish in his head and body.

For some time Sam lay bathed in sweat created by unleashed fury against those who had attacked him. He lay unwilling to move and revive the painful aftermath of physical punishment. How could he ride this out? A police investigation would be launched. The punches to his head he could possibly explain away with a deal of invention, but how to account for the thrashing – a punishment far exceeding his crime?

In the quietness of that small ward, he reviewed the few things he recalled about that attack. The man he was expecting had not been one of the three; his distinctive voice had not said any of the violent phrases directed at him. Sam could make no more sense of them now than he had as they vented their brute force so sadistically. He lay bewildered and uncomprehending. What was happening to him?

At that point he heard Margot's voice asking if he was yet awake, and a man telling her to go in and find out. Sam quickly shut his eyes, intending to keep them closed until she had left. The roundabout was spinning ever faster and his hold on the handrail had slipped a little more.

Seven

Charles Clarkson rose early from a night of wakefulness interspersed with brief periods of troubled sleep. Although he dispensed soporific aids to patients he would not take them himself. Ria had refused them, and the children slept as calmly as usual. Much as he hated to admit it, they found an element of excitement in the present situation. To be fair, the strained relationship with their father did appear to bother them, but they were too young fully to appreciate the blow he had been dealt.

Going downstairs, he saw several envelopes on the doormat. His mouth tightened. More abusive letters. There had been four last night. After opening the first he had destroyed the others, saying nothing to Ria although she would surely be prepared for hysterical reactions from some parents on the base.

Gathering up this fresh batch of hate mail, his head brushed against something as he straightened. Daniel, his artistic youngest, had fashioned an Easter mobile with dangling papier mâché eggs decorated à la Faberge. As he steadied it, Charles realized his hand was shaking. Less than forty-eight hours had passed since he had been accused by that child. It would be a week before the Joint Response team would give their report. A lifetime of waiting.

Deciding to leave Ria sleeping, he breakfasted on tea and a bacon sandwich. Then he pocketed the unopened envelopes and prepared to head for a quiet session with Sam Collier before SIB set to work on him. A fellow feeling perhaps? Charles felt as battered mentally as the pilot was physically.

He got no further than the front door. The word PAEDO had been written in white paint on the windscreen of his Range Rover. Retreating to the small cloakroom at the foot of the stairs, he lost the breakfast he had just eaten, then he sat on the lavatory seat as tears formed in his tightly shut eyes. Dear God, what had he done to Ria and the four wonderful children who gave his life its greatest meaning?

Max drove first to the Medical Centre set on interviewing Sam Collier. He had not received a message advising that the pilot had had to be hospitalized, so he should now be fit for questioning on the events of Monday night. Collier's evidence would surely lead to a swift resolution of the case.

The reception area was deserted, so Max walked through to the small ward where the patient was awake and gazing through the window. His face was black, blue and yellow with bruising, the cuts in his lip and cheek showing red against it.

'Returned to the land of the living, eh?' Max said by way of greeting. 'I almost drove over you on the perimeter road, which would have made you look even worse than you do now.' He smiled and sat on the chair. 'I'm Max Rydal, SIB. Have you had breakfast?'

'They offered what they called the full English. Bit difficult with broken teeth, so I settled for porridge.'

'In much pain?'

'What do you think? I suppose the guy who ran me down drove on?'

'You recall being hit by a vehicle?'

Collier shook his head with care. 'I don't remember anything. It was a shock to find myself here in this state, believe me.'

'When you say you don't remember *anything*, what exactly do you mean?'

'I mean I have no idea how I got hurt as badly as this.'

'Yet you spoke of the guy who ran you down.'

The surprisingly dark eyes gazed frankly at him. 'You just now revealed that you found me on the perimeter road.'

So he was going to play games, was he? 'How much have you been told about your injuries?'

Collier shifted gingerly on the pillows; then said, 'I know they were very edgy all day yesterday about the state of my pupils and internal bleeding. No problem, apparently, because they let me sit up to eat the porridge. The rest I can tell for myself when I move or

156

look in the mirror.'

'Why were you walking along the perimeter road near the Armoury and the classrooms after dark on Monday?'

'I wish I knew.'

'Were you going to meet someone?'

'I've no idea.'

'Is it usual for you to take solitary walks at night?'

'I'd say that's very unlikely.'

'Your wife said you received a phone call and rushed from the house by the rear door.'

'How extraordinary!'

'She also said you told her you would "sort out the bastard once and for all". What did you mean by that?'

'How do I know? I told you I don't remember anything about what happened.'

'Who is the bastard you planned to sort out?'

Collier gave a faint smile which, because of his sutured lip, became more of a grimace. 'A guy banging on about borrowed DVDs he claims I never returned; about my share of a taxi fare I still owe him; about joining a quorum investing in some scheme to make several grand? Take your pick. You know how it is.'

'Sure I do. I also know what happens when patience runs out. Guys get beaten up. Especially if they risk taking solitary walks at night.' Max left a silence to allow his meaning to sink in. 'This was about much more than DVDs or a taxi fare, wasn't it?'

'You're saying someone ran me down deliberately?'

'I'm saying you know exactly what happened on Monday night,' Max said forcefully. 'I advise you to drop this pretence and give me the full details. We'll get the truth eventually, and you'll face a charge of perverting the course of justice if you continue to maintain this attitude. You were beaten up, Collier. Quite bizarrely, and I know you know why. *The truth that has to be told.* Isn't that it?'

Collier sat silently, gazing at Max as if he were talking nonsense.

'What's the last thing you remember?' He clearly caught the man unprepared. But not for long.

'Eating porridge for breakfast.'

'You want this persecution to continue?' Max challenged. 'You're prepared to expose your wife to the danger of suffering a similar brutal attack?'

That brought a swift reaction. 'Leave my wife out of this.'

'Impossible, she's already involved. Have you also forgotten the two weeks of escalating harassment she was subjected to?'

'I knew nothing about that.'

'And the anonymous letters you received. Does your amnesia cover that?'

'What letters?'

'How far back does your loss of memory go?' Max continued relentlessly. 'Do you recall spending four months in Afghanistan? Remem-

158

ber how to fly a Lynx? Know your wife's name, and your mother's? How old are you? Where were you born?'

'What the hell's going on here?' demanded Charles Clarkson from the doorway. 'Who gave you permission to badger my patient?'

Max got to his feet. 'You did. Said he'd be well enough to answer questions this morning.'

'*Questions*, yes. Not Nazi style interrogation. He's had enough. You'll have to leave. *Now.*'

As soon as Max walked from the ward, the door was firmly shut by the doctor whose ruling overrode that of the police in all but rare circumstances. Clarkson had dark rings under eyes which were unremittingly hostile, and he was paler than usual. Max guessed the anger directed against him was due to more than this small breach of protocol.

'We need answers from Collier.'

'He's my patient. You should have obtained my permission before browbeating him.'

'You weren't here. In fact, there was no one in evidence at all. Whoever did that to him could have walked in, finished the job, and walked out again. It *is* possible they haven't let up on him yet.'

'His protection is your job. His recovery is mine ... and you might just have set that back considerably.'

'We need answers from him,' Max repeated doggedly. 'A serious crime against him has been committed and only he can set us on the right track, but he's claiming loss of memory.

Without checking that with you I know that's not the case. He's lying, either to cover his own back or because he's afraid of further retribution if he talks. Contrary to your belief we don't use Nazi methods, which means we have no way of forcing him to give us the info we want. All we can do is wear him down with experienced questioning. It works, but it takes time. I don't think we can afford the time in this instance. The campaign against him has been going on for a month or more already, involving the harassment of his wife ranging from petty inconveniences to attempts to run her off the road in that fancy car of hers. Our main concern has to be to prevent a serious attack on *her*, which I suspect Collier fears. It might be wise for her to go to friends until we've got this sorted.'

'She won't go,' Clarkson said immediately. 'She spends hours at his bedside, even though he's asleep the whole time. She sits quietly drawing patterns on a sketch pad, content just to be near him.'

'Mmm, obsessively devoted, I understand.'

'Really? She's in the early stages of a third pregnancy, the other two having terminated at fourteen weeks. Women tend to need more than the usual cherishing in those circumstances, and this is the critical period once more.'

'Which adds further urgency to our need to get her husband to confess the reason for the punishment attack on him. That's what his colleagues called it, guessing that it was because of the injury to his co-pilot during that daring rescue, but I feel certain there's something more complex behind it.'

Clarkson rubbed his brow wearily. 'I'll have a word with him about his wife's safety.'

'*We* need to question him,' Max insisted.

'All right. Give him a couple of hours peace, then send a woman. She might be less aggressive than you. Collier is the *victim* here, don't forget.'

'He or his wife could be *dead* victims if he doesn't tell us who administered that brutal warning. Bear that in mind, Major.'

Tom decided to escape to Section Headquarters before his family descended for breakfast. Cowardly? Just discretion being the greater part of valour. He and Nora rarely quarrelled, but when they did they never let acrimony remain until the next day. Last night had been different. Maggie had refused to come down for supper. Nora resolved the situation by allowing all three girls to eat in their rooms, thereby diluting Maggie's defiance and easing the atmosphere created by Tom's anger.

Husband and wife ate together, striving to make conversation which avoided any mention of Hans Graumann, their daughters, or Nora's wedding dresses. Tom declined to discuss his own work. This left only the subject of their forthcoming Easter visit to both sets of grandparents, and snippets of regimental gossip, with which to break the tension. Nora was aloof;

Tom was resentful.

As soon as she had finished eating Nora had returned to her sewing machine, leaving Tom to stack the dishwasher then repair to the tiny alcove he used as an office and where he kept his model steam engine collection. Tonight they failed to please him. Were they really boys' toys? Should he be out indulging in more macho pastimes? Quad-bike racing, squash, hang-gliding, shooting rapids in a skiff? Thirty-five was surely the prime of a man's life. He should not be spending his evenings surrounded by giggling girls and acres of white satin covered in sequins and rosebuds.

If he had a son it would be different. They could do man things together; leave the women to gush and sigh over clothes, make-up and posters of pretty-boy 'celebrities' clad in tight black leather, or displaying puny bare torsos. Tom knew his own pecs were more impressive, his shoulders broader, his thighs more power-ful. A body to tingle any woman's spine, Nora frequently declared. So why was she spending so much time fiddling with diamanté, veiling and frilly petticoats?

Staring blindly at the miniature Flying Scots-man, Tom thought of a couple who spent more time upstairs than down; of a woman so crazy about her man she had his pants down as soon as he shut the front door. Was he aware of his amazing good fortune in having that effect on a woman as stunning as Margot Collier?

Tom had still been in that restless, frustrated

state of mind when George Maddox phoned to say, with a wobble of laughter in his voice, that the Duty Officer and Sergeant had just brought in a man found loitering and behaving suspiciously in the vicinity of the Armoury.

'Sneaking around with a torch, sir. He claims he was conducting an investigation into a case of GBH but, as they rightly asked, what was he doing there in the dark alone, if that was the truth. The suspect's details are as follows: Sergeant Philip Maurice Piercey. He claims he's SIB, sir, but he's a shifty-looking bugger.'

Tom was livid. Piercey was a good detective, but an inveterate maverick. Maddox's men were tasked to search that area, if necessary, after Collier had been interviewed in the morning. Piercey was jumping the gun again, seeking personal kudos. In his present mood, Tom had no time for Piercey's antics.

'Where is he now?'

'Duty Officer handed him over to our jurisdiction. That'll be in his report.' The wobble of laughter increased. 'We put him in one of our cells while I contacted you.'

'Right. By the time the paperwork is completed, it'll be too late to call out Captain Rydal to confirm identification and question him. You'll have to keep him overnight, Sergeant.'

'Happy to, sir. We'll dispense with bread and water and give him a good breakfast.'

Only Beth had come downstairs to kiss her father goodnight. Gina had called from the landing. Silence from Maggie. With the sound

163

of a fast-running sewing machine in his ears, Tom had taken a book to bed. His eyes scanned the pages, but his mind registered nothing of their content. Did that scar down his left cheek bother Nora so much? Was it that repulsive? His concern deepened when she slid into bed, gave him a peck on his unblemished cheek, then turned to present her back to him.

He had lain awake after she drifted into sleep, unhappy and angry at the way things were changing; at the way he seemed no longer to be valued by the quartet of females who used to be loving and trusting.

His last waking thought had been that, whatever his heroic appeal might be, Sam Collier was unlikely to excite any woman in *his* present state.

Phil Piercey was absent during the morning briefing. Securing his release from custody, Max had sent him to his quarters to change his clothes and smarten up, after bending his ear with a warning against ignoring authority and acting alone. Feeling a mite of sympathy for the man who would not live down this episode for some time, Max nevertheless understood why Tom had allowed it. Piercey was intelligent and keen, frequently offering interesting slants on a case no one else thought of, but he was opinionated to the extent of regarding himself sharper than his colleagues. Not fully a team player. Yet he had courage and initiative, both valuable assets. It was to be hoped this incident would

164

not result in resentment strong enough to force his transfer elsewhere. Max would be sorry to lose a good detective, and Piercey did not irritate him the way he did Tom.

Max was concerned about his old friend, whose judgement seemed slightly off-key lately. He was surely too young to be suffering what was called a 'mid-life crisis', yet he was certainly bothered by private worries of some kind. His relationship with Nora was very sound, and his girls were level-headed, bright and family-orientated. It could not be Nora's health causing concern, or Tom would have confided the facts by now. That left Tom's own health. Were repercussions from the head injuries sustained four months ago affecting the man's moods and capabilities? It would account for his keeping quiet on the subject. A few casual enquiries when an opportunity arose might bring the answer.

Tom was certainly heavy-eyed and unsmiling this morning. Max was about to add to his grimness by outlining his brief interview with Sam Collier.

'He claims to have no memory of the attack, or even of the phone call summoning him to the RV. The medical dictate forbidding questioning for twenty-four hours allowed Collier time to get his act together. He's cool, he's glib, he's lying his head off. There's something complex behind this persecution of him and his wife. While I'm prepared to accept that a man would tolerate petty instances of anonymous letters and smashed eggs on the doorstep, because reporting them would create worse trouble in our unique military world of living as well as working very closely together, I grow highly suspicious when he allows thugs to deal out bodily violence and still protects their identity.

'Of course, he's also protecting himself and whatever he's done to provoke the attack. We have to persuade him to confess, however serious it is, before a fatal tragedy occurs.' He gave a faint smile. 'I'm sure you're all wondering what my famous guts are telling me. They indicate that these perpetrators are so incensed they won't stop until Collier bows to their demands and "tells the truth that'll remove the blinkers". He's showing no promise of doing that, at the moment, and I strongly believe we should advise Mrs Collier to leave and stay with friends until this business is settled and out in the open. She's very vulnerable right now, and Major Clarkson said her pregnancy is at the critical fourteen-week stage, at which her previous two pregnancies terminated. She has to be protected ... and the unborn child.'

For a brief moment Max was back in an office on a grey, stormy day in England, when they had come to tell him his pregnant wife had not survived a car accident. His thoughts were so occupied, he finally responded to a female voice to find Connie Bush regarding him with bright expectation on her face that reflected her dedication to health and fitness.

'You asked a question, Sergeant?'

'I queried Major Clarkson's estimation of the stage of Mrs Collier's pregnancy, sir.'

'Oh?'

'You said he mentioned the critical fourteen-week period.'

'He did, yes.'

The glow on her cheeks deepened with excitement. 'If he's right, it means that Sam Collier is not the father of that child. He didn't return from Afghanistan until eight weeks ago.'

There was a brief silence as the import of her comment sank in, then Heather Johnson said, with a touch of disparagement, 'So it wasn't a matter of him playing around in Afghanistan, it was she doing the dirty on him while he was serving in a war zone. So much for her supposed hero-worship! A neighbour said she spent those four months in the Seychelles with a group of theatre people, if you recall.'

Max was silently kicking himself for not picking up on something a woman would immediately realize. Had Clarkson made a mistake? If not, this put a new slant on the case. A further complication.

Olly Simpson glanced up from his doodling. 'Shouldn't it have been Collier doing the beating up? The cuckolded husband.'

'Cuckolded by someone from *the theatre world*,' said Connie, with the emphasis used to impress facts on small children.

'Just making a passing comment,' he replied mildly, returning to his abstract scribbling.

Heather looked upset. 'If he's aware of her

167

betrayal he's surely being dealt more punishment than any man deserves.'

Beside Piercey's empty desk, Derek Beeny, looking curiously like a twin with his counterpart missing, said, 'Is *that* the truth that must be told? Guys who resent the recent publicity, and his father-in-law who's pushing him up the ladder, would love that bit of inside info.'

'So, when he refuses publicly to humiliate himself and his wife they beat him up in their attempt to show he's really weak and vulnerable?' put in Heather scathingly. 'That only happens in trash fiction.'

Suddenly entering the briefing he had remained unusually aloof from, Tom snapped, 'You're all indulging in a prurient barrack-room jaw, instead of using your apology for brains in constructive, professional reasoning.'

Connie was reluctant to surrender what she felt to be an important point. 'It's surely relevant to the case, sir. Her present pregnancy must have stemmed from the holiday in the Seychelles, but could a previous one have been the result of a liaison with one of Collier's squadron colleagues? A liaison he's reluctant to abandon and so mounts a campaign of harassment ending in an attempt to run her off the road.'

In his usual laconic fashion Olly Simpson said, 'Maybe she's been the squadron bicycle. They've all had a ride, and...'

'This has gone far enough,' ruled Tom in parade-ground volume. 'A casual statement from Major Clarkson, which could easily be erroneous due to the serious charge hanging over *him* at the moment, has no bearing on the brutal attack we're investigating.'

Good God, thought Max with a jolt, it's more than normal male reaction to a stunning woman. The poor sod has fallen into the honey trap! He decided to take back the initiative.

'As Mr Black says, you're all being side-tracked by what could easily have been a slip of the MO's tongue. Our task is to bring to book whoever grievously harmed Lieutenant Collier. The motive for the attack will emerge – the supposed truth that must be told – but our first concern is to track down the perpetrators, not to unravel the tangle of the Colliers' relationship.

'Major Clarkson will allow a woman to interview his patient this morning. He didn't approve of my "Nazi" tactics. Sergeant Bush can employ her gentler persuasion in an attempt to coax facts from a man maintaining a deter-mined pretence of amnesia.

'I'll set Sergeant Maddox's team on searching the area where the victim was found for evidence of the attack. I want all vehicles own-ed by members of his squadron and attached personnel, and that includes wives' and family cars, examined for blood, fibres or any signs that Collier had been transported in it.

'I want the owners of these vehicles ques-tioned, some for the second time, and I want one of you to get hold of media reports on that rescue outside Kandahar, wringing the core truth from the hype, while another of you gets details of the capture and escape in Sierra Leone that Collier was involved in. Does this "punishment" stem from that? Have any of his fellow captives recently arrived on this base?

'Try to trace the source of the phone call that sent Collier out vowing to silence the bastard. Just a wild hope,' he added with a wry smile. 'Mr Black will study squadron reports on the daily activities of A Flight during November to February in Kandahar, and I will see Mrs Collier. She has to know more than she will reveal.' His mouth twisted in another faint smile. 'My Nazi tactics might work better with her. I shall also do my best to persuade her to camp out with friends or family until this is sorted. Her safety should remove one reason for her husband's silence. We'll get to the bottom of this however tightly he clamps his lips. It'll take longer than if he opened up and confessed, but we'll get there.' He nodded at Connie Bush. 'Do your feminine utmost to wear him down.'

The team members were gathering car keys and mobile phones when Max thought of something else. 'Who's on call here this morning?'

'I am, sir,' said Roy Jakes.

'Right, get me the names and present locations of the four wounded men Collier rescued and flew to safety. Might get something from them that'll throw some light on our darkness.'

Margot Collier made it obvious that she regarded the visit intrusive and highly irritating. 'I'm

170

working on designs for a new ballet and I've already lost a week of creative inspiration. I informed your blundering sergeant major, who precipitately tackled Sam before I had the chance to tell him gently about the harassment, that I have nothing further to add concerning the attack on Monday night. I suggest you concentrate on finding who hurt him instead of persecuting me like this.'

Max saw an entirely different woman from the one who had fainted at his feet. Clad in a beige loose-fitting smock that hid her seductive curves, and with her blue-black hair screwed into a knot, the scowl on her face bare of make-up completed the destruction of his remember-ed image of a femme fatale.

'It's my duty to ensure your safety, Mrs Collier. I'm here to discuss that with you. Can we do it inside the house rather than on the doorstep?'

She walked away along the hall leaving Max to close the door and follow her up the stairs. He was not deluded into thinking he was about to be propositioned, however. The rear bed-room had windows in two adjoining walls, creating a well-lit corner where an angled draw-ing-board such as architects use was placed. On a stand beside it was a large circular container holding an array of glass jars filled with vibrantly coloured paints.

She was working on a dazzling black, gold and silver design that suggested to Max an explosion of fireworks against a night sky. He

171

was fascinated. Even knowing very little about ballet, apart from sharing the common masculine assertion that male dancers padded the front of their tights to produce the maximum effect, Max sensed that real talent had produced what he was seeing. Was *this* why the Colliers spent so much time on the upper floor?

'That's extraordinarily beautiful,' he commented with sincerity.

'Yes,' she agreed. 'Inspiration came last evening while sitting beside Sam's bed. He was sleeping and it was so peaceful.'

'How long have you been doing this kind of work?'

'As soon as I gained my degree in art and design, one of Daddy's friends saw some of my designs and mentioned them to his son who dances for Ballet Romayne. They gave me a small commission right away. I've now become their principal costume designer.'

She had suddenly become a compellingly beautiful woman again. Her dark-brown eyes now contained a core of dark fire, her expression had softened with the onset of artistic fervour.

'You've achieved success very early in your career.'

Her full, naturally pink lips curved in a smile. 'I'm so very fortunate to find fulfilment in both aspects of my life. Professionally with the Romayne, and personally with my darling Sam.'

Max found himself envying darling Sam, but sanity returned to remind him of why he was there. 'I would have thought marriage to an army pilot would hamper your professional life. Surely your studio should be in London, or wherever the ballet company has its headquarters. I've known women who're in routine jobs like teaching, PR, or accountancy, who refuse to move around with their military husbands and fragment their careers. Something highly specialized like your work is even less likely to be compatible with army life. Weren't you tempted to take that into account when you first met Sam?'

'It was love at first sight. I told you that. I *had* to have him.'

'Whatever the cost?'

'Cost? What cost?' She waved a hand at the vivid design. 'I can do this anywhere. I don't have to go to an office, or a school to use my skill. An artist satisfies the creative urge wherever it comes. I've known friends to travel back and forth on a bus or a ferry for a whole day because they have to obey the need to work while the impulse is strong.'

Deciding that this fanciful, to him, arty dissertation had gone on long enough, Max said, 'It's good that location doesn't hamper your inspiration, because I'm here to advise you to leave and stay with friends or family until we've put an end to this campaign against you and your husband. It will ensure your safety and lessen the problems he's having to deal with.'

Margot began walking from the room. 'Wrong! He needs me more than ever now.'

173

Max had to follow her down the flight of stairs, marvelling at how she had instantly changed back to the aggressive woman who had answered his knock on the front door.

'We hate being apart. It's *unbearable* when he has to go to a war zone without me.'

'So you make it bearable by spending those four months in the Seychelles with a group of friends?'

She rounded on him. 'Those *friends* were from the Romayne. We were *working*. And what gives you the right to pry into my private life?'

Max regarded her shrewdly. 'You asked SIB to investigate an apparent campaign of harassment against you and your husband. We're investigating, as you asked. People answer our questions and frequently tell us facts we don't even ask about.'

She put her hand on the door ready to open it and usher him out. 'Your so-called investigation appears to be more a muck-raking exercise than serious probing into those incidents I told you about.'

'Those incidents, Mrs Collier, have paled against the brutal attack on your husband. Our investigation has become a far more serious case; one which, I'm afraid, dictates deeper penetration into the background of you both. We're no longer acting on your application for help. A serving officer has been injured to the extent of making him unfit for action at a time of war. Regardless of smashed eggs on your doorstep, or deflated tyres at the NAAFI, we have a duty to seek out the person or persons who committed this serious crime against him. As a result, we think it's necessary for your safety to leave the base to stay with friends throughout the investigation.'

'No.'

Any enchantment he had experienced upstairs rapidly evaporated beneath growing irritation. 'When you spoke to Mr Black on Monday morning you gave as your reason for finally deciding to come to us your fear of a third miscarriage. I understand you told him that you and Sam desperately want this child. Is that no longer the case?'

Angry colour flooded her cheeks. 'How dare you make such a comment?'

'I dare, because you appear to fluctuate between desires,' he replied calmly. 'You've seen what your enemies – yes, they *are* enemies, Mrs Collier – have done to your husband. Are you yet aware that the attack culminated in a flogging? Have you seen his back? No, I can tell from your expression that you haven't. Perhaps you should take a look when you next visit him. Our concern is that you could suffer similarly before we apprehend those responsible, which would certainly heighten the risk of miscarriage.' Well into his stride, Max said again, 'So I dare to ask about the importance you place on this pregnancy.'

Margot's hands had gone up to cover her mouth as she gazed at Max in distress. 'I don't

175

understand. What do you mean, *flogged*?'

'Exactly what I say. Sam's back was lashed with what we believe was a length of rope.' He took advantage of her silence. 'Perhaps you'll now understand why we consider you should get away for a while.'

'I must see him.'

Max caught her arm as she made to run upstairs. 'Not right now. One of my sergeants is questioning him. He chose not to confide in me, but while he continues to withold evidence the danger to you both will remain.' Still holding her arm, he led her through to the room where two nights ago he had set her unconscious body on the sofa. 'When is the baby due?'

The response came without hesitation. 'Early November.'

That would tie in with Collier's return from Kandahar. If Clarkson's estimate of the present stage of pregnancy was correct, she would have to bluff it out with darling Sam by claiming premature birth. Nothing new there. Many a husband had been thus fooled.

'You owe it to your child, if no one else, to put an end to this persecution,' he said firmly. 'Who made that phone call on Monday evening? Who wrote the letters Sam destroyed? Who tried to run you off the road?'

'I have to see Sam,' she said plaintively. 'I *have* to.'

'Answer my questions!' He knew he sounded brutal but, after Collier's performance this

176

morning, he was losing all patience with this pair.

She appeared to wilt as she gazed at him with tears shimmering in her eyes. *'I don't know.* Sam told me he'd sort it. I should have believed him. It's all my fault he's been hurt. *I've* done this to him by running to you. It's all my fault.'

Enlightenment suddenly dawned. Max folded his arms and gave her a calculated survey from head to toe. 'You shouldn't be designing costumes for the theatre, you should be performing in it. Drop the act, Margot, you've lost your audience.'

For a long silent moment Max was treated to a comparable calculated survey, before she said frankly, 'I had you cast as the simple khaki plod.'

His eyes narrowed. 'Grave error. I'm taking the lead role in this plot ... and *you* are in danger of being charged with withholding vital evidence. Let's have an end to your arty tomfoolery. Start behaving like a responsible woman and tell me all you know about this campaign against the man you profess to love so deeply. Or is that merely an aspect of the histrionics?'

'No,' she said quietly.

'Then fire away ... and give it to me straight this time.'

Eight

Sam Collier no longer looked a hunk and a half to Connie Bush when she entered the small ward. Not surprising after such a beating, but she still was impressed by his composure and by the contrast of blond hair and very dark eyes. She reminded herself that, whatever he had done to provoke retaliation, he had rescued four soldiers under fire. She had previously dealt with men whose basic character verged on the villainous, yet who displayed amazing courage on the battlefield. Was Collier another of them?

Connie smiled and perched on the bed. 'Sergeant Bush, SIB. The Doc has allowed me to talk to you on condition that I don't use Nazi tactics. I won't ask how you're feeling, because that rainbow of bruises on your face gives me a likely answer. Although, I guess it's your back that's giving the most pain. Major Clarkson reckons no lasting damage has been done, so you should be back in the cockpit before too long.'

Collier said nothing while he very obviously studied her dark trouser suit, white blouse and neat hairstyle.

'Andy Richards told us flying is the great love

of your life. How old were you when you first took to the air?'

'Twelve.'

She gave another glowing smile. 'However did you manage that? A kind uncle?'

'Aye, you're right there, but he wasn't a pilot. Our family aren't in that bracket.'

'You're a pilot,' she pointed out.

'At the county fair there was a guy who gave joy rides around the dales for fifteen minutes. Uncle Jack talked him into taking me up for ten pounds less than the usual price.'

'And that lit a flame in you? My friend has a fourteen-year-old brother with the same burning desire. He spends all his free time at a local transport museum helping a former World War Two squadron leader to restore a classic bomber from that period. He can't wait to leave school and join the RAF. I guess flying has to be a real passion. People don't become pilots the way they would drift into selling shoes or ice-cream.'

'Or fish-and-chips. You've carefully avoided that, haven't you?'

Connie reminded herself she was dealing with a man Max had described as cool, glib and lying his head off. He had seen through her attempt to jolly him along before firing the relevant questions.

'*You* avoided joining the family business,' she riposted, using that opening to get down to brass tacks. 'Did it create a break with your parents, cause bad feeling with your siblings?'

'To the extent that they'd fly to Germany to beat me up?' He leaned back on his pillows, winced and sat forward again. 'Use the Nazi tactics, lass. You'll employ them sooner or later.'

Very cool! How glib would he prove to be when she did as he suggested? 'You told Captain Rydal you remember nothing of the events of Monday evening; why you were walking alone in the dark or who had phoned to tell you to rendezvous there. We think you're lying.'

'If you've never suffered from amnesia it's natural to think it's a load of codswallop.'

'Who sent the letters demanding that you tell the truth?'

'What letters?'

'Your amnesia goes back that far, does it?'

Those dark eyes gazed steadily at her. 'How far back is that?'

'Before the harassment of your wife began; before someone tried to drive her off the road at speed.'

There was a definite reaction now. 'I knew nothing about that until she told me.'

Connie pounced. 'She revealed those facts *after* the letters arrived. Your amnesia began much later.'

'She told me about the harassment last night.'

'The medical staff said she complained because you'd slept throughout her visit.'

'Did they? How odd.'

Oh yes, *very* glib. 'When is the baby due?'

He blinked with surprise that she had abandoned the penetrating questioning. 'Early in November.'

'You remember being told about that?'

'Major Clarkson mentioned it yesterday.' Still coolly lying.

'What was it like in Afghanistan?'

'Very hot.'

'Your amnesia doesn't cover that period?'

'Apparently not.'

'It was hot, exhausting and dangerous,' Connie suggested. 'Constant patrols over hostile areas, basic living conditions, forced companionship twenty-four-seven with guys who sometimes riled you, piled on the stress. Is that about right?'

'Aye, lass, like they show it on the TV news.'

'Who did you cross swords with in a major way out there?'

'Several Taliban snipers. You'll have read about it even if Andy Richards hasn't told you.'

He was good, she had to hand him that. 'Your wife spent those four months relaxing in the Seychelles. How did you feel about that?'

'Glad that she was with friends to ease the worry over my safety. It wasn't a holiday. She was working on new designs for ballet costumes. Members of the company were with her.'

Connie suspected he was dominating this meeting with that determination that defied snipers' bullets to rescue fellow soldiers; strength of purpose, coolness under fire and, yes, the well-known grit of the working-class

181

Yorkshireman. She could understand his appeal to a wealthy Sloanite from the artificial theatrical world. A bit of rough? No, an intelligent, down-to-earth, skilful, masculine man. Yet, someone hated him enough to half-kill him two nights ago. And he had no intention of revealing why. Connie was intrigued and sympathetic, against her better judgement.

'You say you were glad Mrs Collier had friends to ease her worry over your safety in Afghanistan. How about her worry over this attack on you? Don't you owe it to her to ensure it never happens again ... with fatal results next time?'

He forced a smile that was more a grimace due to the cut on his lip. 'I'll never walk around the base alone at night, for *any* reason.'

Trying a different direction, Connie said, 'Your wife would have been deeply afraid during those days you were held hostage in Sierra Leone. It could have gone either way, I understand.'

Suddenly, there was a reaction. The coolness vanished. 'That was three bloody years ago. Why bring it up in this context?'

Connie followed that up, sensing a breakthrough. 'Your friends gave their opinion that Margot miscarried because of her fears for your life at that time. She's pregnant again, at the same vulnerable stage. Do you really want to risk a miscarriage? It would be the third, and this time could result in serious damage to her. If you're as devoted to each other as she claims, you'll protect her as selflessly as you protect your fellows on the battlefield.'

He visibly struggled with vying demands, his iron composure badly cracked. Connie watched and silently urged him to give her the means to break this case open, whatever his personal cost.

Finally, he slumped wearily, regardless of the pain to his back. 'There'll be nothing more. It's over.'

'What's over?' she probed gently.

'They've made their point. I've got the message.' It was said in a vague monotone as he gazed into something only he could see.

'The message from whom?'

He took his time. 'It doesn't matter.'

'You don't want them punished for what they did to you?'

Those compelling eyes focused on her once more. 'Just drop it.'

Connie shook her head. 'We can't do that, sir.'

'I'm not laying charges.'

She leaned towards him to impress her words on him. 'It's out of your hands. This isn't a case of neglecting to salute, or using abusive language to a superior. A serving officer has been attacked and rendered unfit for duty when we're engaged in a war situation on several fronts. We have to investigate, whether or not a charge is laid. You're not just the victim, you're the sole witness to the attack and it's your duty to name the perpetrators.'

The coolness returned. He had mastered his

moment of weakness. 'I can't. I don't remember anything about it. I've told you that several times.'

Connie sighed. 'Please don't be foolish, sir. We know you're lying.'

Closing his eyes, he murmured, 'The pain in my head has grown unbearable. Send in an orderly with pills as you leave.'

The morning sick parade had followed the usual pattern. Minor injuries sustained during combat training or sports sessions, mild food-poisoning due to unwise eating, sinus infections, styes, fears of impotence by hopeful fathers, a dose of clap. Charles Clarkson was reaching the end of writing-up his case notes, and was preparing to eject the young detective with Collier who looked like a health freak with no business in a place like this, when his mobile rang. A swift glance showed him the caller was his wife. He got up and walked to shut his office door before connecting with her.

'Something wrong, darling?'

She sounded deeply distressed. 'Charlie, they came here just now demanding to speak to the children. They said ... they said they could be ... at risk. From *you*!'

'*What?*' he yelled. '*Who* came? Who were they, Ria? I'll sort the bastards out.'

'No, Charlie, they said they have to interview the children when you aren't there to influence what they say. I refused to let them come in, but they said they'll return with written authority to enter. Please come home.'

'On my way,' he said through a constricted throat.

He drove to his quarter the quickest way, which included crossing the area where soldiers were being drilled by sergeants with stentorian voices. These broke off in disbelief on seeing a vehicle violating the sanctity of the parade ground. Charles had just one thought; to reach his family before his children could be subjected to questioning that would surely alienate them from him forever.

They would then see his affectionate hugs and kisses, his teasing pats on the bottom or hair-ruffling, as indicative of unhealthy behaviour. They would watch him uneasily, ensure they were never alone with him. Already, they were wary in his presence, knowing he must have done something awful to Stacey to turn their friends against them and make them virtual prisoners in their own home.

Ria looked pale and stressed when he arrived and let himself in. There was an alarming silence throughout the house. 'Where are they?' he demanded sharply.

'Upstairs doing the work we set them.' She gripped his hand. 'They don't know yet. I haven't said anything to them. What shall we do if they come back with the Redcaps?'

Taking her arm he led her to the stairs, saying, 'You and the kids won't be here. You must take them to Portugal today. *Now!*' He almost pushed her up the stairs. 'Forget luggage, the gifts for your parents. Grab their coats and get them out to your car while I fetch the passports, a wad of Euros and the air tickets. Hurry, Ria!'

While he took from his office drawer the thick envelope containing all they needed for their trip to Ria's home next week, Charles heard his wife instructing their children in tones that betrayed her fear, and their voices raised in bewildered protest as they clattered downstairs.

Extracting his own passport and air ticket, Charles walked out to the garage and handed Ria the envelope. He had to clear his throat to speak. 'I can't leave the base, but they won't stop you going through the gate. Park the car at the airport. I'll arrange for it to be picked up later. Exchange the tickets for today's flight. Upgrade to first if you have to, but get on that plane.' He crushed her hands between his own, saying thickly, 'I'll join you as soon as ... for Easter.'

There was pain across his chest as he forced a smile for four children regarding him stony-eyed and silent from the car. 'Bye, kids. See you next week at Granny Sophia's.' He turned back to his wife. 'Go now. *Go!*'

Tom sat in a bare, empty room at 678 Squadron's headquarters with a pile of flight action reports stacked on the table. He felt no enthusiasm to study them. Connie Bush had just put forward a theory that made a great deal of unwelcome sense.

What if Margot Collier had been conducting a

covert affair with a squadron member prior to A Flight's deployment to Kandahar? Shortly after their return, lover is given his marching orders while husband is lauded as a hero with his wife all over him very publicly. Then she announces that she is pregnant. Jealous lover is convinced the child is his and sends letters to Sam demanding that the true parentage be revealed. When that fails, lover harasses Margot hoping to frighten her into acknowledging his right as her child's father and reviving the relationship.

So far so good. It was a common enough situation when husbands' work took them away for considerable periods. Predatory males then closed in on lonely wives. In this hypothesis, the rivals could have been away together. Had Sam and the other man crossed swords at Kandahar? Jerry Lang had made the point that Sam had been pushing himself to the limits lately, as if trying to prove something. Baz Flint had declared Collier was like a man gone beserk during his rescue of four wounded men. What had truly driven him that day?

Taking his thoughts further, Tom recalled the lance corporal who had mistaken him for a journalist saying 'Daddy' was pushing Collier up the ladder in an attempt to make him worthy to join the family. Was that behind the young pilot's refusal to name his attackers, because that was where Connie's theory came unstuck? Charles Clarkson reckoned at least three had been involved in the attack. A rejected, humiliated lover would hardly employ others to beat up his rival to establish his masculine superiority.

So were there two separate issues here? Had the assault on Sam *no* link with the harassment of Margot? The latter could be due to Connie's theory, but the ferocity of the beating of a man generally liked and respected had to have a far more complex explanation.

The nature of the punishment should surely tell them something. *Fifty lashes as the sun goes down.* It smacked of Mutiny on the Bounty, and press gangs. No link to airmen. Tom smiled to himself. He was growing as fanciful as Max. Think more along the lines of a length of rope being the handiest weapon to give a man a lesson he would not ignore.

As he reached for the first of the reports on operations carried out by A Flight in Kandahar, Tom's mobile rang.

'Piercey here, sir,' said the familiar voice undaunted by last night's events. The reason for this was immediately revealed. 'I've traced a car whose boot is smeared with blood and mud. There are also spatters of what looks like blood-stained sputum.'

Tom frowned. 'That's fast going considering you were absent at the morning briefing.'

'I guessed what we'd be searching for and had a hunch,' Piercey said with barely disguised satisfaction. 'The car in question is the blue Audi owned by the AAC guy on UK leave. Cunning, or what?'

'Could be blood from a weekend joint, or an

injured dog,' Tom said brusquely. 'Until forensics check for a link to Lieutenant Collier we can't assume a breakthrough.' He then grudgingly added, 'Let's hope we can show them we're more cunning than they are. Get the crime scene boys on it.'

'Already have, sir.'

Tom could hear the grin in Piercey's voice. 'Don't push your luck, man. Uniform are keeping the cell warm for you.'

Tom disconnected, then leaned back to assess this information. Any locked car could be opened and used with ease by men with military training so, theoretically, any person on this base could have taken that Audi. Tom amended that to any person who knew the owner was in the UK. That would surely narrow the field a little. Was it an attempt to focus SIB attention on 678 Squadron by others unconnected to the AAC?

On a base housing battalions of two line regiments, large units from specialist corps, numerous admin personnel, service families and local civilians, it was not surprising that people tended to mingle within their own group, knowing little of the affairs of those in others. Soldiers who took to the air were even more detached from their uniformed colleagues, both professionally and geographically. Squadron routine and activities were unique to those who fought in the skies, creating intangible segregation, and the siting of their operational headquarters was, of necessity, on the furthest boundary well clear of other buildings.

Reviewing all this, Tom had to accept that the Audi must have been used by squadron members, or by men who served them in support roles. Only they would have access to the leave roster which showed Lieutenant Maine to be in the UK. Then he chided himself for reading too much into Piercey's discovery. As he had told the cocky sergeant, the blood could have come from the Sunday joint.

Turning his attention back to the reports on the desk, he read through about a quarter of them before Max walked in.

'How's it going?'

Erroneously reading impatience in the question, Tom responded coolly. 'Basic stuff so far. Most of it is technical gobbledegook unless you're a flier, and I don't believe there'll be any mention of personal aggro in what are purely factual operational data.'

Max nodded. 'I suspected as much. Piercey can go through the rest. He can't get into trouble doing that.'

Tom swung round fully to face Max. 'He's already jumped the gun. Called in to report traces of blood, sputum etcetera in the boot of the blue Audi owned by the pilot on UK leave. Could be a false lead, but my money's on it being the vehicle used to take Collier to the place where the significant part of the punishment was administered.'

'You see significance in the flogging?'

190

'Has to be,' said Tom, knowing the way Max's mind worked. 'But I can't progress further than ships of the line with billowing sails, and a bosun with the cat o' nine tails.'

Max grinned. 'You've seen too many Hollywood screen blockbusters. Flogging was once a recognized penalty for military offenders, too. I'm also still working on the link here. Once we get that we'll be halfway to a result.' He sat as if intending to stay for a while. 'Do they do coffee here?'

Surprised, Tom nodded and got to his feet. 'They told me tea and coffee makings were in an alcove at the end of the corridor.'

'Get a skivvy to do it, Tom. I've something interesting to impart.'

Having detailed to make coffee the lance corporal he had reported for gossiping in the belief that he was a journalist, Tom returned to the bare room slightly irritated. If Max had info of relevance to the case why not cut the preamble and come out with it, instead of sending him in search of hot drinks? He grew further irritated when he saw the smile on the other man's face and remembered that Max had been with Margot Collier.

'Coffee pronto,' he announced, and sat heavily in the chair he had just vacated.

'Is that midway between espresso and latte?' Seeing that Tom was not amused by his flippancy, Max got to the point. 'You checked Collier's career and discovered that he's a double hero due to events in Sierra Leone. As that

191

hostage affair is three years old, neither of us connected it with this case.'

'It's relevant?' Tom asked sharply.

The girl arrived with mugs of coffee, and a plate of biscuits which Tom rated an apology for her earlier crassness. At her swift exit he repeated his question.

Max avoided a direct reply. 'Neighbours told us the Colliers spend more time upstairs than down, and we all interpreted that the way they did. Given the ravishing Margot's public claims of overwhelming mutual passion, who could blame us for our prurient conclusion?' He took up a mug and commented before sipping the coffee, 'That woman is a consummate actress, my friend. She's had everyone fooled.'

Knowing he was not going to like what he was about to hear, Tom left the other mug on the tray. 'She admitted it?'

Taking a biscuit, Max dipped it in his coffee. 'They spend so much time upstairs because that's where she works. She showed me the bedroom set up as a studio. While she creates, he sits at a desk studying German and French. *Fully clothed.*'

Unsure of his own reaction to that, Tom asked, 'What's the relevance of Sierra Leone?'

'Darling Sam was a changed man afterwards.'

'He would be. They all would be. Only the shrinks who debriefed them discovered full details of their ordeal. Military hostages are forbidden to speak about what really happened. They have to say with as much sincerity as they can muster that they were well fed and treated with respect. Nobody believes the lie, but public conjecture falls drastically short of the truth in many cases. Drug-crazed tribal kids with rifles and a supply of ammo are capable of any obscenity. Collier appears to have risen above the experience.'

'With his wife's help.'

'So I'd hope,' said Tom forcefully, thinking of the support Nora had given him during the last few difficult weeks. 'I still don't see...'

'It wasn't enough. We should have delved deeper into comments that Collier was pushing himself to the limits, that he was like a man beserk while rescuing those four in Kandahar. A man trying to *prove* something.'

Still unsure where this was leading, Tom finally picked up his coffee and drank waiting for elucidation. Was Max hinting that Collier was a potential nut case?

'She's a very complex woman and the complexity is centred around herself. Her husband enters the equation only inasmuch as his actions affect her. And Daddy.' Seeing Tom's expression he wagged his head. 'No, not a dangerously unhealthy fixation like we dealt with at Christmas. General Phipps is merely a doting widowed father who desires all life's blessings to surround her. Nothing but the absolute best for his girl.'

'So darling Sam has to meet that criterion?'

'Exactly.'

'Most people would reckon he has.'

'Not Daddy. Being taken hostage was evidence of deplorable lack of leadership qualities. He betrayed three men by failing to act decisively in an unexpected crisis, subjecting them to a degrading ordeal and besmirching the reputation of the British Army.'

'Besmirching! Good God, he's a Victorian relic. He'd approve of flogging as a punishment, that's for sure. Did she tell you all that in those precise words?'

'She did.'

Absorbing the facts with reluctance, Tom then said, 'I glanced through the official report on the affair. There was no suggestion of blame being accredited to Collier. He was with his air gunner and a pair of mechanics at dusk, out on the boundary of the rough air strip cut through the jungle. They were finalizing an inspection of repairs to a Lynx when a group of trigger-happy kids materialized from the trees and surrounded them.

'Collier attempted to negotiate but was felled with a rifle butt, leaving the rest in no doubt of the threat to their safety. They were spirited away long before their absence was noted. There'd been no report of renegades in the area, so the attack took them totally unawares.'

'Faulty intelligence?'

'No. Seems they were breakaway thugs using their weapons to terrorize people subsisting in small settlements; raping girls and youths, stealing food and anything necessary to support their nomadic rampage. The plan was to demand money for their hostages but they had no idea how to go about it. Collier devised an escape plan before they solved their problem. He received a commendation for that.' Tom frowned and added, 'I'd reckon he displayed enough leadership qualities to satisfy any critic, wouldn't you?'

'*I* would. Daddy stuck by his assertion that Collier should have prevented it ever happening.'

Against his inclination Tom asked if Margot agreed with her father, and was relieved when Max said no.

'But she desperately needed hubby to compensate and reverse the General's thinking. You can guess he was aware of that. You know how women manage to transfer their thoughts without saying a word.'

'Tell me about it,' he murmured, remembering last night. 'The old bastard must be satisfied now that son-in-law has been so extensively celebrated as a hero.' A thought struck him. '*He* organized that overblown media coverage?'

Max gave him a shrewd look. 'I'd say she did. I told you she's a complex creature. Daddy's criticism of her chosen partner is criticism of *her*. She's beautiful, wealthy, artistically talented, widely admired and envied. Daddy adores her, darling Sam is besotted. She's perfect! Criticism is taboo. Collier brought it down on her head; he had to banish it.'

'She told you *that*?' Tom cried incredulously.

'Didn't have to, it stood out a mile. That

woman is manipulative. Her looks make it easy. She manipulated *us*, chum. Smashed eggs on the doorstep, posters under the windscreen wipers? When I quizzed her about that she merely smiled.'

'All lies?'

'It can't be proved either way, but if she was playing some curious game it's turned frighteningly nasty. The doorstep swoon was real enough, and she's now running scared. What began with a few anonymous letters has developed into a bid to rob her of the man she chose to bestow her perfection upon.'

'You believe the letters were fact?'

'Yes, because they were directed at him. He's the real target, as this brutal attack proves. I have a theory and I'd like your thinking on it.' Max put his empty mug on the desk and sat back in the chair. 'Margot told me Sam hasn't fully recovered from whatever occurred in Sierra Leone. He has nightmares, bursts of violent temper, withdraws into himself where she can't reach him. He also hides bottles of vodka about the house.'

Tom was puzzled. 'Why secret drinking when everyone on this base does it very publicly?'

'It's only in the weeks leading up to deployment in a war zone, and for several weeks after his return.'

'Dutch courage?'

'Sounds like it. He needs artificial stimulus to face the enemy, and regular quaffs to unwind once the dangerous period has passed. Was that cool rescue in Kandahar fuelled by vodka?'

Tom frowned. 'How would he get hold of the stuff? Alcohol is forbidden in a war zone, and I can't see how he'd manage to smuggle over there enough for a four-month stint. No, I'd say you're on the wrong track there. Only confirmed alcoholics hide bottles all over the house, and it would be obvious to his colleagues by now if Collier was drinking to that extent.'

'Mmm. We'll have to investigate, although we only have her word for that along with everything else she told us. For the immediate future Collier is effectively grounded, so we'll hold off on that until we can confront him with Margot's claim and get at the truth.'

'Or his version of it,' Tom pointed out. 'He's claiming loss of memory.'

'I think we need a full report of what happened in Sierra Leone. Margot says he's not been the same since that hostage drama, and I'd like to know if the others are still reacting to whatever happened during their captivity.'

'I can't see any possible link between that affair and the recent attack on Collier.' Tom gave Max a mental nudge. 'You wanted to air a theory?'

'Right. Here it is. Anonymous letters start arriving at the Collier home threatening punishment unless some fact is made public. I'd guess they were more explicit than we've been told. Margot is alarmed. Sam makes light of them, but she does her utmost to persuade him to come to us. He's unresponsive, but at the vodka behind her back. The baby she's carrying isn't his, but she wants him and Daddy to believe he's the father. That'll uphold the rightness of her decision to marry a fish-and-chip guy against Daddy's advice.'

'What?'

'I told you she's totally self-centred. Two pregnancies have aborted. She needs to produce a child to complete the perfection of her life. She conceives in the Seychelles, deliberately or accidentally, and returns to Germany hoping her new lover's genes will ensure a full-term pregnancy. Her happiness is inexplicably dashed by threats to her darling Sam.' Noting Tom's expression, he said, 'Oh, she adores him, in her fashion, and desperately needs him to be acknowledged by everyone as the father of the child. It's what she has planned, you see, so it *must* happen.'

Tom took a deep breath. 'You despise her, don't you.'

'That's too strong a word. She's not wicked, just wrapped-up in the concept of what she thinks she is.'

'Is that your theory,' he asked flatly.

'My theory is that she came to you with an invented tale of harassment against her, because she knew SIB would have to investigate. That would scare off whoever was threatening Sam. The move rebounded on her. He's now lying in sick bay after a beating for which she blames herself. It's my guess Collier also blames her. If he discovers the truth about the baby she's carrying, that marriage is liable to crumble. Bang goes Margot Collier's idyllic life.' Max allowed a significant pause. 'She's not the woman you see, Tom.'

He stiffened. 'I take it you mean she's not the woman *one* sees.'

'Of course.'

'Right, you've got under her facade, but where's the link with Sierra Leone?'

'We have yet to uncover that. I said it was just a theory I wanted to run past you. So far we've found no clues to suggest Collier crossed someone in Kandahar, or here in Germany, so we have to look at an event which could have bred aggro that's been smouldering for three years. We need to trace the present whereabouts of his fellow hostages. I'd also like details of Collier's breakout plan.'

'That last is easy. There's a full report available from Records. We already have someone tracing the three captured with him. Unless they're presently in Germany, I'd say your theory is a non-starter,' Tom said firmly, and with secret satisfaction. Max was surely allowing his powers of reasoning to set off a wild goose chase, something not unknown where he was concerned. Still, this time the goose might lay the golden egg. The sooner the better. This case was getting under his skin. He would be glad to see the back of it.

Nine

Connie Bush sat at her desk in contemplative mood. She had been out-manoeuvred by Sam Collier, yet she could not banish the urge to champion him despite evidence suggesting he had done something that warranted vicious reprisals. Her experience at interviewing led her to believe he was basically what his colleagues claimed; a decent, up-front team player. It also told her he was lying in denying any recollection of the assault.

Was he doing it to protect himself or another person? The likeliest one was the fickle wife he was said to adore. Could Piercey's suggestion that she had paid several squaddies to beat up her man be right? No, she had collapsed on seeing the Duty Officer with an apparent civilian on the doorstep at midnight. So Sam was protecting himself which, Connie reluctantly concluded, meant he had done something so serious he was desperate to conceal it.

Sucking the end of a pen Connie reviewed Collier's words before effectively getting rid of her. *There'll be nothing more. It's over. They've made their point. I've got the message.* What message?

While she made a cup of tea and selected two chocolate marshmallows from the comfort food tin, Connie's thoughts returned to the possibility of Margot's baby being fathered by one of her theatre friends. Doc Clarkson's comment about the fourteen-week period, if true, made the possibility fact. Despite his present problems, Connie did not believe he would make an error of six or seven weeks.

Walking back to her desk she considered the idea of Margot being generally promiscuous, having had lovers closer to home. Lovers humiliated enough at being ditched to beat up the man she now publicly claimed to be so crazy about. Could three of them have joined forces for the punishment? It was possible. When their manhood was questioned men acted in ways inexplicable to most women. Flogging a man because his wife had made fools of them? Connie had come across more curious cases.

Munching marshmallows thoughtfully, she recalled Sherilie Fox calling her neighbour a nympho. Claimed it was universally known. Then Connie remembered what else the loud-mouthed woman had said.

Derek Beeny had talked to Ray Fox on the first day of the investigation concerning the harassment of Margot, but the pilot had not been interviewed after the attack on Collier. Why? Feeling the buzz that came at the start of a fresh line of enquiry, Connie brought up on her computer screen all known facts on the man whose wife had caught him watching Margot Collier through binoculars.

Ray Fox had entered the Army Air Corps straight from school and had excelled on the pilot training course. After gaining his wings he had been retained at Middle Wallop as an instructor. Six months ago he had joined 678 Squadron following an incident with a female student pilot. SIB had prepared to mount an investigation, but the complaint had been withdrawn. Connie frowned. Another instance of a woman allowing a man to get away with an offence in order to protect her career. It happened too often for her liking.

She then accessed all the reports and found John Fraeme's statement that Fox and Andy Richards were temperamentally and professionally incompatible in the air, so Fraeme flew with Fox and Richards with Sam Collier.

The wounded Richards had been awarded a DFC for the Afghan rescue. Was there resentment from Fox on that score? But why flog Sam? Because he had made that award possible?

Abandoning that line of thought, Connie reverted to Fox's voyeurism when Margot was gardening in tight shorts. Could she have had a fling with him at some time? They were neighbours. Easy enough for Fox to vault the fence when both partners were absent. Had Margot's pregnancy, and her public adoration of her hero husband, driven Fox to enrol two pals to hold Sam while he vented pent-up fury on a man who appeared to have everything? Growing interested, Connie took up her car keys. Second Lieutenant Raymond Peter Fox was due for another interview.

Connie tracked her subject down at home, relaxing after a two-day night-flying exercise at a nearby NATO base. The reason why he had not been available for interview after the attack. He answered her knock dressed in tracksuit trousers and a T-shirt bearing the words WELSHMEN SING WHILE THEY DO IT. In the first five seconds he had mentally removed Connie's dark trouser suit and white blouse, and was down to her knickers and bra before she could advise him who she was.

Giving a sly smile, he murmured, 'Policemen not only getting younger, bach, they're going in for sex change.'

The flippant words did not cover the signs of unease on a face deeply bronzed by the Afghan sun and ruddy from alcohol. Connie returned his smile. 'And policemen do it with restraints. I'd like a few words with you, sir. Can we go indoors?'

He stood back with a theatrical sweep of his arm. 'Come in to my parlour, said the spider.'

Connie entered the room still cluttered with unironed clothes, chocolate boxes and bottles of nail varnish in rainbow colours. The number of beer cans had increased. Ray Fox looked to be on a bender. She smiled inwardly. If he tried anything he would find himself on the floor before he knew it.

'Your wife out?' she asked, turning as he came up behind her.

He indicated the nail varnish. 'Beauty salon. Mud bath, massage, facial, manicure, pedicure, hairdo. The lot!'

'Expensive afternoon.'

'Tell me about it. Spend, spend, spend!'

'Have trouble settling mess bills?' she probed experimentally.

His eyes narrowed. 'If you've come here to be nasty you can go straight out again, *Sergeant*.'

'I'd like to talk to you about Lieutenant Collier, get your opinion of him. You know he was badly beaten two nights ago?'

'God, yes.' He dropped heavily on the sofa and picked up an open can. 'Can't believe it. Who'd want to...?'

'Please don't drink while I'm conducting this interview, sir.'

'Interview? You said a few words,' he protested loudly. 'Look, I don't know anything about that so why pester me?'

'We're interviewing everyone again, trying to find a reason for such a brutal attack. Can you throw any light on it?'

'No. I already told you that.'

'Do you get on well with him?'

'Yes.'

'But not with Staff Richards?'

His blunt features took on an affronted expression. 'What's the bastard been saying?'

'Your flight commander won't crew you with him. He mentioned a clash of temperaments. Is that right?'

Fox lifted the beer can and drank defiantly before saying, 'He's too slow. Questions everything I say. Shows no damn respect.' He glared up at Connie. 'It's my *life* on the line up there, you know!

'And his.' She got down to his level by perching on a footstool. 'You think he's dangerous?'

He nodded vigorously. '*Bloody* dangerous.'

'Yet Captain Fraeme is happy to let him fly.' There was silence. 'And he's recently been decorated for that daring rescue in Kandahar.'

That clearly touched a nerve. 'A gong for getting shot-up? Passed out, didn't he? Sam had to fly them back. Told you he was bloody dangerous. Set down right where the snipers were hiding. Could've got them all killed or captured.' His glazed eyes stared into space. 'Know what they do to prisoners?'

'So Sam Collier was truly the hero?' Connie probed.

'Had to be, hadn't he? S'what Margot ordered.' His words were growing slurred, his Welsh accent more pronounced. 'Can't blame him for doing anything to keep her happy, can you? What man wouldn't?' He appeared to have forgotten who Connie was and aired his thoughts. '*She* doesn't need mud baths and pummelling with oils. *She's* got it all quite natural, like. And she's got the dosh. Thousands and *thousands*. Sam never has to worry about mess bills, does he? Asks nicely and gets a handout.' He grinned drunkenly. 'Asks *very* nicely, lucky sod. So why can't he share it around, eh? Not asking for much, is it?'

Tardily realizing how very inebriated he was, Connie said encouragingly, 'Just a small loan to tide you over?'

Fox wagged his head slowly. 'A gift, bach, a *gift*. Know his little secret, don't I?'

Connie schooled her voice to remain casual. 'And what's that?'

'If I told you, wouldn't be a secret, would it?' he mumbled with another sly grin. Then he patted the sofa. 'Come over here, be nice to me, and I might whisper in your ear.'

Connie went out to her car and called Tom Black to report a breakthrough in the Collier case.

Max finally located Charles Clarkson at the Rifle Club bar, contemplating a double whisky. The doctor regarded him with caution. 'Have they rightly concluded that she's lying?'

'It's too early for that.' Max perched on the neighbouring stool. 'You've damaged your case by sending your family away. It's likely to be regarded as a sign of guilt by the Joint Response Team.'

'Balls to how they regard it!' he replied explosively. 'I'm not having my kids put through the mangle until they believe their father is a perverted monster. Who do those bloody people think they are? What right have they to ask my innocent children if they're being sexually abused by their father, merely on the strength of the fantasy of an overweight fourteen-year-old in the grips of a feverish virus?'

'All too often it's not fantasy. We have to investigate.'

Clarkson's mouth twisted. 'You can all relax in the knowledge that four badly damaged kids are now safely out of reach of my criminal acts of depravity.'

Although Max sympathized, he ignored the outburst. Not being a father he could not fully appreciate the man's anguish. 'Let's talk about Sam Collier ... in the corner where we can't be overheard.' Max walked there leaving Clarkson to join him at a small table. When they were both seated he said, 'Sergeant Bush interviewed your patient. Her feminine approach brought no more success than my Nazi tactics. He's still claiming amnesia, which we know is feigned.'

'Not necessarily. His head was heftily beaten. The lashes to his back would add to the total shock to his system. Involuntary amnesia could act as a defensive mechanism.'

Max did not argue. He could tell when a man was lying, and Collier had apparently betrayed himself to Connie Bush by vowing they had made their point and he had got the message.

'Has he talked to you about his injuries? If he remembers nothing of the attack he's surely bombarded you with questions. I'd be bloody worried and anxious to find myself in such a state without knowing why.'

Clarkson's hard, penetrating glare did not surprise Max, nor did his assertion that he and his female sergeant were the detectives; he was simply a medical practitioner dispensing palliatives and cures.

'It's your job to discover who put him in my sick bay. Mine is to ease his discomfort. Between molesting young girls, of course.'

Ignoring that last comment, Max said, 'His wife just told me Collier has never fully recovered from captivity in Sierra Leone. He has nightmares, bursts of violent temper, periods of withdrawal when she can't get through to him. It's been going on for three years. During that period you must have...' He held up his hands. 'No, I'm not asking for confidential data, just tell me if he has come to you for help or advice on the problem.'

After some thought, Clarkson said harshly, 'I've seen Collier for his annual medical check, and once for a broken toe.' Again a twist of his lips. 'I've read through his case notes recently otherwise I wouldn't know that. I didn't recognize him when he was brought in by the paramedics.'

'So you've no knowledge of his hang-up over Sierra Leone?'

'No.'

'Can you tell me who debriefed the hostages? You'll surely have a report by one of the psycho brigade certifying his fitness to return to duty.'

'Details of that debrief won't be with the standard case notes. They're highly confidential.'

Max felt it was like communicating through a

bowl of porridge trying to get useful responses from this man. 'But there will be a document with a signature on it, clearing Collier for duty.'

'Yes.'

'I need to see it.'

Clarkson drank the whisky remaining in his glass. 'David Culdrow is at the Medical Centre now. He'll find it for you.'

Max stood and took a few steps towards the door, but was halted by Clarkson. 'Why the sudden interest in events of three years ago?'

Max turned to face the hostile doctor. 'It's your job to ease your patients' discomfort; mine is to discover why that's necessary.' Nodding at the empty glass in Clarkson's hand, he added, 'Go easy on that stuff if you mean to get in a car to drive home.'

He looked a mess. Tousled hair, what trendy guys would call 'designer stubble', and a crumpled T-shirt claiming Welshmen sang while they did it. Max regarded him coldly. In the manner of old Hollywood gangster films, Ray Fox was certainly going to 'sing'before the day was out.

They had brought him in, plied him with black coffee and put him in an interview room with enough bombast to drive away any idea he might have that they were not serious. Connie Bush thought him pathetic, but that was her opinion of most men she came across in her job. Full of hot air until SIB inserted the pin that burst the balloon. She was presently tingling with anticipation and glowing from a sense of satisfaction that she had picked up on evidence no one else had found significant. A comment of 'sharp thinking' from Tom Black, and similar words from their boss turned the afternoon golden although the sun was not out.

Max had decided to conduct the interview himself, along with Connie. This case had got under his skin. Members of 678 Squadron had closed ranks when questioned, and Margot Collier had made fools of SIB. Tom's call had come as he was driving to the Medical Centre irritated by Clarkson, with whom he privately sympathized. That Connie had apparently made nonsense of the Sierra Leone theory was something of a relief. It would have taken days to prove a connection there. Getting the truth from Ray Fox would enable them to close the case before Easter.

Fox began by denying any knowledge of a secret connected with Sam Collier; claimed 'the woman' had made it up. Yes, he believed he might have mentioned that Margot had stacks of dosh, but it was just a figure of speech. Everyone knew she was loaded. Flaunted it, didn't she? Flash car, designer clothes, holidays in the Seychelles.

'And her husband could get a hand-out whenever he asked for one?' asked Max.

'Stands to reason, doesn't it?'

'So Sam's riding high. Beautiful wife, as much money as he wants, influential father-in-law and headlines describing his courage. What more could he need?'

Fox made no comment.

'Haven't you ever envied Sam, resented his trouble-free golden lifestyle?'

'No,' It was said pugnaciously.

'You must be a saint, Ray.'

'How about Margot Collier?' put in Connie. 'You wouldn't be normal not to fantasize about her, Living next door you'd see them together in affectionate situations. Do you ever spy on them?'

Fox flushed; gulped more coffee. 'I'm not into that.'

'Your wife said she caught you studying Margot's bottom in tight shorts through binoculars. How often do you watch her that way?'

He reacted aggressively. 'What's this about?' He fixed a glare on Max. 'You dragged me here because this woman waffled on about mess bills? I paid 'em, so what's the problem?'

'We checked with the Mess President. Once, before you went to Kandahar, and both months since your return, you've had to be pressured into settling. Spending too much time in the Mess hitting the bottle?'

A curious slyness entered Fox's eyes. 'You've got the wrong guy.'

'Have we?'

No response.

'Some other member drinking too much, is he?'

Fox stood. 'I've had enough of this. I'm going.'

'Sit down! We haven't finished yet,' Max told him coldly.

'*I've* finished. I'm not under arrest, so I'm free to leave.'

'I'm holding you for questioning about the brutal attack on Sam Collier two nights ago.'

'*What?*'

'Sit down, Ray, we've a long way to go yet.'

Fox sobered dramatically. He looked deeply shaken as he sank on the hard chair. 'I had nothing to do with that, for Christ's sake! You can't bloody tie me in with it.' He looked wildly from Max to Connie and back. 'What's this woman been saying?'

We've got him, thought Max with satisfaction. 'Sergeant Bush visited you to ask your opinion of Sam Collier. You claimed you got on well with him. You said he only had to ask his wife for money and he got any sum he wanted. You said he ought to share it around. When the Sergeant mentioned a loan, you said a *gift* because you knew Sam's secret. Do you deny that? Is it a secret deserving a vicious beating and dumping on the perimeter road?'

'No. Christ, no! You can't pin that on me.'

'Can you account for your movements on Monday night, sir?' demanded Connie.

'I was out. Driving.'

'Alone?'

'Yes.'

'Driving where?'

'Just around. I needed to think.'

'Were you in your own car?'

'Of course.'

'Have you ever borrowed Lieutenant Maine's Audi?' asked Max.

'What? No. Why would I?' Fox was getting severely rattled.

'So you were just driving around thinking. Thinking about what?'

'The usual things. Work. Money.'

'Margot Collier?' inserted Connie softly.

'No.'

Max said, 'Can anyone substantiate your claim? Did anyone from the base pass you and acknowledge you?'

'I don't know. Can't remember.'

'What time did you return home from this random drive?'

'Late. Sherilie had gone to bed.' His eyes now had a haunted look; he kept licking his lips nervously.

'So your wife can confirm what time you got in?' asked Connie.

'Yes ... *no*. I slept in the spare room.'

'Why was that?'

'She'd ... I didn't want to disturb her.'

'Not even to tell her the results of all that thinking?'

Max shot a question that took Fox by surprise. 'Did you call Sam Collier and ask him to meet you to settle some matter between you?'

'No.' He looked swiftly from one to the other. '*I* didn't beat him up. You can't accuse me of something I didn't do. Would *never* do.'

'We haven't accused you of anything yet,

213

Ray,' Max told him calmly. 'We're just asking questions you don't seem able to answer satisfactorily. We're investigating a very serious crime against one of your fellow pilots. A man you've claimed to know a secret about. We have evidence from Sherilie that you watch his wife through binoculars. You've just now indicated that you have money worries and you feel Sam Collier could share his wife's wealth around quite easily. You can't account for your whereabouts on the night he was attacked. Add that together and it makes you a suspect.'

Fixing the Welshman with a steady, penetrating stare, Max said, 'Did you send Sam a series of anonymous threatening letters? Did you subsequently threaten his wife with random acts of harassment, culminating with an attempt to run her car off the road? Did you arrange to meet Collier on Monday night and demand a large payment to cease hounding them and, when he refused, did you call in your heavies to persuade him you meant business?'

Fox physically sagged, wiping sweat from his face with the tail of his T-shirt. 'You've got it all wrong,' he said wearily. 'I'd like some more coffee.'

While Connie went to fetch some, Max prompted the nervous man. 'You're going to tell us why we've misread your behaviour?'

Fox nodded his bent head. 'I'd never do that to Sam. He's one of us. We stick together. That's why I wouldn't rat on him.'

'By revealing his secret?'

Fox nodded again, and Max sat without speaking until Connie returned with a mug. She then joined Max in silently watching the young pilot gulping scalding black coffee with a hint of desperation. Fox eventually glanced up to face his unsmiling inquisitors and his body sagged further as the silence continued. Swallowing nervously, he spread his hands palm upwards on the desk in a gesture of appeal.

'Sherilie thinks money grows on trees. She sees Margot and wants the same things. She spends a fortune on hair-dos, manicures and clothes trying to match up. We're always rowing about money. I told her before going to Kandahar she could piss off if she's not happy with what she's got. She stayed, of course.' The two detectives sat motionless and silent, which seemed to unnerve him into continuing in brief, concise sentences. 'I've always liked women. She knew that when she married me. I happen to need frequent sex. She knew that, too. She's more intent on creating her "image" than pleasing me.'

He waved his hands ineffectually. 'I met Louise in a bar. She's Dutch. Was staying here with a friend. We hit it off right away. She's everything a man dreams of; everything Sherilie isn't. I've been driving across the border whenever I've had the chance. I was with her on Monday night.'

'She'll confirm that?' Max asked sharply.

Fox looked alarmed. 'Do you need to involve her?'

215

'Yes, we're investigating a serious crime. You need to prove your non-involvement in it.'

Sitting back in his chair Fox ran a shaking hand over his mouth. 'Look, I admit I asked Sam for a sub when I discovered what he was doing. Later, I saw I had access to occasional financial supplements, only Sam wouldn't play ball. He said it was a one-off, but I caught him at it again just two days later. I had another go at him. He paid up, but said there'd be no more.' Fox appealed to them. 'While I was in Kandahar Sherilie ran up huge debts everywhere. No way could I clear them and settle mess bills as well.'

'So you sent Lieutenant Collier anonymous letters threatening to tell what you knew,' prompted Connie.

Fox studied his hands again. 'It was sort of jokey.'

'And when he ignored them, you began to harass his wife. Putting the frighteners on her to persuade him to meet your demands.'

Fox's head jerked up. 'No. Good God, no! What d'you take me for?'

'A man prepared to blackmail a colleague for money.'

That really hit home. Fox's mouth tightened. 'If I'd reported Sam he'd have been grounded indefinitely, and he's a guy who lives for flying. He could get any amount from Margot just for the asking, so he'd simply be protecting his pilot status.' Casting a defiant glare at the two facing him, he added, 'He's bloody lucky I've

216

kept quiet.'

Max took over. 'So you are admitting to sending Sam Collier unsigned threatening letters, putting him under duress to give you significant sums of money?' At Fox's silence, he said, 'Yes or no?'

'I was doing him a favour by keeping his secret.'

'Yes or no?'

'That was all. I had no hand in scaring Margot or beating Sam.'

Unwillingly believing him, Max asked the vital question. 'What was it you were keeping quiet about? Someone decided to beat your neighbour unconscious so the truth would come out, despite your dubious sense of loyalty.'

It was evening before they went to the Medical Centre. The Dutch police had confirmed Fox's meeting with Louise, so he was being charged with blackmailing a fellow officer, with almost certain additional charges for accruing serious debts in local stores and for conducting an illicit affair. Inappropriate behaviour for an officer.

The evening's briefing had been unproductive. Collier's fellow hostages were in the UK, two having left the Army. The four he rescued in Kandahar were also in Britain, not yet having rejoined the Royal Cumberland Rifles here in Germany. Still in a critical condition in hospital was the man who had suffered serious burns, and another with gunshot wounds. The other two remained on convalescent leave.

Only the blue Audi of those vehicles owned by members of 678 Squadron and their families had bloodstains in the boot. Piercey had contacted Lieutenant Maine at the home of his parents in Ipswich, who had confirmed he had been with them all the week.

The two-day task of checking the whereabouts on Monday night of several hundred people had ruled out only a quarter of them. Alibis provided by spouses were considered suspect, and those who had departed very early on Tuesday for the night-flying exercise Ray Fox had been on had only become available for questioning today.

The Audi had been taken into the secure yard behind Headquarters and was undergoing forensic examination.

With patient persistence, Beeny had ascertained that the call which had lured Collier from his house had been made from a public telephone on the base. All this proved was that it had to have been a caller with permission to be on military property. In simple terms, it could have been any one of thousands.

The uniformed boys had identified the spot where the flogging had taken place. Not far from where Piercey had been grabbed by the Duty Officer. No sign of rope or other weapon. It could have been disposed of easily in an establishment like this one and, even if dozens of manpower hours were wasted in a search, the chances of gaining incriminating evidence from it were slim. Their main hope rested on Collier abandoning his determined silence and naming his attackers. Now Fox had revealed the purpose of the letters and the nature of the secret referred to, Collier's stance was surely untenable.

Driving across the base Max apologized for obliging Tom to work late again. 'I hope you'll not get an earful from Nora, although she must be used to keeping meals hot for you.'

'She's up to her eyes in bridal stuff. As I'm not decked out in white satin she won't even notice I'm not there.'

'Like that, is it?' commented Max thoughtfully. 'The Easter wedding rush'll be over soon, and there's your UK leave to compensate.' Getting no response, he asked, 'Everything all right at home?'

'Mmm,' Tom grunted. 'Could do with a bit of male support. Beth's only eight, but she's as bad as the other two where clothes and pop stars are concerned. When I was that age I was making balsa wood models, collecting brochures of sports cars from showrooms and reading spy yarns. They don't do anything meaningful like that.'

Max laughed. 'If any of them did you'd worry that they'd turn out butch. They're *girls*, Tom. It's what girls are like. Have you forgotten how ghastly and boring they were when you were a boy?'

That brought a faint smile. 'I hated one called Freda even more than the rest. Mine aren't like her.' After a pause he added, 'It was great when they were little. They're trickier to deal with now, especially Maggie. She's turning into someone I don't know ... or begin to understand.'

'Par for the course where the fair sex is concerned,' Max stated, pulling up outside the Medical Centre. 'Take Margot Collier. Obsessively hooked on her valiant husband, yet she's driving him to meet her father's rigid standards and carrying another man's child she means to foist on darling Sam. How do you begin to unravel that woman's reasoning?'

Tom unbuckled his seat belt and opened the car door. 'I suggest we check Doc Clarkson's estimate of how advanced that pregnancy is while we're here. He could have got it wrong.'

'Fair enough,' Max agreed, keeping his thoughts to himself. 'You speak to Culdrow then join me with Collier. If fourteen weeks is correct give me a nod.'

Max entered the small room to find Margot sitting beside the bed drawing designs on a square block of plain paper. Sam lay with closed eyes which flicked open at Max's arrival.

Margot put a finger to her lips. 'He's asleep,' she whispered.

'He's just woken,' Max replied, pretty certain the patient had been feigning sleep. Interesting. Why would he ignore the light of his life?

'How are you feeling, Sam?'

'I still don't remember anything, if that's what you mean.'

'I have some news that'll help you get your memory back.'

Sam stared back unblinking. 'I don't think so.'

'Must you pester him like this?' demanded Margot, putting aside her drawing and clutching her husband's hand.

Max ignored her. 'We've just taped a confession by Ray Fox. It's gone some way to helping us find the men who put you in here.'

This brought a strong reaction. Sam sat up, wincing with pain. 'How did you ... what kind of confession?'

Watching with deep scepticism as Margot fussily arranged pillows behind Sam, Max said, 'He's now facing a charge of blackmail. Obtaining money from a fellow officer with menaces.'

'Oh, God!'

'He's admitted writing the anonymous letters you found on your doormat, and he told us how much you paid him to keep quiet about your drinking sessions while on duty.'

'He's lying! It's all lies.' It was a cry of deep distress. 'I've never given him money.'

'He stated that he caught you drinking vodka in your car on two occasions when you were officially on duty. He gave us the dates and times. We checked. You *were* on duty then.'

'He's lying. Why would he do that?'

Max moved closer to the bed. In the low light of that clinical room the young pilot looked a genuinely sick man; eyes sunken in drawn features.

'Ray denied having any hand in Monday night's attack. So far we have no evidence to disprove that. He claimed he would not have reported your drinking despite your later refusal to pay up. He appeared to regard that statement as some kind of mitigation. In our view, his responsibility as a colleague was to offer you help and advice, then report to the CO if you didn't take it.'

At that point Tom came in, his large bulk making the room seem crowded. He glanced at Max and nodded almost imperceptibly. So, Sam Collier had been cuckolded as well as blackmailed and flogged.

Max looked at Margot. 'Mrs Collier, were you aware of who wrote those unsigned letters?'

'I would have told you.'

'Would you?' He let that expression of doubt sink in, then asked, 'Did you know your husband was paying a neighbour hush money?'

'I've told you Ray's lying,' cried Sam hotly.

Max leaned forward and fixed Sam with an intense look. 'You did not pay Fox a large sum on March the tenth, and again on the twenty-fifth?'

'No.'

'You have never drunk alcohol when on duty?'

'Never.'

'You're not in the habit of boosting your confidence with a secret slug of vodka?'

'No!'

'Ray Fox swears you are. And so does your wife, Sam. She told me this morning that you hide bottles around the house before going to a war zone, and for a few weeks after your return.'

Max had never before seen an expression of such emotional anguish as there was on Sam's as he gazed at the woman he loved. Hardened though he was to human behaviour, Max felt like a voyeur of this marital pain as the man in the bed struggled to accept such betrayal. Even so, he deliberately allowed the moment to go on and on, knowing it would bring a turning point in Collier's stance.

Margot looked hardly less moved, and eventually said brokenly, 'I did it to protect you, darling. That's all I've ever wanted to do. *Protect* you.'

Those words increased the pain she was inflicting on this man of proven courage, with their suggestion of mothering an ineffectual nonentity. Wondering if this curious marriage would survive a supposedly premature birth in a few months' time, Max decided to continue the interrogation. Sam Collier was presently at the bottom of a deep, dark hole. Unless he could claw his way out, he was liable to stay there. Ray Fox's military career was virtually over, with a prison sentence to follow. Would Collier also be out on his ear and behind bars at the end of this case?

'I suggest you start being sensible and give us the truth, Sam.'

223

Dragging his gaze from Margot, he said huskily, 'I'd like my wife to leave, then I'll answer any questions you put to me.'

'Sam!' she cried in protest.

Max swung round. 'Please escort Mrs Collier out to her car, Mr Black.'

Tom's hesitation was only momentary before he stepped forward to take Margot's arm in a firm clasp to lead her away. Max then asked if Sam would like the doctor on duty to be present and was given a shake of his head. Similarly to the offer of painkillers or a cup of tea. Waiting for Tom to return, Max then began to unravel the mystery surrounding Monday night's attack.

'You knew Fox was the author of those letters?'

'It had to be him,' Sam replied in a bleak monotone.

'You didn't tackle him about them?'

'I thought he'd eventually recognize the futility of it.'

'You had no intention of handing over any more cash?'

Sam's face appeared to have grown even more drawn. In the pale glow from the light above the bed his deep tan merged with the purple bruising to suggest a dark, expression-less mask.

'I get the shakes. Can't control my hands. A quick slug of vodka sorts it. Ray caught me at it in my car on two occasions.'

'So you paid him to keep quiet.'

It was a while before Sam said, 'Aye, I did. It's never enough to affect my judgement or reflexes, but I'm breaking the rules. I'd be grounded and disciplined. Couldn't risk that.'

Max pondered the significance of that last comment. Couldn't risk Daddy knowing he wasn't toeing the line? 'Why haven't you sought help with the problem?'

'Same reason. I'd be grounded.' He appealed to Max. 'I'm not an alcoholic. I only do it when it's necessary to function properly.'

'Pilots function properly when they're sober,' ruled Tom. 'That's why the rules concerning drinking are in place.'

Max continued the questioning in quieter tones. 'Your wife told me she found hidden bottles in the run-up to your departure for Afghanistan, and for these weeks after your return. How did you manage out there in an alcohol-free zone?'

'It's a long story.'

'Give us the short version,' Tom snapped.

It was a fair time coming, and there was a deal of languor in his voice when he replied. 'What they did to us in Sierra Leone would be nothing compared with the cruelty of those bastards in Afghanistan. Ask the Russians about the obscene torture their men suffered before dying at the hands of the Taliban.'

'All our troops are aware of that, but they don't resort to furtive drinking to give them false courage,' Tom countered, giving no leeway.

Max resumed the interview. 'Are you afraid to go to war, Sam?'

'*No!*' There was enough energy in that one word to make the denial convincing. 'It's like an actor with stage fright. Once he gets out there in front of an audience he gives a faultless performance. I'm naturally hyped-up when the enemy is at the door.'

'So do you regard capture as failure?'

Another long silence. 'I thought you were SIB, not psycho boys.'

'They asked you that, did they?'

Collier raised a hand, then let it flop back on the bed. 'What are you going to do about Ray's evidence?'

'You won't be flying for a while, so it can wait,' Max told him, sitting on the chair Margot had vacated. 'Tell us about Monday night. Who called you arranging a rendezvous?'

'I don't know.'

'Drop that amnesia bullshit,' Tom ordered crisply.

'At the time I believed it was Ray. The caller had a Welsh accent.'

'You'd refused to meet further demands, so why go to the meeting?'

'The voice said "I know what you did, so let's settle the score once and for all". I went because I wanted him off my back.'

'You were prepared to offer a final payment? You had a largish sum in your wallet when I found you in the road,' Max told him.

Collier's head wagged against the pillow.

'Pure coincidence. Mother's birthday next week.'

'Where was the proposed RV?'

'That triangle of no-man's-land at the back of the Other Denominations Church hall. It's quiet and shadowy there at night.'

'Go on.'

He spoke as if reciting words memorized earlier. There was no anger or any other emotion in his voice. What he had seen as Margot's betrayal had clearly left him beyond caring what happened.

'I went expecting to meet Ray. When I arrived there someone walked from the shadows. Before I saw him clearly my arms were seized and roped together behind my back, while the one coming towards me thrust a bag over my head and tied it tightly around my neck. They took me to a car and shoved me in the boot. After a brief drive they dragged me out and force marched me to a place where one of them laid into me with something covered in metal studs while the other two held me. I was practically choking on blood when they untied my arms and pushed me hard up against a wall and lashed my back until I passed out. I don't remember anything more until I woke up here.'

Max weighed up this statement and decided it was probably the truth. 'So you can't identify your attackers.'

'The one I thought was Ray looked a big guy in the shadows. He had a Welsh accent.'

'What did he say? Enough for you to recognize the accent.'

'Much of it was incoherent because of the bag over my head. He was highly excited.' Sam made another weary gesture with his hand. 'Something about getting appropriate punishment for what I'd done. I was beyond taking it in after the first few blows, except that it seemed excessive retaliation for having an occasional slug of vodka.'

'You believed these men were half-killing you because of the furtive drinking sessions?' asked Tom sceptically.

Looking on the brink of total exhaustion by now, Collier said, 'The guys take their safety in the air very seriously. They must believe I invariably go aloft half-pissed.'

'The normal procedure would be to report their suspicions to the Squadron Commander, not to beat the hell out of the offender,' Max pointed out. 'You don't seriously believe that vicious attack was linked to Ray Fox's blackmail. Come clean, Sam. What have you done to prompt such a reprisal?'

Those dark eyes stared back from a brusied and battered face. 'Broken faith with guys who expect me to value their lives as highly as I value my own.'

Ten

The house was remarkably quiet when Tom let himself in. Not even the sound of Nora's sewing machine. A note in the kitchen informed him there was a pork pie with salad in the fridge, or a microwavable risotto in the freezer. They would be late home because Nora had been reliably informed that the supper after the school play would be worth staying for.

Tom stared at the note. He had clean forgotten the school play. He had sneaked away this morning without wishing his girls good luck with their performances. He had not been there to watch, tell them how proud he was of his daughters. Yet again the Black sisters had seen all the other dads smiling and applauding and felt let down by theirs. He had the concept the wrong way round. His family were not excluding him, he was excluding them.

Wandering moodily to the dining room where wedding finery hung on the walls, Tom poured himself a double whisky and drank half while regarding the bouffant dresses sparkling with crystals or sequins. Nora said it was the most important day of a woman's life, the one occasion when she was the star of the show.

He tried to imagine Maggie, Gina and Beth dolled up like fairy princesses, and heard Nora saying he was of yesterday's generation. Would he come in from work one day and find a note in the kitchen revealing that he had forgotten his daughter's wedding, without even realizing she had grown old enough to marry?

Tossing back the rest of the whisky, he poured more. The silence depressed him further. What would life be like without the chatter, the giggles and thumping music; without the noise of a sewing machine running full speed, and the sound of Nora's throaty laughter? He stared morosely in the glass. Was he losing them? Was he regarded merely as 'the lodger' by a family unit complete without him?

Walking back to the kitchen with another whisky refill, he took out the pork pie from the plate of salad, cut it in quarters, then sat looking at it without enthusiasm. Nora usually drew a smiley face and a row of kisses on her notes. They were missing tonight.

Five minutes later, with a cheese and crushed onion crisp sandwich in his hand, Tom sought his model steam engines. They looked the same as when he had last looked at them. He picked up the latest edition of the enthusiasts' magazine from the neat, numbered pile, and flipped through it aimlessly before replacing it. The beautiful, expensive engines did nothing for him tonight. They were unchanging; static. Yesterday's generation toys?

Nora had claimed men fantasized about

young girls when they realized the world was no longer just for them. Not guilty of that; he had three of his own. Had he been fantasizing about Margot Collier? No, that would have involved imagining having sex with her. She had simply revived emotions he had been a stranger to for too long, and undermined his judgement. Max had mistrusted her from the start, and he had been right to do so.

Leaving the sandwich uneaten, Tom abandoned his steam engines and walked out to the small rear garden. There was a full moon and a skyful of stars. He stood looking up at them and acknowledged their power to reduce a man to less than a grain of sand on planet earth. He suddenly grew curiously afraid. Afraid of the certainty of his beloved little girls in white dresses being led away forever by faceless young Lotharios with strong, muscular bodies. Afraid of growing old, of being the day *before* yesterday's generation. Afraid of being left alone, feeble and ailing. Afraid of dying.

Moments later, his troubled gaze lowered to the glass in his hand. Alcohol to numb fear and uncertainty. Dutch courage. In that moment Tom felt at one with Sam Collier, a man who was afraid of capture by the enemy yet had put his life on the line to save four others from that fate. He did not deserve such vicious punishment for calming his raw fear with the occasional furtive charge of vodka.

Dinner in the Mess was over. Max contemplated making do with a mug of soup and a NAAFI sandwich in his room, but he felt the need to get away from military life, mingle with people untroubled by its demands and restrictions. In no mood for Yevgeny's effusive fellowship, Max drove to a small inn on the edge of the forest well away from town.

The case was getting bogged down. Ray Fox had a proven alibi for Monday night and, although he had been squeezing money from Collier, Max believed his claim that he had told no one about the secret drinking. Earlier this evening the theory involving fellow hostages from Sierra Leone had been debunked, partly by Fox's confession and partly by evidence that the men held with Collier three years ago were all in the UK.

He pulled up before the inn, but stayed in the car with his thoughts. Two had left the Army since that drama. Both had a UK address, but they could have come to Germany. Impossible to keep tabs on men who had become civilians. It might be worth having a word with their local police about their present jobs and family situations. Locking the car and crossing to the welcome lights of *Der Bauer*, Max admitted he was now clutching at straws. The manner of Collier's punishment was a clue he had not yet recognized. If and when he did, the solution would surely follow.

A plate filled with veal fricassée and buttered potatoes, with a large salad and a carafe of Mosel wine went a long way to easing his

232

tension. He needed Livya on the other side of the table, sharing his meal, to bring full relaxation. How good it would be to go home each evening to her, to talk things through, hear her reasoning. How good it would be to slip into bed every night and hold her close. How good it would be to have a child, or two, to run in to the bedroom at first light and snuggle in the bed with them.

The waiter came and Max ordered plum strudel with whipped cream. Drinking the last of the wine Max reflected that Tom was a very lucky man. Then he frowned. There was presently an obvious problem with that fifteen-year-old marriage. Caused by Margot Collier, or by Tom's recent illness? If the former, hopefully the rosy-tinted lenses had cleared to show his friend the flawed woman beneath the glamour.

As for the supposed golden couple, beneath the gilded surface decay was fast spreading. Remembering how he had felt on hearing rumours of Susan's affair with a good-looking, audacious corporal, Max empathized with Collier tonight. He understood the pain of betrayal, of vows broken. Max would never know if the unborn boy killed with Susan was his, but there could be no doubt about Margot's baby. Sam had that additional betrayal yet to face.

Driving back to his single room, Max decided he might be better off as things stood. He would have a long, intimate telephone conversation with Livya, make plans for their next meeting, then disconnect and look forward to the same pleasure tomorrow. So he would not hold her in his arms, make love before falling languorously asleep, but he would not be risking silence and a turned back because he had somehow erred. Or because another man had taken his place.

Bright moonlight flooded the room, emphasizing its clinical austereness with sharp contrasts of light and shade. The night duty nurse could see the patient clearly without using her small torch. Two a.m. and he was still awake. She was about to enter and offer a sleeping pill when she noticed the tears standing on his bruised cheeks. She left as silently as she had arrived.

Charles Clarkson left his bed with the intention of making tea. It was pointless to toss and turn any longer. He had had a long telephone conversation with Ria which had been badly unsettling. She was naturally distressed over the sudden departure, and the children were scared and upset. Even being with their much-loved grandparents failed to cheer them. Ria had found it difficult to explain the situation to her parents. They were now tight-lipped and angry, bringing out their familiar comments about the folly of marrying a soldier doctor.

Maybe she should return to Germany, leaving the children in Portugal, she had said. She should have put them on the aircraft and stayed with him. People would think she believed him guilty by running off at a moment's notice, taking the kids beyond his reach. It had been a mistake, but he had given her no time to think of the consequences. Had he yet heard the result of the interview with Stacey? When would he join them? She missed him dreadfully and was sick with worry.

Charles had felt exhausted when the call ended, and he then doubted his wisdom in sending them all away so precipitately. Yet he could not have allowed his loving children's minds to be poisoned by insidious questioning. He *could* not. He yearned to be with them all, offering comfort and reassurance. Small wonder he could not sleep.

Starting down the stairs he became aware of a terrible smell. He soon identified the source. On the doormat was a pile of faeces.

On Thursday there was no new evidence or even new thoughts on the Collier case, so the team faced the prospect of re-interviewing everyone linked to 678 Squadron in the hope of winkling-out something that would bring some enlightenment. Tom took on the task of garnering information and evidence to consolidate the charges against Ray Fox, who had been suspended from duty.

Max visited the staff sergeant heading the team checking the validity of Stacey Laine's claim of sexual assault. Jean Maximus was a shrewd woman with wide experience of handling the abuse of minors. She would not commit herself to a verdict.

'Too early, sir. The girl is unwell and feverish. She's also suffering the usual sense of shame, along with the fear of being the subject of gossip and curiosity as well as the distress of losing her friends. We have to work slowly, build up her trust in us and confidence in herself. This unique military community exacerbates the problems. Every pupil at the school knows every other one, their parents live and work in close proximity so news travels faster than in civilian communities.' She frowned. 'It's a serious charge, and if he *is* using his professional standing to touch and fondle young girls' bodies, it's also despicable. If Stacey is telling the truth, someone must check out the Major's children who are at serious risk. Removing them before they could be questioned damages his claim of innocence, but they are at least safe from harm at his hands, for now.'

Max made no comment. He kept an open mind about Stacey's accusation but, knowing Clarkson's devotion to his family, he did not seriously believe those four were in any danger of abuse. Men who committed crimes against women and children were frequently gentle and loving with their own family. It was tricky to track them down, because all who knew them swore they would never harm a soul.

The subject of these thoughts was at the Medical Centre when Max walked in. Clarkson looked pale and drawn and extremely hostile.

'What do *you* want?'

'I was diverted yesterday on my way to pick up that info about Collier's debrief after Sierra Leone. A signature, a name I can start with and follow up on.'

'Haven't you done enough to hamper the man's recovery? He's deeply depressed after your bully-boy tactics last night.'

'Don't you mean *Nazi* tactics?' Max countered. 'We have to discover who put him in here. His assumed amnesia magically cleared, but he has no idea who attacked him, or why.'

Clarkson's stony gaze bored into Max. 'Which is no different from when he feigned loss of memory, so you're no wiser and my patient's recovery has been set back. Bravo!'

'I'd like that name, please.'

Max thought for a moment that Clarkson was going to refuse, but he eventually got to his feet and went to the filing cabinet. Selecting a thick envelope, he studied the contents with his back turned. Then he meticulously re-filed Collier's medical notes and returned to his desk to write on a scrap of paper which he held out.

Max glanced at the name on it as Clarkson said, 'He won't tell you anything. His patients are guaranteed confidentiality.'

'As it happens, we can tell him something he probably doesn't know. Collier needs further help. That initial debrief didn't completely erase the effects of what happened to him three years ago, and the pressure of his marital demands is putting him under too much stress to cope with his fears.'

Max made to leave, then halted at the doorway. 'You're the medic. I suggest you have a quiet chat with him when the time's right. He's in need of someone on his side just now. His wife broke faith with him last night. It was that, not our questioning, that's heralded depression today.' He leaned further in to the office to add quietly, 'You mentioned that her pregnancy is at the dangerous fourteen-week period. Collier returned from Afghanistan *eight* weeks ago. Think on that, Major.'

Max held the briefing well before supper time. Developments had demanded three late nights, so he decided they all deserved a free evening after hours of interviewing people even more uncooperative the second time around. The case was growing cold now Ray Fox was out of the running.

There was, however, one interesting report. Heather Johnson had tackled Margot Collier while she was still disturbed by the events of the previous evening; events which had spilled over to morning when Sam had feigned sleep throughout her visit. Heather had taken advantage of the woman's volatile mood to get some straight answers.

'She admitted there had not been smashed eggs on the doorstep, deflated tyres or any mysterious resiting of her parked car,' Heather said with a touch of disdain. 'These were not *lies*, you understand, just little touches to bolster her appeal for help in tracing the sender of those letters. The only truth in her statement was the attempt to run her off the road. That had scared her so much she came straight to us before telling her husband, something she later regretted.

'She broke down and condemned herself for having now alienated darling Sam. She had only acted to *protect* him. That's all she's *ever* wanted to do. Oh, and to protect the baby,' Heather quoted. 'It's *so* important for this pregnancy to run full term.' She grimaced. 'It was quite a performance, sir.'

'Everything she does is a performance,' Max agreed. 'She most probably is passionate about her husband, but only in respect of fashioning him into her ideal. One hopes he will accept a lie about a premature birth, especially if the baby strongly resembles one of her theatre cronies. We can charge her with wasting police time on checking out her false claims, but we'll wait until this bizarre affair is completely unravelled. There could be further charges to lay against her.'

The only other offering came from Phil Piercey, who had pursued the sex angle which he felt was behind the beating. All he could come up with was evidence of widespread admiration for Margot Collier from the men, and as much vituperation from the wives. As for his probing into possible sexual adventures in Afghanistan, the best he could offer was that everyone said there wasn't time for anything like that.

'I'll follow up on it tomorrow, when they've

had time to think it over. If it's there, I'll get at it.'

'I'm sure you will,' said Max, humouring the maverick Piercey. 'Fresh input is welcome, however debatable, Sergeant. Let's all take a break this evening and approach the case with fresh enthusiasm tomorrow.'

Dinner in the Mess was a possibility tonight that Max took advantage of. He was weary and slightly depressed. Tired of Margot's play-acting, he disparaged her attitude towards the man who had clearly loved her for herself, not for her wealth or her influential father. It had all been in that look on realizing she had informed against him, knowing it would result in his being barred from doing the one thing he loved best: flying. There had been no suggestion or hint that she had at any time tackled him about his need for alcohol, had attempted to talk him through his fears and offer her support. Her much vaunted passion for darling Sam had not extended to the in sickness and health vow.

She had given SIB the runaround, too. Poor old Tom must be feeling let down and em-barrassed. Max had thought him too hardened by experience to have fallen for her wiles, but she was undoubtedly the embodiment of many men's fancies, and it was spring time when gullible males were known to surrender to headstrong sexual temptation.

Max's own mating instincts were centred on Livya. He had never been a man to play the field. In the three years following Susan's death there had been no woman in his life until Livya had come on the scene last December. Just four months of knowing and loving her, with no more than six meetings since that heady Christmas leave in her company. He longed for her now as he showered and changed in the small room he still could not regard as home. After he had eaten, he would call her and perform a metaphorical mating ritual over the phone lines.

His mobile rang as he was combing his hair. Thinking it would be a police matter, he was surprised to see that the caller was Livya.

'Hi, darling, don't disappoint me by saying we can't have our usual hour tonight. I need it after the day I've had.'

'I can't say too much. I'm not alone.' She sounded tense. Angry, even.

'What's the problem? Are you all right?'

'We're hoping to keep it quiet, but if the press get hold of it, it'll make headlines. I just want to tell you before you read about it over break-fast.'

'Livya, *what's wrong?*'

'Andrew was mugged and robbed of his brief-case this afternoon. It contains highly confidential info.'

'Christ!' Max was totally unprepared for such news. 'Why did he have it with him?'

'Can't go into that,' she whispered fiercely. 'He was taken to A and E by a passing motorist, but they sent him home with plasters and painkillers. There's a huge flap on here to check what's actually missing. I'll be working until the early hours. Sorry to give you this, but I thought you should be prepared to see your father's name plastered all over the tabloids. I'll call you when I can.'

She was gone before he could question her further. He sat heavily on his bed, trying to accept what he had just heard. Throughout his career Andrew Rydal had met danger head-on, taken risks with cool courage, led men with authority and charmed women effortlessly. Like the buccaneer he undoubtedly was, he had sailed successfully through rock-strewn waters for many years, but he had now hit a reef. Sink or swim, the vessel was certain to be damaged.

The house was pleasantly redolent of a savoury, cheesy aroma when Tom parked his car and entered the hallway where Maggie had been embracing Hans too enthusiastically two nights ago. He had seen his daughters since then merely for an hour or so last night. They, and Nora, had remained at the school until the lingerers were ushered out by the caretaker waiting to lock up. Gina and Beth had prattled on in their normal fashion about the play and the disaster over the large, electrically wired Easter egg which had, predictably, failed to open and had had to be pulled apart manually to allow the drama teacher's daughter to emerge dressed as a chick.

Maggie had said nothing until all three went

up to bed. Beth had almost throttled Tom with her loving hug, Gina had kissed his cheek. Maggie had uttered an aloof goodnight and made the walk to the scaffold until she reached her bedroom.

Late though it was, Nora declared that she must work on Monica Purdom's bridesmaid's dress. The wedding was on Saturday and the sleeves were going to be hell to set in correctly. She had not appeared to notice her husband's subdued mood, and when they went to bed after midnight she claimed to be dead beat and turned away to snuggle into her pillow.

There had been the usual breakfast-time hubbub this morning. Tom had always felt alienated by the female activity upstairs, particularly since the day Maggie began menstruating, and he wisely escaped to the peace of the kitchen. Today, the flow of half-dressed girls from bedrooms to bathroom, and the lively chatter between them, seemed to shut him right out of their lives. During breakfast it became more marked, because they still discussed the school play, which he had not attended or shown interest in.

This early homecoming tonight had Tom wondering how, or if, it would be welcomed. Supper was cooking. Had Nora made enough for five, or was she expecting to leave for him the quartered pie and salad he had not eaten last night? It was very quiet downstairs, not even the sound of the sewing machine running. Nora was not on the ground floor.

From Maggie's room came the sound of some music Tom had become familiar with. The girls were watching the DVD of *Pirates of the Caribbean* yet again. Nora must be showering or in the bedroom changing. He decided not to go up. Better to wait in the alcove with his steam engine magazines, and a glass of whisky until she came down to serve supper.

He poured the whisky and was walking back along the hall with it when he grew aware of women's voices coming from the stairs. There was no time to vanish, no place of retreat.

'...the upper rooms of the Country Club, so I have to be able to manage a staircase in these strappy sandals without tripping over the train,' a melodious voice was saying. Next minute, a vision in cream satin came into view and caught sight of him over the banister. 'And here's the best man waiting to ensure everything's going smoothly,' she added with a low laugh.

Nora, in brown trousers and a green blouse, appeared from behind the woman and looked at him in surprise. 'Early night, or just calling in for a few minutes? Tom, you may not have met Major Keyes' daughter, who's being married on Saturday and needs to test her dress before taking it away.'

The two women descended to the hall and faced him. He stared wordlessly at the visitor. Margot Collier surely had a rival in the beauty stakes here. No more than eighteen, auburn-haired with large green eyes and a dazzling smile, this young woman's curves were excitingly outlined by a clinging dress of heavy satin, down the front of which in pale yellow thread was the most beautiful design of water-lilies. With a shock, Tom recognized the work Nora had been doing when he came home expecting her to make lunch for him ... or have a quick session on the bed. The gown was stunning. The girl in it was also stunning, because she was wearing something unique and so lovely it would be classed as 'designer' in the shops.

'Isn't it gorgeous!' the girl exclaimed. 'I'll never wear it again after Saturday, of course, because there'll never be another day as special, but it'll be the dress I'll remember all my life. Even when I'm a great-granny, I'll take out the photos and bore all the kids with a description of my bridal dress they'll have heard umpteen times before.'

Her merry laugh sent a shiver down Tom's spine. When this eager young woman was a great grandma, Tom Black would be no more than a memory in his daughters' minds.

'Mrs Black must have worked like a slave to finish it in time, especially as I was so set on having the waterlilies. She's *so* talented. I told her she should open a boutique. It would be a runaway success. But she says she has enough to do looking after a husband and three adolescent daughters.'

While this was being said she was teetering back and forth on very high-heeled gold sandals, expertly kicking the small train free at each turn.

'It's *perfect*. Thank you, thank you. You *will* come to the church on Saturday, won't you, and bring your girls. We're having it decked with cream and yellow flowers to match my bouquet. It'll look fabulous.' Glancing over the banister, she added with a smile, 'No use asking you to come, Mr Black. Men are only interested in the stag night; think weddings are simply ruinously expensive charades.' She turned back to Nora. 'If Giles turns up hungover and very much the worse for wear on my special day, I'll *kill* him.'

Left alone in the hall, Tom wished he had gone to the Sergeants' Mess for a few beers before coming home. Slumping on the chair in his office alcove, he studied the whisky in his glass and thought about his own wedding.

The lads had done their best to ensure he would never forget his last day of bachelor free-dom by handcuffing him to a rail of the football grandstand, drunk as a lord and wearing just his underpants. They had released him a mere hour before he was to catch the train to Nora's hometown. By lunchtime his father had sobered him up enough to shave, and his mother had given food, and painkillers to offset the raging headache before setting off for the church.

Had he thought the wedding a ruinously expensive charade? While it was being planned, yes, yet when he had seen Nora coming down the aisle in white lace, carrying red roses, as the organ reverberated throughout that ancient church, he had known such joy he had had to swallow back his emotion.

The Adjutant's daughter departed with her finery enclosed in plastic; the pirates were still threatening the Caribbean upstairs when Nora returned from helping to arrange gown and headdress in the car.

'Thank God those shoes have such high heels,' she exclaimed on her way to the kitchen. 'If they hadn't, I'd have spent tonight having to shorten that dress.'

'It looked ... sensational,' Tom offered, getting to his feet.

'She sets it off perfectly, that's why.'

He followed her. 'Nora, I...' He broke off as his mobile rang.

'Tom Black.'

'I'm on my way to the airport,' Max told him. 'Want to check out a few things in the UK. If anything develops you can reach me any time on the usual number. Back in a couple of days.'

The brief message left Tom puzzled. It was unlike his boss to be so vague. What was there at home to check out? A few minutes' thought brought the only answer. Max was still pursuing his wild theory concerning Sierra Leone and meant to interview the men captured with Collier. A wild goose chase which would offer the opportunity to see Captain Cordwell? Sly old dog! It had been obvious her last visit had not gone too well. Another relationship requiring some careful treading.

Nora was busy with vegetables and did not

look up when he arrived beside her. 'Called away, are you?'

'No. Max telling me he's en route to the UK.'

'So you're in charge.'

'The case has gone cold.' He watched her fingers as they peeled carrots. 'I could do that for you.'

'Good. I'll sit and enjoy a glass of wine for a change.' It was so abrupt she left a carrot half-peeled. 'And there are peas to shuck,' she added, pouring wine at the breakfast bar.

Taking over the task, Tom said experimentally, 'Supper smells good. Is there enough for five?'

Nora sat with her wine. 'When have I ever fed us, but not you?'

He swung to face her. 'I didn't mean ... Look, can we talk? Before the girls descend on us.'

'They'll be here any minute. That music signals the end of the DVD. Can it wait?' Her expression was not encouraging.

'Where are the peas?' asked Tom, accepting the inevitable delay with bad grace.

'The girls can do them. Sit and enjoy your whisky.' Her tone was softer, but she did not add the usual endearment.

Tom sat, thought about taking her hand, then abandoned the idea as the familiar sound of a herd of wildebeest on the stairs put an end to intimacy. Overwhelmed by excited chatter about the attributes of Johnny Depp, Tom was almost glad when his mobile rang again. He escaped to his office alcove to take the call.

'George Mitchell, sir. I called Captain Rydal, but he told me to pass it to you. There's been a development with the charge against Major Clarkson. Anneka Chorley and Kylie Stokes, both minors, have just confessed to their parents that he fondled and tried to kiss them during birthday parties at his house. We've *got* him, sir,' he declared, not bothering to hide the malicious satisfaction he felt, 'and their parents are baying for his blood.'

Eleven

The night porter slid back the small glass panel when Max knocked on it in the early hours. 'Yes, sir, can I be of assistance?'

He held up his service identification. 'I'm here to see my father, Brigadier Rydal.'

The man built like a heavyweight boxer studied the document thoroughly, then nodded. 'I'll buzz through to check that he's willing to receive a visitor at this hour.' At Max's raised eyebrows he added, 'It's strict procedure, sir.'

Although the policeman could appreciate the meticulous security, the son was irked at being kept standing in the cold outside the apartment block. Of course, it housed a few celebrities and an unknown number who preferred to keep a low profile and travelled in limousines with darkened windows, accompanied by body-guards.

When Max's mother died twenty-two years ago, the house in Kent was sold furnished. Because he had never married again, and because his military career took him all over the world, Andrew Rydal had seen no point in owning property. On joining the Joint Intelligence Committee, he had moved to this rented apartment near his workplace. Father and son had last seen each other at Susan's funeral; a pair of widowers who hardly knew what to say to each other.

'The Brigadier says to go up, sir.'

The voice broke into Max's bleak thoughts and he walked through the electrically operated doors to the impressive foyer, still heavy with memories. Had he been too hasty in coming here?

The lift glided silently to the third floor while he reviewed his decision. He had not grown close to his remaining parent following his mother's death. School holidays had been spent with his maternal grandparents, now deceased, or in an army hiring wherever his father was stationed. Those times had been very boring. Andrew Rydal was an outstanding sportsman, so his off-duty periods had been filled with manly pursuits. These always attracted female spectators, and Max still recalled the horror of pretty, perfumed women patting his cheek and speaking to him as they would to a pet dog.

The lift stopped; the door slid back. Max remained where he was. There was nothing he could do professionally to resolve the situation. Special Branch officers would tell a military detective to get lost, and he could hardly offer filial comfort after all these years, yet he had left Germany where three army officers' careers were falling apart. A doctor facing serious charges, a pilot who had been driven to black-mail by a wife who lived beyond his means, and another pilot whose whole future seemed destined to spin out of control. Andrew Rydal had also served his country well, but he could be brought down by this. Was that why his estranged son had come?

He stepped from the lift to see his father, dressed in grey slacks and a blue wool shirt, standing ten yards away by his open door. He looked older than he had at Susan's funeral, and had clearly not been to bed yet. Closing with him Max saw the brightness of those shrewd eyes had dimmed, and lines tugged down the corners of his mouth. There was a large pad taped to his left temple, a wide strip of plaster over his left palm. His normal upright stance had developed into a slight stoop. Max was concerned. Livya had spoken of painkillers and plasters, but his father appeared to have taken a bit of more serious aggro.

They shook hands wordlessly, then Max followed Andrew through to an elegant square hall thickly carpeted in blue, which led to a large, airy room furnished with settees, armchairs and assorted glass-topped tables. The ornaments and pictures blended well with the opulent room, their provenance surely reflected in the rental charge.

Andrew turned to Max. 'Drink? Coffee, tea?'

'Coffee will be fine.'

The older man nodded and headed for the kitchen. 'Beds are always made up in the two spare rooms. Choose either. I take it you need somewhere to kip down for a night or two.'

It was not a question, so Max walked through to the first guest room, dumped his bag and took off his overcoat before using the green marble bathroom so elaborate he felt guests should immerse themselves in asses' milk, water being too mundane.

When he returned to the main room the central glass-topped table bore a tray with cups and saucers, and a large cafetière. His father was shaking biscuits from a packet on to a plate, but he glanced up to ask, 'Are you in need of real sustenance?'

'No, I had a meal on the flight.'

He grimaced. 'Airlines' muck!'

'It sufficed.'

'Good flight?'

'Usual Lufthansa efficency. Bit different over here. The car hire desk was unmanned; taxi driver wanted an infamous amount to bring me to central London. "Late night surcharge, guv'nor", so I defiantly opted for the Piccadilly Line. Reached Osterley. Everyone off the train! Work on the line ahead; buses waiting to take passengers onward.' Max gave a wry smile, taxi fare from there cost me almost as much as from Heathrow.'

Andrew depressed the plunger, then poured dark coffee and handed a cup to Max. They sipped in silence. He remembers that I like it black and sugarless, Max thought with surprise, yet we can only communicate with social chit-chat. He studied his father as they drank. A man of impressive physique with well-defined

253

features, green eyes and dark wavy hair not yet showing any grey. I've inherited his height, stature and colouring, mused Max, but not his irresistible charm. Is that why I feel awkward in his company? He dazzles where I probably just glimmer.

'Over here on a case?'

Max came from his thoughts and answered automatically. 'Yes, yours.'

It brought a strong reaction. 'Don't be crass. There's not the slightest connection with SIB Germany.'

'I'm not here wearing my red cap,' he returned quietly.

The comment hung between them for long moments, and Max saw the lines of strain deepen. 'I suppose some well-meaning contact over here decided you should know before it hits the headlines.'

Max hesitated, then decided it was not the right moment to reveal his relationship with Livya. 'That's right.'

'You've made an unnecessary journey. I can handle this, believe me. I've dealt with...'

'This isn't a military operation. For once, you're not in command. Difficult though you'll find it, you'll have to sit tight and do nothing while others attempt to limit the damage that could result from this theft.'

'And you count yourself one of these "others", do you? They'll never let you join their team. You'd be too biased in favour of the military.'

254

'And I'm a blood relative,' Max returned curtly. 'No, I don't aim to muscle in on the investigation.'

Another long moment of awareness between them until Andrew got to his feet. 'Let's have a man's drink.'

Max said nothing while his father poured whisky in two cut-glass tumblers and added a splash of soda to each. 'Too much coffee rots the brain,' he said with a faint smile as he handed Max a glass. 'And this stuff rots the liver but what the hell!'

Max eventually broke the silence his father seemed content to maintain. 'Care to tell me what happened?'

Gazing steadily into his glass, Andrew said, 'All these years of meticulous observation of probity, one moment of carelessness. Just once a junkie comes along and sees the price of a next fix in my hand.' His gaze lifted to face Max. 'I refused to let go, but he yanked with desperation. If the thing had been fastened to my wrist he'd have had my hand off. Then he clobbered me with something. It was bloody hard, stone he had as a handy weapon, perhaps. Went down on my knees, still holding the briefcase. That's when he put his boot in my guts, over and over until I collapsed. Next thing I was aware of was a young city type bending over me and insisting on driving me to the nearby A and E. I was then empty-handed.'

On the verge of embarking on the series of questions he would normally put to the victim

255

of such an assault, Max refrained. It would be almost insulting to ask if this senior officer had notified his department immediately of the loss of documents, and where he could be contacted in the next hour or so.

'Familiar scenario,' he commented instead. 'I'd guess the city type witnessed the whole thing, along with others, but was relucant to intervene. Pity he didn't instead follow the junkie. It might have given a lead to where he was getting his supplies.'

Andrew raised his eyebrows. 'Typical police thinking. Leave the old fool to sort himself out and chase the villain.'

Managing a suggestion of a smile in turn, Max said lightly, 'The city type would have known ladies would flock around to help. They always have, as I recall.' After a pause he said, 'What was in it?'

Andrew took another sip of his whisky then hesitated before answering. 'I'd attended a high-powered conference. It broke and I called my driver to bring the car round. We set off, but I remembered something I needed to pick up from here on the way back to the office. It's impossible to park outside this place, so I told Barnes to drop me at the corner and I'd take a taxi when I was ready to return. I called the firm I always use. They said they'd divert one returning from dropping a fare. Ten minutes, tops, they promised. I went down, had a brief chat with Eric, the security guy, then saw the taxi arrive. The bloody thing dropped two

residents, then drove off. It wasn't mine. The junkie came up behind me as I stood there. The rest you know.'

'There wouldn't be a connection with the taxi driver? Guessing you'd be outside waiting.'

'It's not your case,' came the chilly reminder. In retaliation, Max gave a reminder of his own. 'You still haven't said what was in it.'

'Documents relevant to the conference. Not top secret, but highly confidential. Could be damaging in the wrong hands.' He got to his feet signifying the end of confidence. 'My responsibility. Should have returned to the office in the staff car. No question of apportioning guilt. It rests squarely on my shoulders.' He walked towards the bedroom area. 'Breakfast makings are in the kitchen. Help yourself whenever.' Pausing to glance back at his son, he said quietly, 'There was no need for you to come, as I've outlined ... but I appreciate the gesture.'

The king-sized bed was so comfortable Max would have slept well into morning, if Tom had not called to confirm that two more girls had accused Charles Clarkson of sexual advances. It was unwelcome news. Max prided himself on his ability to read people's character. He had been right about Margot Collier, but badly wrong about the Medical Officer. Clarkson's career with the Army was virtually finished. How the General Medical Council would deal with him Max was not qualified to judge, but

the man's entire future looked rocky. What a fool to throw it all away for want of a little control. This was the doctor whom he had suggested should attempt to help Collier face his demons.

Taking a lengthy shower, Max put on the dark-green bathrobe hanging on the back of the door, and went in search of coffee. Andrew was reading the *Daily Telegraph* at the breakfast bar, with a tall glass of orange juice and a basket of croissants before him. He was drinking coffee and indicated the cafetière as he bade his son a serious good morning.

Max poured the strong, dark coffee into a bone china cup which stood in a matching gold filigree-patterned saucer. After drinking some, he said, 'It always tastes infinitely better from fine china, so why do we so often use thick mugs?'

'Sleep well?'

'Very, until my sar'nt major woke me with news I'd rather not have heard.' He drained his cup and refilled it, asking carefully, 'Anything in there about what happened?'

'No. Won't know about the tabloids until I get a call from the office. They'll check.'

After slight deliberation, Max asked, 'How are you feeling this morning? Physically.'

'Hearty aches in the gut and head, but the painkillers will soon kick in. Ready for breakfast?'

'Soon as I've shaved and dressed ... if I can trace my things in that vast room. I'll take this

with me.'

Picking up the cup and saucer he walked towards the bedrooms, then pulled up short as the main door opened and Livya walked in, key in hand.

'Andrew, there's nothing...' Her words tailed off as she realized the man in the bathrobe was not who she had expected to see. When she registered who he actually was, she halted in obvious confusion.

Pulse racing with reaction, Max said coldly, 'My father is in the kitchen. You doubtless know where that is.'

She recovered her poise very swiftly. 'Why didn't you tell me you planned to come over?'

'You cut the connection too abruptly.'

Moving to where he stood, she said quietly, 'I have a key so that I can fetch things if they're needed, and keep an eye on it when he's away.'

'You don't have to explain your arrangements to me.'

'Oh, I think I do,' she countered. 'Right now, you're certain your suspicions are justified. Well, have your moment of smugness and wallow in it. I'm here on a matter more vital than your bruised ego.'

She stepped past him and headed for the kitchen. Still shaken, Max then noticed she held beneath her arm a thick pile of newspapers, which made sense of her words to Andrew when she reached the elaborate kitchen.

'We've been through them all very thoroughly. No mention, thank God.'

Max took refuge in the bedroom, his emotions in turmoil. A key to this apartment? Was it usual for a captain to have such access to the home of a brigadier? Livya had early in their relationship revealed that his father insisted on her using his name when they were off duty; hated being called 'sir' over the dinner table or on a long flight. Would he be as lenient with a male subordinate? Max doubted it, so was it Andrew Rydal's natural charm towards women that made him uncomfortable with protocol in any dealings with them that were not wholly military?

He nicked his cheek in two places while shaving, and stuck small pieces of toilet paper on them to stop the bleeding while he dressed in beige shirt and trousers, with a chocolate-brown sweater. He fussed needlessly with the few items he had brought in his holdall to delay the moment when he must emerge and see them together. How would Livya play it when they came face to face in his father's presence? How would *he* play it? The delaying tactics were to allow him time to decide.

Demanding of himself whether he was man or mouse, Max went out to settle the situation one way or another with the woman who meant a great deal to him. She was pale but composed, sitting on a high stool at the breakfast bar opposite Andrew, drinking orange juice. Tabloid papers lay fanned out on the veined marble surface.

If she had had little sleep, as she had forecast

in her phone call, it was not apparent. Her strawberry-pink skirt suit and cream silk shirt were immaculate; her make-up expertly applied. Although deliberately not in uniform for this call at a senior military officer's home, she wore her hair neatly coiled at the nape of her neck.

Andrew glanced at Max and, for the first time since his arrival, smiled at him. 'No need to introduce my estimable ADC because you two met up at the Chess Championship just before Christmas.'

'That's right,' said Max, 'and we've been meeting regularly ever since, haven't we, darling.'

There was a brief silence before the other two reacted to that bold statement. Livya's colour rose a little as Andrew said lightly, 'Courtesy of Lufthansa, I take it.' Then he added, 'Ah, the contact who spilt the beans yesterday ... with an ulterior motive.'

Although Max hardly knew his father, he was experienced enough at reading reactions to surprise to feel certain the news had not disconcerted Andrew. He was less sure of Livya's response to having their affair announced, yet he knew her intimately. However, as he had frequently said to Tom, women were better than men at disguising their feelings.

'There was no ulterior motive,' Livya said evenly. 'I called Max to alert him to the probability of unpleasant headlines. The last thing I expected him to do was to drop everything and

261

hop on a plane. From my reading of the situation here, it's very uncharacteristic behaviour.'

Her dark gaze challenged Max. He had revealed the nature of their relationship; she had just made it plain she knew of his with his father. Score even, but she did not appear angry over what he had done. Nor was there any evidence of dismay because Andrew had accepted the news so unemotionally.

'My father behaved uncharacteristically to precipitate this situation,' said Max with a relieved smile. 'It's a facet of Rydals you've not yet come across.' He went to sit on the stool beside her, and kissed her cheek. 'Let's make inroads into these croissants.'

Livya's presence made all the difference. Conversation flowed easily, more coffee was made, and a fruit bowl was brought across from the worktop by Livya to compensate for the croissant calories. Andrew and Livya were very easy with each other, and Max could see why women liked his father. Andrew Rydal treated them with old-fashioned courtesy. Connie Bush and Heather Johnson would be charmed, both being accustomed to the tough attitudes of their male contemporaries.

Livya soon declared she must get to the office where work was piling up. This put Max in a quandary. What to do now? His surprising impulse to visit his father appeared to have run its course, and with Livya's departure he and Andrew would be back to wondering what to say to each other. There was also work awaiting him in Germany.

Knowing he needed some time alone with Livya before he took a flight back, Max was on the point of suggesting they met for lunch when the doorbell rang. Livya went to discover who the visitor was, arousing a fresh faint shaft of disquiet in Max at this sign of her familiarity with his father's home and affairs. Yet an ADC's duties involved such familiarity, which Max would accept without question if the ADC was a man.

The disquiet evaporated when Livya returned with the visitor, playing her official role to perfection. He was tall, handsome and dressed in a dark grey suit bearing the unmistakable mark of having been made for him by a leading military tailor. The regimental tie of discreet oblique stripes would have been bought from the same establishment proud to count members of the royal family among its clients. Andrew was on his feet; Livya stood quietly just inside the kitchen door. Max, isolated beside the massive refrigerator, recognized Major General Sir Preston Phipps with a jolt of pleasure. He had encountered 'Daddy'. What a piece of luck.

'You've always been the lucky sod who invariably lands on his feet, Andrew,' Phipps said without preamble. Then he noticed Max and narrowed his eyes. 'Who's this?' It was snapped out in commanding manner.

There was momentary silence, which Max decided to end to save any embarrassment for his father and Livya. 'Max Rydal, SIB, sir.'

'And who the hell authorized *you* to meddle in this business?' he challenged after absorbing that information.

Oh, yes, definitely a man to use the word *besmirch*, thought Max. 'I'm in the UK to interview several possible witnesses in a case we're investigating, so I cadged a bed for the night. I'm on the point of leaving.'

Phipps's eyes narrowed further. 'Not yet! I want to talk to you.' He turned back to Andrew. 'You haven't made him aware of this, have you?'

'I heard about it through police lines of communication,' Max said swiftly, carefully avoiding Livya's gaze. 'A supplementary reason for coming here last night instead of booking in a hotel.'

Andrew now stepped into the breach. 'A lucky sod, you said, Preston. You've brought good news?'

Phipps glanced at Livya and Max, then nodded. 'We're all in the know, but *this* goes no further than this room.' He walked forward to sit on one of the high stools and pushed the fruit bowl aside as if clearing a space, yet he did not fill it with anything. He fixed his attention on Andrew.

'There are still a few of our compatriots with honesty and integrity. One of them, at five this morning, handed in to his local police station a folder containing documents he thought could not possibly have been discarded in the small skip outside the end house by anyone living

264

in his street. They were marked HIGHLY CONFIDENTIAL and bore a fancy badge heading. He felt they must be important to someone.'

Max heard an involuntary cry of delight from Livya, before Andrew, looking slightly dazed asked, 'Photocopied?'

'Bert Philpotts, ticket dispenser at Elephant and Castle tube station, isn't the type to own a photocopier or any kind of sophisticated camera as shown in TV spy junkets. One has to assume your druggie hadn't enough nous to realize a tabloid would buy those fifty pages for the price of a fix every month this year, so he chucked them in a nearby skip and progressed to a pub to sell the expensive briefcase, pigskin gloves and Mont Blanc pen.' He drew in his breath. 'As I said, a lucky sod who invariably lands on his feet. But, by God, you came very close to disaster this time, man!'

Still registering awed relief, Andrew said, '*Two* worthy citizens. Someone at the cop shop could have seen the potential Bert Philpotts and my mugger missed.'

'I was told a stalwart cockney sergeant recognized our logo and guarded the folder until it was collected by one of our couriers.' The tight lips relaxed into the semblance of a smile. 'Demanded his credentials, then phoned Barker for a description before agreeing to hand the stuff over. We should recruit him. He's wasted down there at the E and C.'

Livya broke into the two-sided conversation

to say she would head for her office if she was no longer needed. 'Will you be along later, sir?' she asked Andrew very correctly. 'If not, I'll attend the meeting with Rex Ingram and deliver my report this evening for you to go over and mark for action.'

'Yes, do that,' ruled Phipps before Andrew could speak. 'The Brigadier needs to recoup at home today.' He turned on Max. 'Now then, give me a sitrep on your progress in the case of grievous assault on my daughter's husband.'

Max swiftly considered what to do about Livya, who had been peremptorily dismissed. He was fully prepared to excuse himself from answering until he had had a private word with her, but would she resent his bringing her personal relations into what had become an official situation? Deciding that she would, he silently watched her walk from the kitchen towards the main entrance.

'Well?' demanded the authoritative voice with a touch of impatience, but Max was watching Livya's pantomime with her mobile phone telling him to call her in an hour's time, and unconsciously smiled.

'Something amusing about a hero being beaten senseless, Captain?'

'No, sir.' Choosing his words carefully, Max outlined the difficulties they were facing because Collier was unable to give descriptions of his assailants, and so far the possible suspects all had alibis.

'We have DNA and fingerprints, but they're

only of use once we have enough evidence to pull someone in on the charge.'

'You've been at it for five days, man. It *has* to be someone on that base. Not too hard to find who bears him a grudge, surely. How much experience have you had at handling serious cases?'

Before Max could respond to the insulting comment, Andrew said, 'Preston, he knows his profession as well as we know ours. He'll get the bastards, take my word.'

Momentarily thrown by this unlooked-for defence from his father, Max was subjected to further attack from the man who reportedly had once dubbed the victim weak and unworthy of the role he played in military service.

'Who are these witnesses you've come over to interview?'

Obliged to support his earlier lie, Max said off the top of his head, 'The men your son-in-law rescued in Kandahar. They might throw some light on the situation out there.'

'*No!*' It was as sharp as the crack of a rifle. 'Taboo! D'you hear that? Leave well alone.'

It was not advice, it was an order. One that took Max aback, despite the fact that he had no intention of tracking down the injured men. 'Can I ask why, sir?'

As Phipps opened his mouth, Andrew spoke swiftly. 'The Colonel of the Royal Cumberland Rifles has been outspoken about the paucity of equipment for his men serving in the Middle East, so the families of the men rescued by

Lieutenant Collier are preparing a court action against the MoD because the protective jackets they should have been wearing had been given to a foot patrol tasked to take out a rocket site.'

'Hence why one was ablaze when Collier reached them?'

'He died on Tuesday from burns that failed to respond to treatment. The whole of his back became suppurated due to some defect in his immune system. His young wife and parents are whipping up support against the MoD.'

'How are the other men he rescued?' asked Max.

His father continued to respond. 'One is still at Headley Court rehabilitation centre. Shattered kneecap.'

'The remaining two are in Norway,' Phipps interceded brusquely. 'Not as a means of getting them out of the limelight, as their wives are claiming. They're due to go this year and it's an opportunity for them gradually to ease themselves back to the demands of normal duty before the rest of the detachment arrives there in May.'

Max frowned. 'We've heard nothing of this.'

'Why should you expect to be privy to such info? It's not an SIB matter,' Phipps replied with some disdain. 'And you haven't heard it now. You understand me, I trust?'

'Perfectly, sir. Is it permitted for me not to hear the grounds these families think they have for bringing a case? Out of interest in the legal aspect.'

With a glance at Phipps, Andrew said, 'You'll read about it in the tabloids once they contact the press. Soon, no doubt. They're claiming their men were inadequately protected against enemy attack. Your colleagues in Kandahar are investigating and compiling a report which you'll have access to, eventually. It's pretty certain to uphold their claims.'

'That's all very well, Andrew, but what these women don't realize is that the available funds have to be spent, and equipment distributed, where it will be most effective,' said Phipps, rapping his knuckles on the breakfast bar to emphasize his point. 'When I was out there on that fact-finding tour I was canvassed on all sides by men wanting extra equipment, more ammo, better gear, better food, better facilities. You name it, they said they needed it! The fact that the American troops have it all, and more, doesn't help.

'The Cumberland Rifles officers bombarded me with requests for upgraded body armour, tougher boots and more men to do the tasks they were expected to carry out. I told them I'd list their needs as a priority. When I spoke to other groups, they had their demands, too, and I told them I'd note them as a priority.

'Trouble is, as you're well aware, there's only so much finance available, and we have troops in too many hostile zones to equip them all to the hilt. But you can't lower morale by stating bald facts when men are under extreme stress. I told Collier that when we had our brief private pow-wow during my visit.'

Max picked up on that interesting fact in a diatribe he had heard all too often. 'You were in Kandahar during Lieutenant Collier's tour of duty, sir?'

Phipps turned in surprise, proving he had forgotten about Max over by the refrigerator. 'I was, yes. Before his bold rescue of those very men whose wives are kicking up the deuce of a fuss. Their husbands could have been captured and murdered. They've forgotten that, haven't they? Forgotten how damned important it is to maintain air cover in desert areas where aircraft are the vital lifeline for men on the ground. They move troops swiftly, they ferry essential supplies to vulnerable outposts, they pick up the sick and wounded to transfer them pronto to the medics, they overfly convoys, make invaluable reconnaisance forays and, not least of their tasks, attack from above when ground troops are pinned down. Yes, aircraft *must* be kept fully operational, which is why I rated them top priority on my list of recommendations. I'm glad to say my findings were acted upon and Six Seven Eight Squadron got their spares and upgraded night vision goggles well before they returned to Germany.'

Although Max was aware of that commanding voice continuing as the speaker rode a hobby horse at a brisk trot, his attention was elsewhere. He had chased wilder geese than this one, but it was flapping its wings enticing him to follow, and he had nowhere better to go.

Twelve

The sun had set two hours ago, but he made no attempt to put on any lights. Darkness epitomized what his life had become. It would stay that way far into the future. Suspended from duty, metaphorically under house arrest in a hostile community, the night was his only friend. *Wrong!* His other friend stood half empty on the table beside him. It would be totally empty soon.

Ria had phoned an hour ago. Was there any news? Oh, yes, *was* there! But he had bluffed through her concerned questions, giving the reassurances she sought because he could not bring himself to tell her the truth.

Gulping more whisky, he pictured Anneka Chorley and Kylie Stokes; the first tall and willowy with knowing brown eyes, and Kylie too flirty for her own good. At the kids' Christmas party in this house, both had worn such brief skirts it was possible to see a flash of lacy knickers when they bent over. Knickers so small their buttocks had swelled beneath them. Asking for trouble. And those close-fitting T-shirts bearing suggestive slogans!

The girl-women today thought nothing of

blatant sexuality. Ria was a good Catholic reared in the less permissive Portugal, so she kept their two respectably clad and well-behaved. Ginny and Zoe grumbled, but the family bond was strong and they were nevertheless popular at school.

The real teaser, of course, was Maeve O'Halloran. Smokey dark hair, deep-blue eyes, breasts as prominent as a pair of peaches, skintight hipster jeans leaving three inches of bare golden flesh between them and a low-cut top. She had followed him into the bedroom pretending she thought it was Gina's, but making the lie pretty obvious. Ria had seen her and swiftly sent her packing. When a man eventually took Maeve as a partner, he would be getting more than second-hand goods.

He thought of his own two girls. They would surely grow into elegant, bewitching women like their mother. The others would look old and well-worn by the age of thirty or so. He was only thirty-nine. The past few days had put years on him. He felt like an old man; an *ancient*.

After today's double charge by SIB he had contacted his own medical protection society again, informing them of the new development. They had advised him to behave with great circumspection until the girls' accusations had been fully investigated and a case mounted. He had phoned a legal friend for advice, but Derek had sounded cautious. The original charge might have been contested successfully, but three such accusations would be more difficult to dismiss.

That pronouncement, and Ria's distress, had sent him to that eternal antidote to misery: alcohol. He had been drinking steadily since that first sundowner. There was a full bottle in the cabinet for when this one ran dry.

As time passed, a series of dream memories flitted through his mind. Ria young, vital and irresistible. Wild, unprotected sex. Baby after baby, until energy and bank balance were at an all-time low. Reason had then battled with religious dictates and won. No more children; cautious sex.

Family scenes faded beneath dark, violent images of suffering. Bosnia. Physical exhaustion, emotional turmoil. The children had been the worst cause of his ethical torment. Innocent victims of their elders' savagery. He had been restricted by the same doctrine as the peace-keeping force forbidden to step outside their neutral role, forced to watch atrocities being committed by both sides and do nothing.

Suddenly, dreams seemed to have become reality. The crash of breaking glass, missiles raining down. A heavy blow to the side of his head, shooting lights in darkness until only darkness remained.

Max had expressed regret over the further charges against Charles Clarkson when Tom had called this morning, but he had not revealed his reason for taking off for the UK so urgently.

273

If Tom was honest, he welcomed Max's absence in order to get a few things straight in his mind.

The Collier case was on a back burner while painstaking questioning was continuing without enthusiasm. Meanwhile, two lesser cases were being finalized ready to present to the relevant commanding officers. A relatively quiet period for Tom.

The wedding outfits rush was slowing. Nora had delivered those to be worn tomorrow, and had just two straightforward bridesmaids' dresses and an amazing purple bridal gown to complete before the Black family set off to visit both sets of grandparents for Easter. She was confident the work would be done in time for her to pack for their trip to the UK. The girls always put out far too much to take with them, so Nora had to do some pruning. Tom invariably packed sparingly, his military training having taught him to travel only with the essentials.

Last night there had been a partial thawing of Nora's attitude, but she was still at the sewing machine all day and too tired for him to attempt more than a kiss and a hand on her nightgowned hip as he lay facing her back. Just as well, perhaps. Call it spring fever, Easter madness, the sight of all that wedding finery, but he had a ridiculous urge to seduce his wife in a small hotel well away from urban civilisation after dumping their brood with the grandparents. Pretend they were of *today's* generation.

Friday. School would close for the Easter holiday. The house would be noisy with three girls planning what to do with all that free time, and the sewing machine racing. No point in hurrying home. Better idea to have a couple of beers in the Sergeants' Mess first.

Not such a good idea after all. The bar was practically deserted, the two members present being among those who steered clear of Redcaps believing it a mistake to get too friendly in case indiscretions slipped out during alcoholic revelry. Tom doggedly drank his planned two halves, then drove from the base to the rented house a short distance from the main gate.

He parked in the drive, glancing at the shuttered house opposite. The Graumann family had left early for Easter, thank God. But they would return, and that boy would be all over Maggie again. She had not forgiven him for sending Hans packing; the rift remained. Hopefully, being with the grandparents would lessen her wounded susceptibilities.

Entering the house, Tom was struck by the absence of a welcoming aroma of supper cooking. Not salad and cold meat again! He really fancied something hot and tasty tonight. The sewing machine was racing away in the dining room, but there was remarkably little sound upstairs. Not even evidence of *Pirates of the Caribbean* being rerun for the umpteenth time. Strange.

He decided to raid the fridge for a cheese sandwich before greeting Nora. It would give him the opportunity to suss out what he was to be offered as an evening meal. Before he reached the kitchen door he was halted by Maggie calling to him. Surprised, he looked up to see her at the top of the stairs.

'Dad,' she said again.

'Yes?' At her hesitation, he added, 'Is there a problem?'

'I ... Can I talk to you?'

Delighted that she was offering the olive branch, he smiled. 'Of course. I'm going to make a sandwich. Let's have one together in the kitchen.'

'Can you ... could you come up? I've got something to tell you.' She bit her lip. 'Please come up.'

His delight fast waned. Good God, what was she about to tell him? He could now see that she was troubled and unhappy; a thirteen-year-old in a plaid skirt, red skinny jumper and calf-high black boots who had turned into the little girl who had trusted him to solve all her problems in the past.

Climbing the stairs swiftly, Tom's throat grew dry with apprehension. Young girls were so vulnerable. Why had Maggie waited for him to come home rather than consult Nora, who was surely better equipped to advise her? Reaching the landing Tom found his daughter had retreated to her bedroom which, being the eldest, she had to herself. Growing seriously worried, he entered what was usually regarded as private property seeing nothing of the paraphernalia of most modern teens or the beloved stuffed toys of childhood. Once he was there, Maggie closed the door alarming Tom further.

'What's wrong, Maggie Blackbird?' he asked gently, using the pet name of old and taking her hand.

She gazed up at him, near to tears. 'It's *awful*! I've been waiting all afternoon to tell you. I almost called your mobile, but I thought you'd be angry if you were doing something really vital.'

'I'm here now,' he soothed, swallowing his fears. 'Let's sit on the bed and talk, eh?'

Once they had settled side by side, Maggie had difficulty finding words. After a few moments, Tom said, 'Have you told Mum about it?'

Maggie shook her head. 'You're the only one who can put it right. Oh, Dad, I don't like doing this, but I know it's right to tell you.'

'Of course. Whatever you've done I promise to try to understand and not be angry. Just bring it out into the open, sweetheart.'

She glanced up quickly. 'It isn't anything *I've* done. It's *them*.'

All at sea, Tom demanded, 'Who?'

Maggie now avoided his eyes and concentrated on their linked hands. 'Everyone at school knows about Stacey Laine and Major Clarkson. People have been laughing about it, specially the boys. They've been saying nasty things about Ginny, Zoe, James and Dan.' She gulped back tears. 'Even their close friends have been joining in. Some of them. It's *horrible*!'

Tom squeezed her hand. 'They're ignorant, that's all. Don't worry about it. The Clarksons won't be coming back to Germany, so it'll all blow over. After the holidays they'll find something else to titter about at school.' He bent to look at her downturned face. 'Is that the problem?'

She shook her head, then blurted out short, emotional sentences. 'I heard them talking. This afternoon. Anneka and Kylie. Laughing about it. They made it up. All of it. He didn't do it. None of it.'

'Hey, hey, slow down,' said Tom, frowning. 'Anneka Chorley and Kylie Stokes? What were they talking about that you overheard?'

Maggie's head drooped further. 'They didn't know I was there. They were talking on their mobiles to Stacey about how they'd done it. Done what she wanted, so she'd be all right now. Everyone would believe her and stop thinking she was to blame. Then ... then they went into details of what they'd told the Redcaps he'd done to them. The Doc.' She looked up then, eyes red-rimmed. 'Dad, they thought it was a joke, saying they wished he really had done what they said because he was super cool. *They told a load of lies.* They said Redcaps were stupid enough to believe any-thing. That's why I knew I must tell you what they'd done. I wanted to shout at them that Redcaps are clever and ... and very brave.' She threw her arms around him and began to sob.

'Oh, Dad, I do love you. I hate it when we're not speaking and ... and you're far nicer than any of *their* dads.'

Tom called Jean Maximus, head of the JR team questioning Clarkson's accusers, but could do no more than leave a message asking her to call him soonest. He then punched in Connie Bush's number, but had to do the same. When he tried Heather Johnson he was in luck. She and her friend Connie were at the swimming pool. Connie was just finishing her last five laps; Heather was drying off in the changing room.

Tom related what Maggie had told him. '*I* can't act on this, of course, and my daughter's name mustn't be mentioned at any stage,' he added. 'You two interviewed Stacey at the outset and concluded she was fantasizing. I have full confidence in your judgement and in my daughter's truthfulness. These girls have conspired to support Stacey's lies, for that's what fantasies are. I want you to interview Anneka and Kylie tonight. Nip this distasteful business in the bud. They might well be going away for the Easter holiday and I want Major Clarkson exonerated before any further harm is done to his reputation and career.'

'I'll fetch Connie from the pool and we'll get straight on to it,' Heather promised. 'Trust us to handle it with sensitivity, sir.'

'I do,' said Tom firmly.

'Will you advise Major Clarkson of this development?'

279

'No. Until the girls confess, it's merely conjecture. The Joint Response team will have to issue an official verdict before we can dismiss the charges, but I'll return to base shortly to advise the Commandant of the situation. He might decide to have a private word with the Major suggesting new evidence has come to light which may well throw doubts on witness statements. Give me a sitrep after you've talked to the Chorley and Stokes girls.'

'Will do, sir.'

Having told Nora he would be back in time to set out for dinner with their friends – the reason why there was no appetizing aroma in the house – Tom drove back to base feeling lighterhearted than he had all week. His eldest was his little girl again, and his two women sergeants' judgement had been vindicated. He sincerely hoped the Commandant, Colonel Trelawney of the Royal Cumberland Rifles, would give Charles Clarkson a hefty hint that his ordeal might soon be over.

The parents of those three girls should read the riot act to them for inventing such damaging fiction. Because they were all minors it was not possible to charge them with wasting police time and making slanderous charges against an innocent man, but they had caused untold anguish besides almost certainly forcing an entire family to relocate and wrest four children from their friends and school.

Tom contemplated sending an e-mail to Max, then decided to wait until morning. Whatever their boss was doing so secretly in the UK could occupy him without interruption until tomorrow, by which time there could be a definite resolution to the Clarkson case.

The base was busy. Soldiers were coming from or going for their supper, heading for the Recreation Centre or the sports venues, loading cars for the drive to the UK on Easter leave, setting out for the town in search of beer and girls. Tom drove carefully through the centre of the base towards the senior officers' accommodation, passing the Medical Centre. Some of his feel-good sensation evaporated. They badly needed a breakthrough in the Collier case.

As if by thought transference his mobile rang at that moment and Tom pulled over to take the call, thinking it might be from Max. He was wrong.

'Good ee-vening, Tom. Here is Klaus Krenkel,' came the voice of the boss at the local *Polizei* headquarters. 'Am I disturbing you for the dinner? I apologize.'

'No need. I'm in my car. How can I help you?'

'Indeed, it is I who will help you, I think.'

'Oh, yes?'

'We have been much busy this week with very serious case, that I only today have had dealing with the question you ask four day ago about the threat to the lady of the pilot.'

Casting around in his mind for something that made sense of this, the only connection Tom could come up with was that it must concern

281

Margot Collier. 'You have some news on that?' he asked experimentally.

'It will be helpful only a little, I think. You ask if we have know of a man in blue Audi who bothers ladies driving alone to frighten them.'

Tom sensed his well-being was about to fade further as the German advised him that they had been aware of this practice for quite a time, and his men were constantly looking out for the dangerous driver.

'He is not always in one place, so it is not easy to find him. We have reports from many ladies over a wide area, which makes the difficulty. I can tell you most strongly that we will catch and punish him.'

'I'm sure you will,' Tom said automatically, his mind registering the fact that their certainty of the absent Lieutenant Maine's similar car being used for the assault on Collier was undermined by this piece of information.

'Thank you for letting me know,' he muttered. 'As always, if we can be of help to you at any time, get in touch.'

He sat for a minute or two a few hundred yards from the Medical Centre, now certain the blood Piercey had found in the boot of the Maine Audi would prove to be from a joint of beef, removing their one clue to Collier's attackers. Back to square one.

No longer feeling buoyant, Tom got under way intent on reporting to the Commandant, then returning to seek solace from his family. He was so lost in his thoughts he did not immediately register the significance of the crowd when he turned in to the lamplit street. When he did he acted swiftly. Stamping on the brake, he snatched up his mobile and called the Military Police post on the base. Corporal Lewis took the call.

'Sir, we've already been contacted by Major Clarkson's neighbours, but I'm undermanned at the moment. Two patrols are out in town where there's a serious barney in the park between squaddies and pseudo-Nazis. The third vehicle is over at the female accommodation dealing with a reported drunken male intruder. I'll divert them right away.'

'Make it faster than that. This could be a dangerous incident,' Tom snapped.

Clarkson's house was surrounded by an angry mob screaming obscenities and hurling all manner of rubbish at the walls and windows, a ground floor one already having been smashed almost in its entirety. The patrol vehicle would take a while to cross from the female accommodation, so Tom did the only thing he could to attempt to diffuse the situation. Switching the lights to full beam, turning the radio on full volume and winding down the windows, he put the car in motion to cruise slowly at the crowd with the heel of his hand on the horn.

It was enough to draw the attention of those on the periphery, but the diversion was only momentary and the women soon turned back to their vituperation of a pervert who tampered with innocent children. Tom then saw why. In

Clarkson's shadowed front garden were three women, probably the mothers of the girls behind this deplorable affair. They were shouting vitriolic accusations of perversion. Lights from upstairs windows of neighbouring houses highlighted their vicious, vengeful expressions.

Their undivided attention was on the house, and Tom's heartbeat quickened when he saw the subject of their anger appear at the smashed window. Clarkson's head was bleeding and he swayed unsteadily as he gazed blankly at the scene in his garden. An almost feral shriek arose as the female tide surged forward.

Christ, they'll batter him senseless, breathed Tom, scrambling from his car where the radio was still pounding out pop music full blast. Instinct overruled all else as he ran forward to fight a way through the pressing bodies. The 'weaker sex' when roused were a match for any man, even one as big and muscular as Tom.

As he struggled to reach the house, the sound of their raised chanting voices against the amplified music, and the bright lights piercing the darkness of night, combined to revive memories of the chase through a packed Christmas market for the obsessed woman who then attacked him with a weighted traffic cone and split his head open.

That mental revival caused him to renew his efforts to prevent further persecution of this innocent man. In the midst of the shifting mob he could smell the sweat of their hostility, the sourness of their breath as they yelled demands to kick him where it would ensure children would be safe from him.

He felt he was losing the battle when he grew aware of commanding male voices ordering the women to fall back. It was suddenly easy to break through the front rank and cross the grass to the window where Clarkson still stood as if mesmerized. Taking up a protective position before the window, he did not see the large stone pulled from the border of the flower bed and meant for the besieged doctor. It hit Tom's left temple exactly where the traffic cone had caught him four months ago. As he dropped to the ground, the high excited voices, the raucous music piercing the night, the surging bodies all suggested he had travelled back in time.

Arriving back at the base, Max drove directly to the Medical Centre to interview Sam Collier. Throughout a delightful lunch hour, extended to two because Livya had deemed she was entitled to compensation for working halfway into last night, and during his return flight, that goose had continued to flap its wings regardless of Max's reasoning that geese did not come a lot wilder than this one. A few words with Collier would either set it in full flight or kill it.

Three hours before midnight and night medical staff had little to do with only a single patient to tend. The light in Collier's room had been dimmed to allow him to settle for sleep, but the pilot was sitting wide-eyed against supersoft pillows when Max entered quietly.

'Sorry to bother you this late,' Max said with a smile. 'I've just flown back from the UK and need to check a few things with you. It won't take long.'

Collier simply made a weary gesture with his arm to signify assent. He still wore a defeated look.

When the orderly withdrew, Max sat facing the bed wondering how to approach the questioning that could possibly bring a solution to why this man had been treated so brutally.

'Is the back healing satisfactorily?' he asked.

'So they say.'

'Good.' The niceties dealt with, Max embarked on the vital inquisition. 'This morning I unexpectedly encountered your father-in-law while investigating an unrelated case.'

Collier's heavily bruised face became an expressionless purple and yellow mask. He made no comment so, after a moment or two, Max continued.

'During your stint in Kandahar, General Phipps spent a day or two there while undertaking a fact-finding tour of Afghanistan. Correct?'

Sam nodded.

'His aim was to assess the situation and list what, in his opinion, was needed to accelerate stability and the withdrawal of our forces?'

'Aye.'

'He was swamped on all sides with requests for equipment, weapons and additional manpower?'

Sam said nothing, but his body had tensed and those dark eyes grew flinty.

'Six Seven Eight Squadron badly needed the latest updated night vision goggles and vital spares for aircraft servicing?'

Sam nodded again.

'So you had a word with the General during a private family get-together and persuaded him to prioritize the Squadron's needs above all the others?'

A short silence. 'A private family get-to-gether? Where the hell did that fantasy come from?'

'You didn't have a short personal session with your wife's father?' Max asked sharply.

'Oh, aye, he took me aside to remind me of my obligations to her and the family; said I had every opportunity out there to make my mark and erase the disgrace of Sierra Leone.' It burst from him with surprising heat. The first time Max had witnessed any vitality in this man.

Having been told of Preston Phipps' attitude towards the hostage crisis in Sierra Leone, Max had no need to question that statement, but it threw him, nevertheless.

'So you didn't use your marital link to pres-surize the General into obtaining much needed equipment for you and your fellows?'

'I've just said.' Sam waved his arm in the familiar gesture Max recognized as one of futility. 'Look, the only personal sessions I ever have with my father-in-law are brief and to the point, with him doing all the talking.' Suddenly roused up, he added, 'If you have some idea that I use our relationship for my own ends, you don't know me. I didn't ask for commissioned rank; it was bestowed without reference to my wishes. I don't want anything from him. I'm my own man. Something he refuses to acknowledge. And he's not the only one, I've just discovered,' he added, the fire in him dying.

Any sympathy Max might have felt had to be smothered beneath the demand of flapping wings that had not been stilled by Sam's words.

'But you got your spares and the NVGs shortly after his visit.'

Adjusting to this return to the original subject, Sam nodded. 'John Fraeme must have put forward a strong enough case, I guess. Made life easier for us. Caused some aggro, naturally.'

Max sat forward. 'Who from?'

'The Infantry. We understood, but everyone out there has to fight their own battles.'

'Aside from the one against the enemy?'

After a moment of tense silence, Sam said quietly, 'Once you know who your enemy is.'

John Fraeme was watching a DVD with his wife when Max called on them. There were obvious signs of small children; toys neatly stacked in a box, playpen in the corner, the faint smell of baby powder and warm milk. Apologizing for arriving without telephoning first, Max said he needed only five minutes of Fraeme's time to get confirmation of several vital facts.

'I've just flown back from the UK and want to progress tonight some new evidence regarding the assault on Sam Collier.'

Once more Max was struck by the aura of controlled command Fraeme radiated, even dressed casually in jeans and a polo shirt. Asking his wife to freeze the DVD, he led Max to the dining room where there was a computer on a desk in the alcove. The large pile of documents and manuals gave an indication of why this pilot was so self-assured; why he was in command of A Flight. Fraeme was a real career soldier.

He turned now to Max with interest lighting his eyes. 'New evidence garnered in the UK? How come?'

'My source is unimportant, and this might lead nowhere, but we've exhausted all other possibilities so I must follow it up.'

'Shoot,' he invited, folding his arms in a typical listening pose.

'Simple answers to a few simple questions,' cautioned Max with a faint smile. 'While you were in Kandahar, General Phipps paid a flying visit on a fact-finding tour.'

'Yes.'

'He was bombarded with complaints and requests for those essentials the troops felt they needed in order to do the jobs they were sent out there to do.'

'Yes.' Fraeme was resolutely giving simple answers.

'Your REME engineers and mechanics were

short of spares to keep A Flight fully operational, and your aircrew still had not been issued with updated NVGs.'

'That's right.'

'After the General's visit, they were supplied?'

'They were.'

'To the dissatisfaction of those who didn't get what they believed they'd been promised?'

'That's an understatement.'

'Real aggro?'

Fraeme nodded. 'Foot soldiers tend to mouth-off at us at the best of times. It simply became more personal. One more goad to put up with along with the heat, the spartan conditions, the fear, the separation from family and the feeling that we weren't fully appreciated by the great British public.' He gave an apologetic smile. 'Forgot for a moment you wanted simple answers.'

'How was it more personal?' asked Max cautiously.

'There was the usual crap about Sam having a word with his dad-in-law to swing it for us.'

'And had he?'

A short derisive laugh. 'I like to think I did that. I used some pretty strong language to the General. All Sam got from him was another bollocking. The interchange was short, and so far from sweet Sam disappeared until his temper calmed.' He gave Max a frank look. 'He takes so much stick from that man, any suggestion that he rides on his back for favours makes Sam so angry he has to absent himself until he manages to cool it. God knows what the outcome of this affair will be. It's sure to be regarded as another sign of weakness; allowing it to happen.'

'I think your friend will have more to worry about than his father-in-law's approval when he gets back on his feet,' Max said. 'Why didn't you mention all this when I asked three days ago if anything specific concerning Collier had happened in Kandahar?'

'A few exaggerated accusations? Normal for dealings with RCR personnel who know his background. Anyway, as I recall, you concentrated on the compatability of crew members, and on the depth of my friendship with Sam. Nothing else.' Fraeme looked bemused. 'You surely don't believe...?'

'There's no limit to what I believe after eight years in this job.' Moving towards the hall, Max acknowledged the truth of the man's words. At first, they had concentrated on relationships within 678 Squadron, because Margot had implanted the belief that their persecutor was a member of it. He should have picked up earlier on the possible connection between the flogging and the RCR casualty with his back aflame.

Back in his car, Max made a quick call to the Royal Cumberland Rifles Officers' Mess, to discover the lively Ben Steele was Duty Officer.

'Twice in three days, Ben? Overdoing it

somewhat, isn't it?'

The young lieutenant laughed. 'I'm not after brownie points. I've a hot date over Easter, so I changed duties with Jason who has a hot date tonight.'

'Not with the same girl, I hope.'

Ben laughed again. 'The Easter Bunny won't be calling on her with chocs and flowers if it is.' A short pause. 'From your tone I guess there's no problem for me to sort out.'

'No, just a little info about your regiment.'

'I'm no encyclopaedia on the subject. You'd do better to consult Colonel Trelawney.'

'I will when I've got everything straight. Ben, you had two companies in Kandahar over Christmas.'

'They came back last weekend.'

The goose wings flapped faster. 'Thanks.'

'That's it?'

'I hope so. I really bloody hope so.'

Max disconnected and checked the time. Ten o'clock. No, it would not wait until morning. He turned the car and headed for the main gate and the house Tom shared with his family. Twenty minutes to reach the short cul-du-sac. Lights were on in every room, which was a good sign. When Nora answered his knock, Max reversed that thought. Her tone and expression as she invited him in told him something was badly wrong.

Thirteen

Tom opened his eyes to sunlight beyond the drawn curtains, and an antiseptic smell in his nostrils. He rolled his head on the pillow to check the clock, then groaned. There was a swelling on his skull that he believed had gone down weeks ago, and it was as painful as ever. He put up a hand to touch it cautiously. His fingers encountered a large padded dressing. He thought that had been dispensed with weeks ago, too. What the hell was going on?

He grew aware of being watched. On the far side of the room the door was standing ajar and three young faces, one on top of the other, were peering at him. They swiftly vanished, and high voices cried, 'He's awake, Mum.'

Then Nora was beside the bed with his three lovely daughters. They all smiled at him, that concerned, loving smile. It made him uneasy. Whole family clustered around the bed. Surely he wasn't on his way out.

'Feel like any breakfast?' Nora asked in her normal manner.

Good. Everything must be all right. You don't ask a dying man about breakfast. 'Cup of tea?'

'And a bacon sandwich?'

The thought of bacon made his mouth water. 'Great.'

'I'll make it,' chorused the girls, and they rushed away squabbling over the privilege.

Nora sat on the bed still wearing the loving smile. 'The Doc said he'd come by this morning just to check all's well.'

It was as if a switch had been tripped by that word 'Doc'. He knew why he was lying in bed when everyone else was up and dressed. 'How's Major Clarkson?'

'About the same as you, I imagine. They stuck a plaster on him the same time as they did yours. He'd been hit by a brick shied through his window. Jim Lewis and Pete Stevenson took him off somewhere for the night. Said he'd stay there until the investigation was over. Connie Bush hinted to me it wouldn't be too long.'

He took in the significance of that. 'Good. The sooner he goes off to join his family the better.'

Nora regarded him thoughtfully. 'Whatever made you take on single-handed a mob of incensed mothers?'

'It comes with the job, love. Even if he had done what those girls fabricated, he was entitled to a defence in a court of law. We don't allow mob rule in this country.' She was still giving him a quizzical scrutiny. 'He appeared at the smashed window bleeding from the head, and stood there swaying, clearly confused about what was happening. I was afraid they'd do him further harm.'

'So you took the bullet meant for him.' She leaned down to kiss him gently. 'If the cavalry hadn't arrived just then, I suppose you'd have made a heroic last stand,' she teased.

Gazing up at her he knew nothing had really changed. She had just been busy, and he had been seduced by spring fever. He took her hand. 'Would there be time before they bring breakfast for us to have a bit of a cuddle?'

'In your present state?' she replied with a happy laugh. 'Heroes in fiction might well fight a furious battle, then return to jump straight into bed with the girl waiting at home, but the truth is they'd demand a hot bath, a huge meal and a long sleep. The girl would come later. As she will in this case, chum,' she added getting to her feet.

'The sewing machine?' he asked flatly.

'Two more days. After that? Rest and build up your strength. You're going to need it.'

Max drove to the junior officers' quarters where Captain Crane had agreed to talk to him immediately after breakfast. Short, with wiry straw-coloured hair, Rory Crane was a bundle of nervous energy with grey eyes that reflected the strain of six months in a desert war zone. What he lacked in stature was compensated for by a deep, rich voice and a very assured manner. This presently projected coolness. It was nothing new to Max. Regimental officers invariably grew cagey when SIB began asking questions about their men. Closing ranks!

'Is this likely to take long?' Crane asked, leading the way through a hallway cluttered with skis. Not difficult to guess where this family was going for the Easter break. On reaching a small back room, he turned to Max. 'How can I help you?'

Max declined to be rushed. 'Sorry to learn Rifleman Pomeroy died of his wounds earlier this week. Something lacking in his immune system, I understand.'

Crane's pale eyes glittered angrily. 'Something lacking on his body when facing possible enemy attack! He'd still be alive if he'd been correctly equipped.'

So the aggro was felt through all ranks. Max avoided being drawn into that dialogue. 'You might be aware that we're investigating a brutal attack on the pilot who picked him and three others up and flew them safely to the field hospital at Kandahar.'

'I had heard, yes. And so?' Crane's coolness was now only just short of hostile.

'And so I'd like to talk to anyone in your company who was close to those four, particularly Pomeroy.'

'We're all on leave. I've no idea where individual men are right now.'

'Just give me names. We'll track them down.' When Crane made no immediate response, Max said crisply, 'Obstructing the police in the course of their enquiries is an offence. Please do as I ask, Captain Crane.'

No man to succumb to threats, Crane replied

with frost icing each word. 'I can't see the connection between the RCR and your enquiries, Captain Rydal.'

'Don't play games with me,' snapped Max, losing his temper. 'Of course there's a connection. Collier saved four of your men from probable slow death by the Taliban. On Tuesday evening he was savagely beaten around the head, then flogged. His back is a mass of raw weals. Pomeroy's death resulted from suppurating burns to his back. Pomeroy died on Tuesday. *Now* d'you see the connection?'

'You're not suggesting...?'

'*The names*,' Max reiterated.

Crane spun on his heel and walked to a desk where he scribbled briefly on a scrap of paper. He offered it to Max without a word. There were half a dozen names on it.

'Thank you. One more thing. Are any of these men Welsh?'

'The obvious one; Lance Corporal Jones. Is that all?' Crane asked, real hostility now apparent.

'For the moment.' Max walked back towards the front door, then turned to Crane on the step outside. 'Your men were victims of an acknowledged enemy. Collier was the victim of people he's entitled to believe are friends. You've put up a spirited defence of your men. It's my job to do the same for him.'

Max wound down the car window to clear the interior stuffiness, breathing deeply to ease his temper. It was a warm spring morning; the kind to tempt people out for the day. Yet it was still early, and soldiers on leave tended to stay in bed until hunger drove them out of it. With luck, Lance Corporal Jones was not extra hungry today.

He punched out Connie Bush's number on his mobile. She had been waiting for his call, and Max read out the names Crane had given him then waited while she located details of their accommodation on the computer. Max then told her to meet him outside the block housing three of Pomeroy's pals, including the Welshman Jones.

It was with mixed feelings that Max drove across the base. The goose was nowhere near as wild now. In fact, the likelihood of its being caught was strong. He wished Tom could have been with him. He had chosen Connie because she had pinpointed Ray Fox by some astute reasoning, and also because she clearly had sympathy for Sam Collier.

Connie was waiting when Max arrived. She was dressed in a navy trouser suit and white blouse, which set off her glow of health. A valuable member of his team whom he greeted with a smile.

'Sorry to pull you in on Saturday, but this can't wait. Another few days and these men could take off for the long Easter weekend.'

She glanced up eagerly as they approached the entrance to the three-storey block. 'Have we cracked it, sir?'

'We'll see, shall we?'

They climbed to the second floor and walked along the corridor to a room that could be divided into two by a heavy brown curtain. The familiar smell of sweaty bodies, unwashed socks and the fug created by sleeping without opening a window greeted them. They were also treated to the sight of two unshaven young men sitting on their beds in underpants, chatting easily with the curtain drawn back to open up the room. They paused to stare at these two civilians intruding on their territory.

One of them, a great beefy fellow, said aggressively, 'Piss off! This is a private area, see. Only residents allowed.'

Max identified himself, registering inner excitement. This gorilla spoke with a Welsh accent. 'And this is Sergeant Bush. We'd like a word with you, Lance Corporal Jones.'

It was as if someone had thrown a bucket of icy water over him. The bombast ebbed. He looked completely dumbstruck. 'What about, sir?'

'I think you know the answer to that. Get some clothes on. We're taking you to Section Headquarters.' Seeing the man's wild expression, Max added, 'Don't even think it. We'll stand here while you dress ... and make it snappy!'

While his room mate scrambled into jeans and a T-shirt, the other lad watched in bemusement, but Jones had had time to recover from the shock and began muttering about police brutality and his rights.

'Know a lot about brutality, do you, Jones?' asked Connie.

His head shot round. 'What?'

'Play violent computer games, do you? Log on to websites showing gang warfare? Dream of transferring to the SAS?'

'You shut your...' He broke off, remembering who this young woman was. 'What's this about? I'm on leave, see. Just back from fighting the bloody Taliban. You've no right to come here...'

'Shut it, Jones, and zip your fly,' Max instructed. 'We'll read you your rights when we get to our headquarters.'

They did that, once the bull-like Jones was seated opposite them at a table in an interview room. Max opened the questioning. 'Where were you on Tuesday evening, Corporal?

Jones made a great play of thinking. 'Ah, yes, I was in the NAAFI bar.'

'When did you arrive and leave?'

'Dunno. Went there straight after supper.'

'And left when?' asked Connie.

'Late.'

'Then what?'

'Bed. After six months in bloody sweltering tents it's a treat to sleep in reasonable comfort. We were all bloody knackered, see.'

'Who were you with?' asked Max.

'Plenty of witnesses,' came the smart answer.

'Names, so that we can check your alibi.'

'Alibi?' Caution returned. 'I don't need no alibi. What you trying to make of nothing?'

300

'Who were with you, Corporal?' Max repeated.

'Mossy Peat and Flinto. Jim Flint.'

'*Mossy* Peat?' queried Connie.

'Steve.'

'Your mates?'

'Yeah.'

'Like Mike Pomeroy was?' Max said quietly.

Jones visibly stiffened and stared back at Max.

'Mike Pomeroy was your best mate who'd died that day of wounds received in Kandahar. Is that why you and Peat and Flint were in the bar? Drowning your sorrow? Drinking to his memory?'

Jones was uncertain how to reply, still shaken by the course this interview was taking. 'What you getting at?'

'We're getting at what you were doing on Tuesday evening,' said Connie. 'The evening Lieutenant Collier of the Army Air Corps was brutally assaulted.' She paused. 'The pilot who rescued your best mate Pomeroy from Taliban bullets.'

'Yeah, and got a gong for it. Real bleeding hero!' Jones said sneeringly.

'You don't think he deserved recognition for what he did?'

'I ... it's nothing to me what he got.'

'He risked his life for someone you were close to.'

Jones fidgeted in his seat. 'Look, I told you where I was on Tuesday. That's it. I was with mates in the NAAFI.' He stood. 'I got to get on with things I planned for today.'

'Sit down!' ordered Max. 'We haven't finished yet.' He waited until Jones reluctantly resumed his seat. 'How much did you drink that evening?'

'What? I dunno. Several pints.'

'Several?' Connie sounded sceptical.

'That's about usual.'

'Not a few more than usual because you were upset about Mike's unfortunate death?'

Jones suddenly fired up, saying explosively, 'There weren't nothing *unfortunate* about it. It were bloody *murder*, see. Mike didn't stand no chance. No more did Cracker, Simmsy and Jacko.'

'Murder?' repeated Max questioningly.

'What else can you bloody call it when you're sent out without the full protective gear?'

'That was the general opinion, was it?'

'Too right, it was. We were all set to get the gear. We was told it was priority. Then that bastard...' He stopped, and silence hung in the air while Max and Connie stared unwaveringly at him until he looked down at his hands.

'Which bastard?' prompted Max.

'I got nothing more to say.'

'While you were in Kandahar did you hear a rumour that Lieutenant Collier had used his family connection to reverse General Phipps's decision to prioritize the RCR demand for protective gear, and instead recommend that Six Seven Eight Squadron be given all *they* needed?'

Jones's head came up. 'What you getting at?'

'I'm suggesting that you and your mates had an issue with Lieutenant Collier in Kandahar. Am I right?'

Jones began to look deeply worried. 'Weren't just us.'

'So it was a widespread grouch throughout your company?'

Jones seized on what seemed to be a means of diverting attention from himself. 'Our Colonel went public about it. It was in all the papers.'

'*He* blamed Lieutenant Collier?' asked Connie incredulously.

'Well ... not exactly him. But he must've known what we all knew.'

'So when you returned here last weekend and saw that pilot again, your resentment revived. Then you heard that Mike Pomeroy had died, and your resentment spilled over into active hostility against the man you believed had indirectly caused Mike's suffering and death. You, Mossy and Flinto went to the NAAFI bar to deaden the pain of losing such a special mate,' suggested Connie in sympathetic manner. 'You talked about it, drank to Mike's memory, and grew more and more angry over the fact that he shouldn't have died. And all the time you knew whose fault it really was. A man who'd even been in the line of fire during that rescue and emerged unhurt.'

'And the bastard got a medal and all that bleeding publicity. We all do our bit out there, but he gets turned into a bloody hero because he's crafty. Knows which side to butter his bread. Marries a bloody general's daughter, don't he? Makes sure he's going right to the top the easy way,' Jones raged, caught up in Connie's gently persuasive scenario.

'So you, Mossy and Flinto decided to teach him a lesson. For Mike, whose back had burned raw and who had died in great pain.'

The silence almost crackled with tension until a surprising sound broke it. Jones began to sob deep in his throat. His shoulders started to shake, his head bowed so low his tears were hidden. Max and Connie sat still, saying nothing and knowing a full confession would follow.

They had cracked it, but there was little sense of triumph. Men who faced months of tension, stress, debilitating heat, spartan conditions, boring food and very real danger formed powerful bonds with their friends. Losing one was akin to losing a brother. Grief exacerbated by alcohol bred an undeniable urge for revenge.

And there was the second tragedy of a man who had been cruelly punished for an imagined act of nepotism by a man who treated him with scorn. Another painful truth Sam Collier had yet to learn.

Tom looked much the same as he had just prior to Christmas when Max arrived late that afternoon: large dressing bound to his head, pale face, and a mug of tea on the table beside his chair. Nora and the girls had just returned from the garrison church, where the bride had worn a stunning dress embroidered with waterlilies. Nora made tea for Max and brought slices of cake for them both, then left them to talk.

'News that'll please you, Tom,' Max announced with a smile. 'Connie and Heather feel certain Jean Maximus can wind up the case against Clarkson by Easter. When they visited Anneka and Kylie they faced angry fathers, who did their best to prevent the girls responding to a gentle suggestion that the truth had a way of coming out during an investigation, so it was best to make sure they told us what had *actually* happened. The dads insisted their girl never told lies, she was the *victim*. Why hadn't we locked up the pervert instead of bullying young kids?'

'The mothers were out throwing insults and rubbish at Clarkson's house, of course,' said Tom.

'And hefty stones at you. Ironically, their fathers' ranting did what our girls were aiming for. Anneka and Kylie grew so agitated they broke down and admitted Stacey had given them money to say what they had, and had promised not to tell on them.' Max picked up a slice of cake. 'Maggie's name has not been mentioned, or even hinted at, so tell her not to worry on that score.'

Tom sighed. 'I've been a bit hard on her lately. You've no notion how proud I am of her sense of morality.'

'Has she?' Max asked carefully.

'Yes. We've reached an understanding on several subjects.' He frowned, puckering the dressing. 'Girls are so tricky to rear.'

'Which is why Nora does most of it,' responded Max with amusement.

Tom gave a reluctant laugh. 'Guilty as charged.'

They drank tea in companionable silence for a few minutes. Then Max gave the big news he had come to impart, revealing that a chance encounter with Preston Phipps had triggered the possible meaning of Collier's flogging. Skimming over events that had led to that providential meeting, Max then recounted the interview with Lance Corporal Jones, a large man with a Welsh accent.

'We'll bring in Peat and Flint when they return to base tonight. Jones has landed them heavily in it, so we'll have no problem bringing a solid case against all three. In Jones' statement he admits they blamed Collier for not getting the equipment promised by General Phipps, and when they were swamped with tales of his heroism in the media their aggro grew. The award of an MC added further fuel to the flames of their anger. Even out in Kandahar they vowed to sort him out one day.

'As soon as they arrived back here they began to devise a plan. They'd phone him with an enigmatic message to arrange a meeting. They would grab and hood him, then drive to the far side of the base to give him a going over and leave him to walk back as best he could. Flint had been a joy rider in his early teens and knew how to steal a car.'

Max was halted at that point by Tom's account of the call from Klaus Krenkel of the *Polizei*. 'Did Jones and co. try to force Margot off the road?'

Max shook his head. 'The first and only time they were in Maine's car was last Tuesday evening. Flint thought using a vehicle owned by a member of the squadron added piquancy to their plan. He chose one at random, unaware that Maine wouldn't be blamed because he was in the UK.'

'So she must have been targeted by the German weirdo.' Tom gave a short laugh. 'The one lie she didn't tell us! I guess she knew someone in the squadron owned a blue Audi, and jumped to a conclusion that set us off along a dead end. Life is eternally entertaining, isn't it?' He leaned back wearily. 'You say these three riflemen vowed even before they returned to Germany to bash Collier?'

'They did, but their initial plan was simply to rough him up, possibly leave him with very sore balls.'

'But Pomeroy's death that day made the whole exercise more deadly?'

Max nodded. 'Fuelled by alcoholic bravado Jones came up with the notion of whipping their victim until his back was as raw and agonizing as Pomeroy's had been. And the basic punch-up turned into a lambasting with a handkerchief wrapped around a fistful of gravel. Far more effective as a punishment.

'The revised plan went ahead. They weren't aware of Ray Fox's sideline, of course, which aided their ruse to get Collier to their RV. Flint had appropriated Maine's Audi and they drove to the REME workshops with a hooded Collier in the boot. That's where the plan backfired. Far from reducing his back to pulp, they had to abandon the attack because he collapsed. He's a big, heavy man. They couldn't hold him upright once he was unconscious, so they decided to dump him in the road and scarper.'

Max picked up his half empty mug and took a short drink of tea. 'Jones said when they'd sobered up having relieved their anger, they realized they'd lost control of the situation and maybe *killed* their victim. Remorse soon faded when they heard he was being treated in the Medical Centre, and that we were swarming over the AAC lads. They were sharp enough to know we'd find evidence in the boot of the Audi, and it added to their revised glee that that would definitely concentrate our attentions on the squadron. Not for a minute did they believe we'd ever get on to them, so they hadn't bothered to consolidate a defence strategy.'

Max smiled and leaned back in his chair. 'Case solved. Connie's female sympathy and apparent understanding undermined Jones very quickly. Funny how very big men often break under gentle questioning faster than small men. Connie Bush is a first-rate interviewer.'

There was a short silence before Tom said, 'There's one point left to explain.'

'Yes? What's that?'

'What did you go to check in the UK?'

Max got to his feet. 'You look knackered. I think you should have a rest or Nora will be after my guts. Enjoy your Easter leave with the grandparents and return fighting fit.' He pulled some Euros from his pocket. 'Buy Maggie an extra chocolate egg and tell her she's well and truly her father's daughter.'

The day before Good Friday. The team had finished collating all evidence in the Collier case, ready to present to Colonel Trelawney after Easter. Jones, Peat and Flint faced trial, a prison sentence and discharge from the Royal Cumberland Rifles. Sadly, nothing would ever convince them Sam Collier was blameless. They would tell the story even to their grand-sons, and still believe it.

Max had sent the rest of his team off and was about to leave Headquarters himself, when Charles Clarkson walked into his office. The Medical Officer looked like a man who had had little sleep. He was dressed in a dark suit with a light raincoat over it to protect him from the showers alternating with sunny periods.

'I'm on my way to the airport. I'll be in Portugal tonight with my family. Sergeant Maximus knows how to contact me, if needed.' He offered his hand. 'I owe you for getting at the truth and establishing my innocence.'

Max gripped his hand. 'We're compelled to investigate any charge, regardless of our personal convictions. I'm sorry you're leaving us. Every success in your new posting.'

'Time to move on, perhaps. Liaising with you has been an education, Max. Goodbye ... and thanks.'

Max sat for a few minutes after Clarkson left. The base was losing a first-rate doctor because a young girl had allowed her hormones to run riot. So often with that type of case there was a 'no smoke without fire' attitude that remained despite a not guilty verdict. He hoped the Clarksons would settle happily elsewhere after this unpleasant affair. He also hoped the man's replacement would be of equally high standard. SIB frequently worked alongside a medical officer, so a good rapport was a bonus. Max and Clarkson had had their ups and downs, but they had respected each other.

He locked his safe, his office door and the main door before setting the security alarm and walking to his car. Because Tom was on leave he had to remain on stand-by while others enjoyed the Easter break. He might drive out to the river to take out his skiff on Sunday, as he usually did. Rowing was one sport his father had never taken up. Was that why he had?

His room in the Mess seemed no more welcoming than it ever had, but he was getting used to it. There would be few members dining in tonight, which suited Max well enough, although the successful result in the Collier case had brought friendly approaches from men who had hitherto kept their distance. It had also brought an invitation to dine with the officers of 678 Squadron next week.

Sam Collier was due to be discharged from the Medical Centre on Monday. Max knew Rex Southerland was aware of Collier's hang-up over captivity, because it was in his report on Ray Fox's blackmail activities. As the commander of 678 Squadron, Southerland would have to take whatever action he thought fit on that score. Max believed a few sessions with the psycho boys would probably sort that out. He had no idea who or what would sort out that intense marriage.

He had not seen Collier since telling him his attackers had been arrested. The young pilot had seemed to be still in a state of detachment, uninterested and uncaring until he heard why he had been beaten and dumped in the road. Max could not pinpoint the emotion showing on that bruised face, but it was a dark one. Although his professional dealings with Collier were at an end, he would attempt to keep track of his future.

After showering and dressing for dinner, Max called Livya for their usual long exchange of news and sweet nothings. She told him she would drive to her parents' home for Easter.

'No chance of Steve McQueen arriving on a Harley Davidson as he did at Christmas?' she teased.

'I wish.'

'Our venerable chief is highly chuffed that you've removed his daughter's fear and anxiety over the attack on her husband. He seems immune to the probability that he was the indirect cause.'

'He would be,' grunted Max. 'Not a man I warmed to at all.'

'On that subject, I must warn you that Saturday's papers, and almost certainly the TV news, will carry a full account of the case against the MoD being brought by wives and families of RCR troops serving in war zones. You'll have reporters swarming all over you tomorrow. Can you keep Collier's name out of it?'

'Not up to me, Livya. The Garrison Commander controls media activity on base, but there are always leaks. It's impossible to monitor private phone calls. Even "Daddy" can't do that.'

There was a short silence from her, then she said carefully, 'Andrew has to come over there for a two-day conference next week. We'll be overnighting a mere seventy Ks from you. He thinks it would be nice if you could join us for dinner.'

Max was taken aback. Did he really want to do this?

'There might be a heavy case under way.'

Another silence from her. Then, 'A hand is being held out. If you don't take it now, you never will.'

He thought quickly. His plan for himself and Livya, if successful, must bring closer contact with his father. Surely her wish for him to accept this invitation meant she shared his plan for their future. Warmth invaded him, and his tone softened.

'I'll come.'

Sam walked slowly and cautiously from the hospital. Energetic movement was still painful; headaches were frequent and debilitating. They had discharged him from the Medical Centre a day early because Margot had undergone yet another miscarriage. He had bottles of pills, tubs of antiseptic cream, and an appointment with Dr Culdrow seven days hence.

He should have used a taxi, but he had instead decided to drive Margot's Jaguar because the seats were so well-cushioned. He now sat behind the wheel absorbing what the gynae-cologist had just told him. An abnormality that prevented his wife from carrying a foetus beyond fourteen weeks. Margot had just mis-carried another man's child.

Twenty minutes passed before he could bring himself to turn the key in the ignition and drive out to the road that led to the autobahn. He could not go back to the house where they had lived together, where her costume designs lay around that room upstairs, where she had teased and excited him so lustily after doing the same with someone else in the Seychelles. He never wanted to enter that house again. He never wanted to see or touch her again.

Running up on to the autobahn, he headed away from the base, driving fast, his head pounding. He was on autopilot. His thoughts were wild. The roundabout had finally flung him off into the dark void.

He had stepped on to it at an airshow, and his life had been spinning faster and faster towards this final humiliation. He had given up membership of the Blue Eagles, a source of pride and delight. He had been reviled and insulted by her father until she had become obsessed with redesigning her 'Samson' to Daddy's requirements. And he had still loved her.

Sierra Leone. Rape by crackhead kids armed with machetes and rifles because his blond hair excited them.

The first miscarriage after his safe return. Safe? He was haunted by the pain and degradation of that obscene act, while his procreative ability was being questioned. And he had still loved her.

A second miscarriage. The genes of a fish-and-chip lover must be below standard, of course.

On stand-by for Afghanistan. Nightmares about being taken captive again. The Taliban went far beyond rape. He could only still the shakes with alcohol.

Ray Fox and his demands. It would all come out and he would be grounded; a pilot once skilled enough to perform complicated manoeuvres before the public.

A vicious, calculated beating by ignorant oafs for something he had not done. As humiliating as the rape. Something sparked off by the man who had derided the weakling his daughter had married. And he had still managed to love her.

Until this final betrayal.

The road now cut through countryside bursting with the overture to Spring. Sam saw nothing but an empty road and the distant curve that ran beside the high brick wall of a large estate. He accelerated. A hundred metres from the curve he gripped the wheel steady and closed his eyes as the car hurtled towards the wall.

When he stamped on the brake and skidded with a scream of tyres to a halt, his eyes were still closed. The growing silence echoed the growing calmness within him as he sat contemplating his decision made during that hiatus between life and death. He was not yet ready to see how close he was to the wall.

Yorkshiremen did not give up. He could go back to the beginning. Rid himself of wife and father-in-law, thereby ridding himself of the resentment of his fellows. He could seek medical help for those nightmares. He could ride out the period of grounding, then take to the air again to prove how good a pilot he was. At twenty-six he had enough time to aim at a second crack at the Blue Eagles. Life was out there waiting for him to rejoin it.

Slowly, he began to smile. Besides, he had a medal to collect from the Queen.